Shadows in Calusa Cove

The Aegis Network: The Everglades Divison
Book 2

Jen Talty

Chapter One

One Month Earlier

Trent Mallor shifted his pickup into park and stared at Karl Simpson's truck, which was crooked in Trent's driveway. That told Trent everything he needed to know about how this conversation would go.

Karl leaned against the driver's side door, arms crossed, with that easy grin that used to mean trouble was about to get fun. Now it just meant trouble.

Slipping from behind the wheel, Trent made his way across the gravel drive, doing his best to keep his attitude in check.

"Mallor." Karl pushed off the truck and spread his hands wide. "Looking good, brother."

Trent stopped a few feet away, keeping distance between them. "I'm not your brother." The last time they'd seen each other, about six months ago, it hadn't gone well. "What do you want?"

"Can't a guy visit an old friend?"

"We stopped being friends the moment you took a gator from my property."

Karl's grin flickered but didn't die. He was a big man, gone slightly soft around the middle but still carrying the kind of muscle that came from wrestling reptiles for a living. His sun-weathered face was a map of every bad decision he'd ever made, and there'd been plenty.

"Come on. That was years ago. Water under the bridge."

"I don't think so." Trent laughed, but there was no humor in it. "Besides that, I spent six months on probation because I took the heat for you. Had to grovel to every conservation officer in the state to get back in their good graces. And what did I get from you for my trouble? Nothing except the expectation that I'd do it again."

"Not true, and I said I was sorry."

"You said it was a misunderstanding."

Karl shrugged. "Semantics."

They'd been friends once. Good friends, even. They'd done the Python Challenge together three years running, hauling invasive Burmese pythons out of the Glades for bounty money and bragging rights. They'd pushed boundaries, cut corners, done things that came close to crossing lines that shouldn't be crossed. Young and stupid and convinced they were invincible.

Then Karl had gotten greedy. Started dealing in animals he had no business dealing in. When the wildlife officers came knocking, it was Trent's name on the paperwork, not to mention he'd been caught with an illegal python kill by Karl, because Trent decided to clean up the mess.

He'd taken the heat. Kept his mouth shut about Karl's involvement because he still believed in loyalty back then. Still believed that the code meant something.

It didn't. Not to men like Karl.

"Look," Karl said, dropping his voice like they were co-conspirators instead of former friends. "I didn't come here to rehash old shit. I came here with an opportunity."

"Not interested."

"You haven't even heard what it is."

"Don't need to." Trent crossed his arms. "Whatever you're selling, I'm not buying."

Karl stepped closer, his eyes bright with the kind of excitement that always preceded disaster. "I've got clients. The kind with deep pockets and specific needs. They're looking for someone with your skills—the snake work, the gator handling, the whole package. We're talking more money than either of us has ever seen."

"No."

"Just hear me out—"

"I've heard more than I wanted to already." Trent's voice went flat and hard. "My days of skirting the law are over. I've got a business to run. A mother to take care of. I'm not throwing that away to help you make a quick buck off whatever shady deal you've cooked up this time."

Karl's expression soured. "You've gotten soft. That's what this is. Gone all respectable." He said the word like it tasted bad.

"Maybe. Or maybe I just got smart enough to stop making the same mistakes."

"This isn't a mistake. This is the score of a lifetime."

"Then go find someone else to help you score it." Trent jerked his chin toward the truck. "Get off my property. And don't come back."

For a moment, something ugly flickered behind Karl's eyes. The kind of look that made Trent's instincts sit up and pay attention. But then it was gone, replaced by that easy grin again—though it didn't reach his eyes this time.

"You're making a mistake." Karl climbed back into his truck. "A big one. But hey—your funeral."

The engine roared to life, and Karl backed out of the driveway with more speed than necessary, kicking up a spray of gravel and crushed shell. Trent watched until the truck disappeared around the bend, then stood there a moment longer, letting the tension drain from his shoulders. The last thing his mom needed was him coming in with a shitty attitude.

His phone buzzed in his pocket.

Dove: *On my way with food. Tell Dolly to keep her mouth shut when I cross the bridge.*

Despite everything, Trent smiled. Dovelynn Quinn had a way of doing that—cutting through the noise, making him forget, even for a second, that the world was full of men like Karl Simpson.

Trent: *She's not the one you need to worry about. It's the little ones that'll sneak up on you.*

Dove: *Sometimes I really hate you.*

He chuckled, and it felt so damn good.

Trent: *See you soon.*

He pocketed the phone and headed toward the house just as the hospice nurse stepped out on the porch. "I thought I heard you come home."

"How's she doing?"

"She had a good afternoon. Didn't eat much but tried. We talked for a bit—she was lucid, in good spirits."

"It sounds like there's a but in there."

"Her vitals are declining. Slowly, but steadily." She touched his arm, the gesture practiced but not unkind. "I know I've said this before, but—it's time to start thinking about final arrangements. Having those conversations while she's still able to participate in them."

He rubbed the back of his neck. "My mom's always been a planner and she's let me know what she wants."

"Good. That's good, because she really doesn't have much time left." She squeezed his arm and let go. "I'll be back tomorrow morning. Call if anything changes overnight."

He watched her stroll to her little SUV and drive away. He stood on the porch for a long moment, watching the sun bleed out over Mallor's Landing in shades of orange and copper, spilling across the water like something wounded.

The gators were settling in for the night, their dark shapes drifting through the moat like fallen logs come to life. Somewhere in the cypress stand, an owl called out—one low note, then silence.

Inside the house, his mother was sleeping. Or

pretending to sleep. It was hard to tell the difference these days, and he'd stopped asking.

The sound of an engine tickled his ears. Seconds later, Dove's truck rolled down the drive.

His heart beat a little faster as she emerged from her vehicle and walked across the bridge, glancing left and right, all while scrunching her forehead. It was adorable. The trained Army sniper, an expression of fear and awe sweeping across her face. It was rare for Dove to show any vulnerability, but he saw through her defenses. Through her tough exterior. They weren't all that different, except he retreated, where she surrounded herself with people.

She appeared at the bottom of the steps, a plastic container in her hands and a careful smile. "I can't believe I'm bringing food to an alligator farm."

"Technically, the farm is the commercial side. This is a natural habitat."

"That makes it worse. They're wild, and you let them come live here by choice.

He chuckled. "They can't get to the house."

"Right, but I had to cross that damn bridge, and all I saw were eyes in the water. One of them opened their mouth," she said, with a shudder. Lifting the container, she said, "Chicken and rice. Nothing fancy, but it's good for the soul."

Trent took the container, the heat of it seeping through the plastic into his palms. "You didn't have to do this."

"I know."

"I mean it. You've already—"

"Trent." She said his name the way she always did—like a period at the end of a sentence. Final. Not up for debate. "Take the soup. Feed your mother. Stop arguing with me."

"Yes, ma'am."

She rolled her eyes, but there was something soft underneath the gesture. She was so beautiful, with her blond hair, blue eyes, petite frame, and toned muscles. She might be only five-foot-five, but no one should let her size fool them because she was a lethal weapon all by herself.

She was also sweet and kind.

He opened the door, and it creaked on its hinges the way it had since he was a kid. The cicadas were loud tonight, their chorus rising and falling in waves that washed over the property like a pulse. Out in the moat, one of the gators bellowed—probably Dolly, complaining about the heat or the humidity or whatever else gators complained about.

Dove hesitated and chose not to step inside.

That didn't surprise him.

"How is your mom? Really?"

Trent glanced over his shoulder toward the living room, where his mother was propped up on the couch with a blanket over her legs despite the warmth of the evening. She grew thinner every day. Fading like a photograph left too long in the sun.

"She has good moments," he said. "Though, fewer of them."

Dove nodded slowly. She didn't offer platitudes. Didn't tell him it would be okay or that miracles happened or any of the other useless things people said when they didn't know what else to say. She just stood there, solid and present, and let the truth of it sit between them.

"I appreciate everything you've done," he said. "The soup. The company. Sitting with her when no one else was around." He shook his head. "You didn't sign up for any of this."

"It's what friends do." She reached out and squeezed his arm, her grip firm and warm. "I'm here for you. And for her. Whatever you need—I'm just a phone call away."

Friends. When it came to Dove, that word confused him. He set the soup on the table by the door and looked at her for a long moment. The light was doing something to her face, softening the sharp edges.

He leaned in and kissed her. Brief. Gentle. More gratitude than passion, but not entirely without heat. She kissed him back the same way, her hand coming up to rest against his chest for just a moment before she pulled away because they'd agreed to be just friends.

"Go feed your mom," she said quietly. "I'll check in tomorrow."

"Okay." He sighed. It was for the best that she pushed him away.

She headed down the steps and across the yard toward her truck, moving with that particular grace she had—the one that said she was always aware of her surroundings, always ready for whatever came next. He watched until her taillights disappeared then went back inside.

His mother was watching him from the couch, a knowing smile playing at the corners of her mouth.

"Don't," he said.

"I didn't say anything."

"You were thinking it."

"I'm allowed to think whatever I want. It's one of the few pleasures I have left." She patted the cushion beside her. "Now come sit with me, and let's eat whatever that sweet girl brought over."

Trent retrieved two bowls from the kitchen and ladled out the soup, the smell of garlic and herbs filling the small space. He handed one to his mother and settled onto the couch beside her, careful not to jostle her too much. She was fragile these days. Breakable in ways she'd never been before.

She took a sip and made a small approving sound. "This is good. She can cook."

"It's soup, Mom. Not exactly gourmet."

"Good soup is harder than you think." She took another sip, studying him over the rim of the bowl. "I like her."

"I know you do."

"She's good for you."

"We're just friends." There was that damn word again.

His mother laughed—a real laugh, the kind he hadn't heard from her in weeks. It dissolved into a cough, and he reached for her automatically, steadying the bowl in her hands until the fit passed.

"Sorry," she said, catching her breath. "It's just—the look on your face when you say that. Just friends." She shook her head, still smiling. "You keep telling yourself that, sweetheart."

He didn't argue. There was no point arguing with Linda Mallor when she'd made up her mind about something. Never had been.

"Why don't you turn on the news?" his mother suggested.

"Sure." He pointed the remote at the television, and the first thing that popped up was Stacey Mohawk. God, he really didn't like that woman. She wasn't a very good reporter. She preferred gossip and spinning stories for sensationalism to digging her teeth into something real.

"Turn it up." His mother lifted her spoon, then blew on the liquid and took a small bite.

"You want to watch Stacey?"

"I want to hear the story about Garrett Dutton. He's running for State Senate," his mother said. "He used to be a US Marshal, and he knew your father."

That caught his attention. "He doesn't look old enough to have been a marshal when Dad was set to testify." Trent had only been fourteen when his father left Mallor's Landing after witnessing a politician and an executive from Gulf Coast Energy Partners pass papers they shouldn't have. And then he witnessed a murder. A few months later, while under the protection of the US

Marshals office, specifically, a man named Aaron Slade, Jack Mallor died in a freak car accident, changing Trent's life forever.

"I don't know the details, but I believe he was fresh out of training." His mom took another small bite. At least she was eating. "I only met him once. When he came to pay his respects."

"I don't remember him at Dad's funeral."

"It was a few months later. When you were away at football camp. I guess he'd been on another detail and couldn't come to your father's service. It was nice of him, but I'm not sure I'm gonna vote for him." She set her bowl aside. "If I'm still around—"

"Why don't you like him as a candidate?" Trent had promised his mom he'd be realistic about her condition, but he just didn't want to hear it now that they were so close to the end.

"He supports the mining of limestone. Says we need to do more and would be willing to do it in the Glades."

Trent stared at the television for a few moments, listening to Stacey ramble about Dutton, and it was obvious she was in his corner. Well, Trent wasn't. The mining of limestone was a controversial topic because of the environmental damage it caused, even though it was considered necessary for construction materials.

"I've heard enough." He turned down the volume and set his bowl aside. "Dutton sounds like a slick politician, and Stacey looks like a woman on a mission to get him elected... or on the hunt for a husband."

"As long as she stays away from you." His mom patted his leg. "Trent, dear," she said, and the way in which her tone dropped made him go still. "I need to ask you something."

"Anything."

"Are you happy here? Running Mallor's Landing?"

The question caught him off guard. "What do you mean?"

"I mean exactly what I said." She turned to look at him fully, her eyes—still sharp despite everything else that was failing—searching his face. "You've spent your whole life on this property. Running the business, taking care of the habitat, keeping everything going after your father—" She stopped, swallowed. "After your father died. You were just a boy, and you stepped up. Became the man of the house before you'd even finished being a child."

"Someone had to."

"That's not what I asked." She reached over and took his hand, her fingers thin and cool against his skin. "Do you feel trapped here? If you wanted to leave—to experience something else, somewhere else—I'd understand. I'd be okay with it."

"Mom—"

"I have a buyer." She said it quickly, like she'd been holding the words in her mouth and they'd finally spilled out. "Someone interested in purchasing Mallor's Landing."

Trent went very still. "What?"

"It came in last week. I wasn't sure if I should

mention it, but..." She gestured toward the end table beside the couch. "The letter's in the drawer."

He set down his bowl and retrieved the envelope, his movements mechanical. The paper inside was thick and expensive, the kind lawyers used. He scanned the contents, his jaw tightening with every line.

The offer was good. More than good—it was generous—a little over fair market value for a property like this, with all its complications and restrictions.

And the name at the bottom was one he recognized.

"The Hendersons," he said flatly. "I took them out on an eco tour two months ago. They asked a lot of questions about the property. About how to manage the alligator farm with the wild habitat. How permits work and if the two worlds ever crossed. I thought they were just curious."

"They seem like nice people. They said they wanted to preserve the land, keep the natural habitat, including the moat, as well as continue with the commercial business, keeping the employees."

"That doesn't sound like a couple who wants to retire, and I'm not interested in selling."

"Trent—"

"Absolutely not." He shoved the letter back into the envelope and dropped it on the coffee table like it had burned him. "This land was my grandfather's. Then it was my father's. Then yours. And when you—" His voice cracked. He forced himself to continue. "When you pass, it'll be mine. I intend to keep it that way."

His mother was quiet for a long moment, watching him with an expression he couldn't quite read.

"And after you?" she asked gently. "What happens to it then?"

"What do you mean?"

"I mean you're not getting any younger, sweetheart. And unless you're planning on settling down and having children—" She paused, and that knowing smile crept back onto her face. "Which brings me back to Dove."

"We're not doing this again."

"She's perfect for you. Smart, capable, not afraid of hard work or hard truths. And she looks at you like—"

"I like Dove. I do. But we're not a couple. And I don't see us being anything other than friends."

His mother sighed, but she let it go. "I just worry about you being lonely. This place..." She looked around the room, at the photos on the walls, the furniture that had been here since before Trent was born, the shadows that gathered in the corners as the light outside faded. "It's full of ghosts. I don't want you to end up haunted."

"I love it here. I don't want to be anywhere else."

"But if you're not going to sell, and you're not going to have children—what happens to the land when you're gone?"

He'd thought about this—more than he'd ever admit. "We have managers who'd love to take over the commercial part. I have thought about parceling that off someday when I'm too old to deal with it." He shrugged. "The natural habitat, well, I'd talk to Fletcher. See if there's a way to have the National Park absorb it. Keep it protected. Or maybe Fallon could see if Fish and Wildlife could use it for educational purposes."

His mother's wrinkles seemed to soften, especially around the eyes. "That's a good plan. Responsible." She reached over and cupped his face in her palm, the way she used to when he was small. "I love you, you know. So much. And I am so proud of the man you've become."

His throat tightened. "I love you, too."

He shifted on the couch, wrapping his arm around her thin shoulders, pulling her gently against his side. She came willingly, her head finding its familiar spot against his chest.

"Shall we continue with that show? What episode were we on?" he asked, reaching for the remote.

"Fourteen, I think. The one where they finally find the treasure map."

"Right." He queued it up, the familiar theme music filling the room as the opening credits rolled. "This is the good one."

"They're all good."

"True."

She settled against him, her breathing slow and shallow, her body impossibly light against his side. On the screen, characters laughed and argued and chased adventure, living lives that would never end because they existed in a world where the worst thing that could happen was a cliffhanger.

Trent held his mother and watched without seeing,

his chest tight with a grief that hadn't fully arrived yet but was on its way—barreling toward him like a freight train he couldn't stop and couldn't outrun.

She had days left. Maybe a week if they were lucky.

He pressed a kiss to the top of her head and held on tighter.

Chapter Two

Three Weeks Later

The Spanish moss hung from the live oaks like mourning veils, swaying in a breeze too faint to feel.

Dove stood apart from the small cluster of people gathered around the fresh grave at the family burial site on Mallor's Landing, her black shirt already sticking to her skin in the late morning humidity. She rubbed her hands over her black jeans. It wasn't funeral attire, and she stood out like a northerner in the winter with pasty skin. But she didn't own a dress. And the other pants she had in her closet were either for workouts or camo, and Dove figured Linda would forgive her.

The minister had finished his final prayer ten minutes ago, but no one seemed ready to leave. They lingered the way people do at funerals—shuffling feet, murmured condolences, the awkward arithmetic of grief. Dove didn't do this part of life well. Hell, she didn't do the living part of life well. Hadn't in a long time, if ever.

The only place she'd ever felt like she'd fit in had been the Army, but even there, she'd had walls. Big ones.

An Army therapist once told her that she used sarcasm and sex to mask her feelings of being misunderstood, unaccepted, and alone. That she hid behind her weapon and her walls because the idea of being vulnerable was scarier than being killed.

Dove hadn't been able to argue any of those points.

Through the scope of her rifle, from an overwatch position three hundred feet away, she'd watched helplessly as her entire team got blown to hell. Her entire world had shattered. Everything she believed about herself crumbled into a big pile of dust. With no passion left for much of anything, she'd left the Army. Encouraged by her favorite uncle, a US Marshal, she took a job with the Aegis Network.

It was there that she began to piece herself back together and find new purpose.

But it was Calusa Cove and its people who showed her how to rebuild her life and tear down her walls. Across the grave, she watched Trent. He stood stiff with his broad shoulders square between his father's tombstone and the freshly dug grave for his mother. He filled out his dark shirt and slacks with thick muscles. His wavy hair touched the back of his neck, and he'd styled it, something he normally didn't bother with, but that his mother would have appreciated. His hands were fisted at his sides like he was holding himself together by sheer force of will. She wished Trent could find a way to punch through the layers of brick he'd formed around himself.

While the entire town had attended Linda Mallor's funeral service at the church, her final send-off was a small affair. A couple of dozen people—just those Trent considered family—milled around the gravesite. But she suspected that Mallor's Landing would be a revolving door for the next few hours.

A few more people strolled toward the access road to their vehicles. Only a few remained.

Buddy Ballard, Dove's boss, stood with his arm around his girlfriend, Fallon, her auburn hair vivid against the dark fabric of her dress. Juniper from Massey's Pub was there, dabbing at her eyes with a tissue. Silas Monroe stood alone near the back, hat in his hands, looking like he'd aged ten years since Dove had seen him last week.

And then there were the Hendersons. She doubted Trent had invited them to the gravesite, so she had to wonder why they were here. Hopefully, it wasn't what she suspected.

Trent stood at the head of the grave like something rooted, immovable as the cypress trees lining the water. He'd shaken hands and accepted embraces and said all the right things, but it was clear in his gaze that he was somewhere else entirely. Someplace no one could follow.

Dove watched Buddy lean in and say something to him, watched Fallon rise on her toes to press a kiss to his cheek. Trent nodded at whatever they said, his expression unchanging. Then they stepped away, Buddy catching Dove's eye and giving her a small nod as they passed.

She was about to go to Trent when the Hendersons approached.

Dove hadn't ever met them before and only recognized them because Trent had pointed them out once before. They were in their mid-fifties, maybe. Well-dressed in that understated way that whispered money without shouting it. The woman had silver-blonde hair swept back in an expensive-looking updo. The man wore a suit that fit too well to be off the rack.

Dove stayed where she was, watching. The woman spoke first, reaching out to touch Trent's arm. He accepted the contact stiffly, his shoulders drawing back almost imperceptibly. The man said something. Trent just stood there. Dove had seen warmer responses from a closed door.

That was enough for Dove to move.

She crossed the distance between them, her boots sinking slightly into the soft earth with each step. She came up beside Trent and slipped her hand into the crook of his elbow, a casual gesture that was anything but.

"Hey," she said softly.

Trent smiled. It was weak, but it was something.

The couple turned to look at her. Up close, the woman's smile was pleasant but Dove had learned over the years that meant nothing. The man's handshake, when he offered it, was a little too firm. Like he was trying to prove something. Or maybe make a statement.

"Beau Henderson," he said. "And this is my wife, Emma. We were just offering our condolences to Trent.

Linda was always so kind to us whenever we visited Calusa Cove. She was such a sweet woman."

"That she was," Dove agreed.

"We live a few towns northwest," Emma added. "But we've been coming here for years. Such a charming community. But I don't think we've ever met."

"I'm sorry." Trent cleared his throat. "This is my friend, Dove Quinn."

"It's nice to meet you," Dove said. "Though, the circumstances suck."

"Exactly what my mom would've said." Trent patted her hand.

"A sense of humor is a good thing," Emma said, her smile faltering slightly. "We should let you get back to your guests. But—" She paused, exchanging a glance with her husband. "If you ever change your mind, our offer still stands. No pressure, of course. Just know the door is open."

They walked away before Trent could respond, picking their way through the headstones toward a silver sedan parked on the access road.

Dove waited until they were out of earshot. "They didn't just offer to buy Mallor's Landing again, did they?"

Trent exhaled through his nose, watching the Hendersons' car pull away. "I believe they did just that."

"Did you even invite them here?"

"Nope." He ran a hand over his freshly shaven face. A rare thing for Trent. He always sported a little scruff. "My mom thought they were nice." He shook his head.

"But she's rolling over right now knowing they just showed up and did that."

"I'll look into them."

"Don't waste your time. They can offer all they want, but my answer will never change." He leaned in and kissed her cheek. "Besides, I've got bigger fish to fry."

"What does that mean?"

"Fucking Karl," Trent mumbled. "Asshole texted me this morning asking me to meet him later. Says it's important. That we need to talk, and that I should remember he saved my life."

"The shady dude you used to be friends with?"

"Yup." Trent sucked in a breath and let it out with an aggressive sigh.

"How did he save your life?"

"Python wrangling when I was a senior in high school. I got cocky. Was showing off and I didn't realize there was another snake. It got the upper hand, and Karl saved my sorry ass." He took a step back and planted his hands on his hips. "He likes to hold it over my head like I owe him. He knows I was burying my mom today, and yet, all he can think about is whatever get-rich scheme he has going that involves me doing something illegal. Not gonna happen. I have half a mind to meet him just to punch him in the face."

"Last thing you need is the police chief tossing you in lock-up for the night."

"You're right, but planting my fist in Karl's face would feel good." Trent ran his fingers through his hair.

"For about thirty seconds," Dove said. "I can look into

him. Maybe tail him for a day and see what he's got cooking and give that information to—"

"You're sweet, but it's not worth the effort. Karl will go away on his own. He always does if you ignore him long enough. It's nothing."

Dove opened her mouth to argue, but something caught her eye. Movement in the cypress stand at the edge of the cemetery. A shape that didn't belong—too vertical to be a tree, too still to be an animal.

"If it's nothing," she said slowly, "then why is there someone watching us from those trees?"

Trent followed her gaze. His body went from tense to coiled in the space of a heartbeat.

"If that's Karl, I'll...Stay here," he said.

"I do love it when you get all alpha on me, but I'm a much better shot. Besides, dealing with shadows lurking in the dark is what I do for a living."

They moved together, crossing the cemetery in long strides. The figure in the trees seemed to realize he'd been spotted. He shifted, started to retreat—slowly at first, like he was trying to convince himself he hadn't been seen.

Then he bolted.

"Shit." Dove took off running.

The man had a head start, but she was fast. Trent was faster, his long legs eating up the distance, dodging bushes and low-hanging branches. But the stranger knew where he was going. He cut through the cypress stand like he'd mapped it beforehand, his dark clothes making him hard to track in the dappled shadows.

By the time they burst through the tree line onto the dirt access road on the other side of the private cemetery, he was already behind the wheel of a dark SUV. The engine roared to life. Tires spat gravel.

Dove squinted at the license plate as the vehicle fishtailed away. "Can you read it?"

"No." Trent breathed hard, his hands on his hips. "Looks like it's covered in mud, and that's not Karl's vehicle. He drives a white pick-up."

The SUV disappeared around a bend, swallowed by the trees.

"But would he have known about this road?" Dove asked. "I've been out here a dozen times, and I didn't know there was access so close to the water."

"Not many people do. We've always kept this part of the property private, but it connects to a county road about a mile east. No gate on that end, which is why I put one here." Trent stared at the empty road, his expression dark.

"Could or would Karl have hired someone?"

"It's possible, but Karl doesn't like to spend his own money on things, and why would he? What would he have to gain by sending someone to spy on me?"

"If he's trying to get you to do work for him, or someone else, it could be that he's trying to gather intel to use against you."

"I suppose," Trent said. "Let's go check out the gates."

They jogged back to Trent's Jeep—the old one he used for knocking around the property, more rust than paint at this point. He cranked the engine, and they bounced down the access road toward the main gate.

"I wanted to thank you again for all that you've done." Trent shifted the manual transmission and quickly glanced in her direction. "I don't think I could've gotten through these last few weeks without you."

"You would've been fine. You had Fallon, Buddy, and so many other friends." Dove had done her best to make herself useful. It wasn't that she didn't feel valued as a friend, she did. But Trent had grown up in Calusa Cove, where Dove often still felt like an interloper. Though, she was trying to change that narrative. This was the first place she'd lived where she wanted to make it last.

Not to mention somewhere along the way, she'd developed feelings for Trent.

"Maybe, but you've really been there for me, and considering that things were awkward for a bit, I wanted you to know how much it's meant to me."

"Don't think twice about it," she said. "It's what friends do."

Trent slowed the Jeep, downshifting to second. "The gate's open." He rolled the Jeep to a stop and sat there for a long moment, staring at the chain-link fence. "That padlock should be securing the gate. No one knows that combination except me and my mom—and before you ask, no, I never gave it to Karl." Trent pulled out his cell and tapped on the screen.

"What are you doing?"

"Texting the weekend manager at Mallor's Landing Alligator Center," he said. "While those buildings are clear across the other side of the property, and none of my employees have the combo, I need to ask them if they've noticed anything strange."

"Do you trust all your employees?"

He jerked his head back. "Yeah. All locals. I don't have many, but the ones I do have, I've known my entire life. A few have worked here longer than I've been alive."

She raised her hands. "Just asking." Deciding to move on to a different set of questions, she asked, "When's the last time you changed the combo?"

He was quiet for a beat too long. "Never."

"Not a great security system. Is there any way Karl could've guessed it?" she asked, because he was the best suspect. And because focusing on being an Aegis Network Agent kept her mind from spiraling over some of the dumbass choices she'd made the first few months she'd lived in this quaint small town.

The biggest one was treating Trent like a good time boy, only needing him for sex. Of course, when they first met, she hadn't a clue what emotional attachment was.

"It's random numbers." He rubbed a hand over his face. "They don't mean a damn thing. No sentimental value. No birthdays, anniversaries, nothing like that."

"Is it possible your mom gave it to someone? Maybe recently?"

He laughed, but there was no humor in it. "Her last few days, she wasn't exactly coherent. She'd talk to people who weren't there. Thought she saw my dad once —said he looked good. Healthy. Said he came to check on her, to say goodbye, and that he was sorry." His voice caught slightly, then steadied. "She also thought I was still living with Fallon, so take that for what it's worth."

Dove reached over and put her hand on his arm. He didn't pull away. "I'm going to dig into this," she said. "The Hendersons. That guy in the trees. Karl. All of it."

"It's not—"

"I'm doing it regardless, so you might as well not waste your breath arguing." She squeezed his arm. "But you need to change this combination. Today. And you need to call Dawson."

"I just buried my mother." The words came out raw. Scraped from someplace deep inside. "She was the last family I had. Can I have one goddamn day before I have to deal with the chief of police? "He stopped, jaw clenching.

"I know." She kept her voice soft. "But someone was watching you, today. Someone who knew how to get onto your property without being seen, and maybe it was Karl. And while the Hendersons might be a nice couple, I don't like how they keep asking to buy Mallor's Landing."

He stared out the windshield at the open gate, at the empty road beyond. His hands gripped the steering wheel hard enough to turn his knuckles white. "Fine," he said finally. "I'll call Dawson. But not today. Tomorrow."

"Today."

"Sometimes, you're worse than my mother. Definitely worse than Fallon."

"I take that as a compliment."

"I suppose, in a way, it is." He turned to look at her, and for a moment she saw everything he was holding back—the grief, the exhaustion, the anger that had nowhere to go. He looked like a man who'd been hollowed out and was running on nothing but fumes and stubbornness. "Okay," he said quietly. "Today."

She nodded and settled back into her seat, keeping her hand on his arm.

They sat there for a while longer, the Jeep idling, the gate hanging open like an unanswered question. Somewhere in the distance, a gator bellowed.

Dove didn't know what was coming. But she knew it wasn't good.

And she knew, with a certainty that settled into her bones like cold water, that whatever had started today wasn't going to end easily.

Chapter Three

Three Weeks Later

Trent had been nursing the same beer for forty minutes, and it had gone warm a while ago.

He didn't care. Drinking wasn't the point. Sitting here, in public, surrounded by people—that was the point. That was the promise he'd made to his mother right before she took her last breath.

Try harder. Be better. Less sharp-edged. Less alone.

Some nights, the promise fit like a sweatshirt. Tonight, it dragged like a blade against bone. Not because he didn't want to crawl out of the grief that had swallowed him, because he did. He was tired, and the last thing he wanted was to slip back into living on the fringe between right and wrong like he had for so many years after his father had died.

However, the town notice sat on the table in front of him—taunting him—creased from where he'd folded and unfolded it a dozen times. He'd found it tacked to the bulletin board outside the general store this morning, right between a flyer for the church bake sale and a lost dog poster.

NOTICE OF PUBLIC HEARING: Sovereign Resources Inc. hereby provides notice of intent to file for mining permits in the Calusa Cove watershed region. Proposed limestone extraction operations would be located in Sections 12, 13, and 24 of Township 53 South...

Section 24. That was right next to Mallor's Landing. That was his home.

Trent had read the notice so many times that the words had lost their meaning. Mining permits. Limestone extraction. Environmental impact assessment. It all sounded so clean, so clinical, as if they were only talking about paperwork instead of blasting and excavation, and artificial lakes carved into land that had been wild since before humans had a name for it.

He knew the impact of mining. He'd seen the aftermath up near Lake Okeechobee—moonscapes where wetlands used to be, water tables poisoned, wildlife scattered or dead. The companies always promised minimal impact. They always promised restoration. And then they took what they wanted and left the land bleeding.

Bad enough he'd just buried his mother. Now, some corporate bastards wanted to gut the only thing he had left—the only connection he had to his father. The very same thing his father died trying to protect.

Worse—it brought all the guilt he'd carried for the past twenty years to the surface like heartburn collecting in the center of his chest.

He took a slow swig and scanned the bar. Massey's Pub hadn't changed since he'd been a kid. Same warped floorboards groaning under every step. Same ceiling fans chopping through air too thick to move on its own. Same neon Budweiser sign buzzing in the window like a dying insect, throwing red light across the bottles lined up behind the bar.

The place smelled like it always did—spilled beer soaked into wood, fried grouper from the kitchen, and underneath it all, the river. Always the river. You couldn't escape it in Calusa Cove. The water got into everything. Your clothes, your skin, your dreams—though he wasn't sure he knew what he wanted anymore.

Trent sat at a high-top near the back wall, one shoulder angled toward the door out of habit. As he scanned the bar, contemplating whether he was actually going to try his hand at being social or not, his gaze landed on the Hendersons' three tables away.

Shit. This couple was going to drive him crazy. They'd left him alone after his mother's funeral, but two days ago, they decided to send him a letter with another offer to purchase Mallor's Landing. They tried to sweeten the deal by suggesting he stay on as the alligator farm's manager. As if being employed on his family's land was enough of an incentive.

Beau eased from his seat and sauntered across the bar. "Good evening, Trent. How are you doing?"

"Fine. Yourself?"

"Just came down for a long weekend. We're staying at Harvey's Cabins. What a wonderful little establishment."

"Can't go wrong there." Trent took a sip of his beer, reminding himself that his mother would expect him to be kind. That being a dick got him nowhere in life.

"I'm sorry to bother you, but we were wondering if you've had a chance to look over our offer."

And there it was—pushy asshole. "I don't mean to be rude, but no amount of money or job opportunities would make me want to sell my home—or my business. I'm sorry."

"I hope you'll take another look." Beau stretched out his arm toward Trent. "It's a good offer."

"The answer will always be no." Trent took his hand and shook it. "Have a nice evening."

Beau returned to his table and hopefully, that was the last he'd hear from them regarding the sale of his home.

Juniper's laugh rang out from behind the bar, sharp and bright, cutting through the low murmur of conversation like a bell through static. She stood with her elbows planted on the scarred wood, leaning into an argument with Fallon, Buddy, and Sterling that had apparently been going on long enough to draw an audience.

"I'm just saying," Juniper, the owner of the pub, said, jabbing a finger at Buddy, "you don't mess with a name that's part of a town's history. Massey's means something."

Buddy Ballard, an Aegis Network operative and Fallon Reeves' boyfriend, lifted his beer, unimpressed. "Massey's means a criminal nobody wants to remember and a sign that's been repainted so many times you can't read it from the road."

"It's got character." Juniper crossed her arms.

"It's got termites." Sterling laughed at his own joke. For a confident, badass former CIA agent now employed by the Aegis Network, Sterling lost his ability to act like an intelligent man whenever he was around Juniper.

Sterling shifted against the bar. "I don't understand why you don't rename the place Juniper's Pub. You own it now. And it's a cool name. Fits in with the vibe around Calusa Cove."

"It is a good name." Buddy smiled. "Besides, some have already started calling it Juniper's."

"Especially Sterling," Fallon teased.

Trent didn't laugh. On another night, he would've. He'd lean against that bar, engrossed in conversation. But the notice sat in front of him like a summons, and the beer had gone sour in his stomach.

He watched the group from his corner, something tight and nameless sitting in his chest. The four of them looked easy together. Comfortable. Like people who hadn't spent the last three weeks learning how to breathe around a gaping hole in their life.

Fallon caught his eye across the room. Her smile was soft, but questioning. As if to say, *Are you okay over there?*

He lifted his bottle a half-inch and smiled.

She pursed her lips, which meant she was worried. However, she knew him well enough to know that if he were about to lose it, she'd be the first person he called. Fallon turned back to Juniper without pushing, and he was grateful.

However, he wasn't thrilled about the reporter making her way through the maze of people and heading right for his table.

Stacey had a sweet smile and kind eyes, but nothing about Stacey was genuine. Everything about her was a mask, and she didn't care about anyone but herself. It shouldn't shock him that she hadn't managed to find her ticket out of Calusa Cove. At first, she was all about her career. All about that big network job. Now, it was about finding a rich husband so she didn't have to work anymore, and she could settle down and have children.

"Good evening, Trent." Stacey leaned against the table, which pressed her breasts together. She tapped her finger on the notice. "Isn't that exciting? I've heard such wonderful things about Sovereign Resources. They're going to bring a lot of jobs to our community, and I heard that Congressman Dutton plans on making an appearance. I'm hoping to get an interview with him."

"Good for you." He folded the notice and shoved it in his back pocket. "If you'll excuse me, I'm getting ready to head out."

"You don't sound too excited."

"Because I'm not," he said. "I don't mean to be rude, but I don't have the time for this."

"You get a pass because of all that you've been through." She stood tall. "Take care of yourself." She turned and disappeared into the crowd.

He pushed aside the warm beer and was reaching for his wallet when the door swung open, and in walked Dove.

She stood silhouetted in the doorway for half a breath, doing that thing she always did, scanning the room corner to corner before letting herself settle.

Dove spotted Buddy and Sterling first, lifted a hand in greeting. She wore form-fitting jeans, a dark tank top, and a killer smile. She was one of the most beautiful women he'd ever laid eyes on. And she was smart and funny—everything he admired and almost everything he might want in a partner.

But she had an aversion to reptiles, and those were not only his bread and butter, they were also his passion.

Her gaze swept the back wall. She paused, smiled, and stood for a long moment without moving a muscle.

Trent had spent months telling himself the thing between them was over. Finished. Nothing more than a few dozen nights that didn't mean anything and a mutual agreement to walk away before it got complicated.

His body hadn't gotten the memo.

Dove headed straight for him.

A man followed.

Tall. Sixty, maybe sixty-five, but carrying it well. Silver at his temples, steel in his posture. A faint hitch in his gait—so slight most people wouldn't notice, but Trent did.

And his stomach dropped.

"Hey," Dove said.

"Hey, yourself."

Her mouth curved into a playful smile. "You look like hell. More than usual."

"Been a day." He fell into the easy half-teasing. He

was sure he didn't look like his normal self, and his mood had been crappy for the last few hours.

Dove's hand came up to rest on the older man's arm. "Trent, this is my uncle. U.S. Marshal Aaron Slade."

"Outside of this one, everyone calls me Slade," her uncle said, offering his hand.

Trent shook it because his mother had raised him with manners, even when he didn't feel like using them. "I remember you," he blurted out. "You came to my father's funeral." Trent's heart pounded behind his ribs as the guilt rose higher.

Twenty years ago, Trent had no idea what he'd seen. All he knew was that he'd witnessed two men who should be on opposing sides of the table having a secret meeting, and it looked friendly. More than friendly. He told his dad, and next thing Trent knew, his father was involved in a federal case as a witness. A few months later, he was dead, and Trent couldn't help but feel as though it was his fault.

Dove's eyes widened slightly, cutting between them.

Slade nodded slowly. "I'm surprised you remember—you were young."

"I was fourteen." Trent kept his voice even, but something hot and old was coiling in his chest. "Old enough to remember the man who told my mother that the marshals service would find whoever leaked my father's name as a key witness before a trial even began. Old enough to notice when that promise turned out to be empty."

"That leak had nothing to do with your father's

death. Only the unraveling of the case." Slade didn't flinch, nor did he look away. "However, we never stopped looking. The investigation—"

"Went nowhere." Trent did his best to keep his voice from rising. "Twenty years of no answers."

"It's not for lack of trying—especially on my part."

"Maybe not, but we weren't ever told anything." The words came out sharper than he'd intended. He took a breath, forced his shoulders to relax.

Slade was quiet for a long moment. "I failed your father." He held Trent's gaze steadily. "I've carried that ever since. It doesn't change anything, but I want you to know that there isn't a day that goes by that I don't think about what happened. About what I could have done differently. And since I'm here in Calusa Cove, I'd love the chance to sit down and have a conversation with you."

Trent wanted to say something sharp. Something cutting. Something about how that didn't change the fact that Jack Mallor had trusted the marshals service and they'd gotten him killed.

"It was a long time ago," Trent said. The words felt like stones in his mouth. "I honestly don't want to rehash it. It's in the past. But I do have a question for you."

"I'm happy to answer it. Could we do it over a cup of coffee?"

"I just want to know your thoughts on Garrett Dutton," Trent said.

"I'd rather—"

"It's not an essay question. Just a general impression is all I need." Trent resisted the urge to fold his arms across his chest.

"He was a decent marshal, and I worked with him on a couple of cases. Your father's included. He always had political dreams, and he chased them, but I didn't know him well. Is there a reason you're asking about him?"

"He's running for Senate, and one of his campaign points has to do with limestone mining, which could affect Calusa Cove and my property."

"I did hear that." Slade nodded. "Why don't we sit down—"

"Slade, you old dog. Didn't know you were coming down this weekend." Buddy appeared at Slade's elbow, oblivious to the tension.

"Surprise visit," Slade said, turning away from Trent with a look that indicated he wasn't done. "Wanted to see what kind of trouble my niece has been getting into, especially because she hasn't invited me since she moved here from Jacksonville."

"I'd be lost without her," Buddy said. "Mostly."

"She certainly keeps us on our toes." Sterling shook Slade's hand.

"That's frightening." Slade looped an arm around Dove's shoulder, kissing her temple as a father might.

They fell into easy conversation—shop talk, war stories, the kind of shorthand that people developed when they'd worked adjacent to the same world for long enough. Trent caught fragments of it—old cases, mutual acquaintances, jurisdictional headaches that had apparently been funny in retrospect.

He let the words wash over him without engaging as Buddy, Sterling, and Slade made their way back to the bar where Juniper and Fallon were sipping wine and laughing.

Dove stayed.

"You doing okay?" she asked quietly.

"Good days and bad. Today was somewhere in between." He hadn't seen much of Dove since the funeral. Since she'd spent the night at his house. Since they once again agreed they were better off as friends. That time, it was him waking up in the morning, sitting on the edge of the bed, handing her a cup of coffee, and telling her he was sorry. That he shouldn't have taken advantage of or used her like that when he was hurting.

In usual Dove fashion, she shrugged it off as if she knew exactly what he was doing and was a willing participant in his need to bury his pain in human flesh, which just made him an asshole. But she kissed his cheek, got out of bed, and made him pancakes like it didn't matter.

Only, it did.

"You were a little hard on my uncle."

Trent picked at the label on his beer bottle, not meeting her eyes. "I understand my father's death was an accident. But you have to understand it was also all over the news. Federal witness name leaked before the case fell apart. Investigation launched. Lots of handwringing and promises made to find who did it, because it was that leak, along with the destruction of evidence, and the death of another witness that destroyed the case. But then the news cycle moved on, the investigation went cold, and my mother spent the next twenty years wondering which of the people who'd sworn to protect her husband decided they didn't want this case to go to trial. And now one of them waltzes into town while an—"

"It wasn't my uncle."

"I never said it was. I'm just telling you what happened and where my head's at."

She stepped closer—close enough that he could smell her shampoo—something floral and clean that didn't belong in a place that smelled like beer and river mud. "My uncle never told me the details about the accident that nearly put him on desk duty. The one that's haunted him for twenty years. He warned me when I joined the Army that the job had costs."

"My father was one of his costs." Trent shrugged, but the motion was stiff. "My mother liked him. Appreciated his presence at the funeral. She never believed he was the one who leaked the name. But every time I think about that day, I just..." He shook his head. "The system was supposed to protect my dad. Instead, someone within that system betrayed him and everyone else involved in that case. And no one ever paid for it." And that was the biggest reason he'd kept what he'd seen to himself for two decades. Not to mention, he wasn't even sure of what he saw.

Dove reached out and curled her fingers around his bicep, her grip warm through his shirt. It was a small touch. An innocent touch. But it sent heat spreading through his chest in a way that had nothing to do with the humid air. "I'm sorry," she said. "For what happened to your father. For what your family went through. And for ambushing you with my uncle without warning."

"You didn't know."

"I should have. I knew my uncle worked in South Florida witness protection for most of his career. I knew your father died while in witness protection when you were young. I should have put it together."

"It's not exactly cocktail conversation. 'Hey, did your uncle happen to be involved in my father's death?' doesn't come up naturally."

Her mouth twitched despite the heaviness of the moment. "I'll add it to my list of icebreakers."

"Right after 'do you have any twelve-foot alligators I should know about?'"

"That one's already on the list."

The tension in his shoulders eased a fraction. This was what Dove did—pushed until he pushed back, then kept pushing until the pushing turned into something that almost felt like a conversation.

It was annoying as hell. It was also the only thing that had worked in weeks.

"I'm fine," he said. "Or I will be. I just need time to figure out what fine looks like now."

"You don't have to figure it out alone."

"I'm not. I've got the gators."

"Reptiles don't count."

"Tell them that. They'll be offended." He winked, then touched his back pocket, where the folded notice burned a hole in his ass. "Besides, I've got bigger problems."

"Are you talking about the Hendersons? Because it hasn't gone unnoticed that they're right over there."

"No. Not them. Though they are a little relentless. But I think I finally have them understanding that Mallor's Landing is not for sale."

"I hope so," Dove said. "I want you to know that I still haven't given up on finding the intruder from your mother's funeral. I've been looking into Karl. He's shady, but for some reason people like him."

"He's got charisma." Trent chuckled. "Dawson hasn't been able to find a single clue, and nothing else has happened since—including the fact I haven't heard from Karl, although that doesn't mean anything."

"The whole thing still bothers me. People don't show up to spy on a funeral and then duck and run."

He pulled out the flyer and handed it to her. "I'm more concerned about this."

"What is this about?"

"Blasting. Excavation. Destruction of the Glades." The words came out flat. "They'll gut the whole ecosystem. Kill everything that can't run fast enough. Then they'll leave, and whoever's still around will spend the next fifty years trying to undo the damage. And a former US Marshal who was on my father's case, now running for office, is promoting it."

"Wait. First, aren't the Everglades protected from this? And how do you know this politician protected your dad?"

"My mom told me one night when Stacey, the vulture, was reporting on it. I don't like it, never have, but now they want to do it right next to Mallor's landing."

"What can you do?"

"There's a public hearing in a few days. The company will lay out its plan. Talk about environmental impact assessments. Economic growth. The overall need for what they are doing. They'll probably hand in their request for permits and all that bullshit." He glanced around the bar. At all the people he'd known most of his life. The people who loved this town and no matter how poor and backwards Calusa Cove was, they still wanted it to stay exactly the same. "I'll fight them. I don't care if it takes everything I have. They're not touching the Glades, or anything near my land."

"Good."

He blinked. "Good?"

"You needed something to grab a hold of and fight for." She squeezed his arm once, then let go. "Grief is easier when you've got somewhere to put the anger."

He stared at her. This woman, who hated gators and loved guns, and somehow kept showing up exactly when he needed someone to push back against.

"That's surprisingly wise," he said.

"I have my moments."

"Rare as they are."

"Watch it, Mallor."

Dove's expression eased as she leaned into him again. "I stopped by your house yesterday."

Trent blinked, and his pulse did a little dance in his

wrist. "Really? Keep doing that and I might think you have an ulterior motive."

"You've been withdrawn, and I promised your mom I'd check on you." She pursed her lips. "So, get your mind out of the gutter."

"Kind of hard not to go there," he said slowly. "I mean, you don't like coming to my place. With the water. And the gators."

She grimaced. "They hissed at me."

"They hiss at everyone."

"Not like that. One of them did that thing where they puff up and make that sound—"

"Bellowing."

"It was terrifying."

"It was a greeting."

"Sounded more like a threat."

"Dolly likes you. She just has a weird way of showing it." Trent missed these back-and-forth exchanges with Dove.

Dove stared at him like he'd grown a second head. "You're insane."

"Probably." He drained the last of his warm beer, grimacing at the taste. "But I'm insane in a place where the gators know me, and I know them. That's worth something." Trent set the empty bottle down and pulled a twenty from his wallet. "I should head out."

Dove's eyes went to the door, then back to him. "It's early."

"Early for you. Late for me. I've got feeding time at dawn, and Dolly gets cranky when I'm behind schedule."

"Crankier than the bellowing?"

"Much." He leaned in and kissed her cheek, letting his lips linger a moment longer than strictly necessary. "I appreciate you checking up on me. I really do. But I'm hanging tough."

"I know." She didn't move out of his path. "Call me. Tomorrow. Or the next day. Just... let me know you're okay."

He hesitated. There were a dozen reasons not to promise her anything. They'd agreed to keep a distance between them. They'd agreed that whatever they'd been was over after he'd gotten shot. Then again, after his mother took ill. And again, after the funeral.

"I will." He walked away before Dove could say anything else, or he suggested she follow him home.

The parking lot was half-empty, his truck sitting alone under a light that flickered every few seconds, moths throwing themselves against it in suicidal spirals.

He stood on the wooden porch for a moment, letting his eyes adjust. Letting the noise of the bar fade behind him. Letting the silence of Calusa Cove settle into his bones the way it always did, familiar and strange at the same time.

His mother had loved this town. Loved the water, the birds, the way the sunset turned the sky into fire. She'd spent her whole life here, raised him here, buried his father here.

And now she was buried here, too.

His father had died trying to do the right thing. He'd fought for what was right and lost everything. Now, some faceless corporation wanted to take what was left—the land Jack Mallor had loved, the home he'd built, the legacy he'd left behind.

Trent wasn't his father. He wasn't noble or brave or willing to sacrifice himself for abstract principles.

But he was stubborn as hell, and he'd be damned if he let anyone destroy the Everglades without a fight.

Chapter Four

The road to Mallor's Landing curved through the Everglades like a scar.

On either side, sawgrass stretched toward the horizon, silver-tipped under a moon that hung fat and low over the wetlands. The sky was enormous here, unpolluted by town lights, thick with stars that most people never saw anymore.

Trent let the night air wash over him. It smelled like water and mud and rotting vegetation—the perfume of the swamp, his mother had called it. She'd loved that smell. Said it reminded her she was alive. His throat tightened like it always did when he thought about these things.

The river appeared on his left, black as oil, its surface broken by the occasional ripple of something moving beneath. Gators. Fish. Snakes. The usual residents.

His headlights cut tunnels through the darkness, illuminating the road ten feet at a time as he moved further away from civilization and deeper into the swamp. Trees closed in, cypress and mangrove crowding the edges, their branches reaching over the pavement like fingers.

The gate to Mallor's Landing appeared out of the dark.

Trent slowed, his headlights washing over the chain-link fence, the rusted padlock, the hand-painted sign that had been there since his father put it up thirty years ago.

Mallor's Landing. Private Property. Trespassers Will Be Eaten.

His father's sense of humor. The gators didn't actually eat trespassers.

Usually.

He pulled up to the gate, shifted into park, and stepped out to deal with the lock. The metal was still warm from the day's heat. He worked the combination by feel, the way he'd done a thousand times before, and pulled the chain free.

The gate swung open with a creak that echoed across the water.

And something answered.

Trent froze, one hand on the gate.

The sound had come from inside the property. A low, guttural rumble that he felt more than heard—the kind of sound that vibrated in your chest and made ancient parts of your brain sit up and pay attention.

Gator hissing.

He stood motionless, straining to hear over the thrum of insects and the distant slap of water. The moat that surrounded the main house was a hundred yards ahead, invisible in the darkness but present in his mind like a map drawn from memory. A few adult alligators had made that moat their home, and a few others visited frequently. He knew each of them by name, by size, by temperament.

They weren't supposed to be hissing like this.

Trent got back in the truck and pulled slowly through the gate. Dawson Ridge, the local police chief, was constantly on him to replace the old fence with a new, modern, motorized one. Not only did Trent not have the funds, but he also didn't see the point. The gators and a well-placed, cheap security system were enough.

The gravel drive crunched under his tires, impossibly loud in the silence. His headlights swept across the palmetto scrub, catching the glint of something small that darted into the underbrush. Possum. Maybe a raccoon.

A light. Thin and sharp, cutting through the darkness near the water's edge. Then another, sweeping in a slow arc across the far side of the moat.

Flashlights.

Trent killed his headlights.

The darkness crashed back in, absolute and immediate, and for a moment, he couldn't see anything at all. He sat motionless, letting his eyes adjust, letting the shapes of the world resolve out of the black.

The house emerged first, a darker bulk against the night sky. Then the outbuildings—the equipment shed, the feeding station, the observation platform he'd built three summers ago when he'd started taking tourists out for educational programs.

And there, near the water, two figures. Moving carefully along the bank, flashlight beams swinging low, avoiding the house.

Trent eased his truck off the gravel and onto the grass that bordered the drive. He shifted into park and cut the engine.

Retrieving his pistol from the glovebox without taking his eyes off the distant figures, he checked the magazine by feel. Full. He chambered a round and stepped out of the truck, easing the door closed until the latch caught with a soft click.

The night pressed in around him, thick with moisture and the electric hum of insects. Somewhere in the moat, a gator slid into the water with a sound like a whispered curse.

Trent pulled his phone from his pocket, shielding the screen's glow with his body, and dialed Dawson's number.

"I've got company, and they weren't invited," he said without preamble when the line connected.

"How many?" Dawson's voice was sharp, and he didn't ask questions about why Trent was calling.

"Two that I can see. Maybe more."

"Location?"

"East side of the moat. Near the old dock."

"On my way. Eighteen minutes."

The line went dead.

A lot could happen in eighteen minutes.

Trent hesitated, thumb hovering over the screen. Then he pulled up another number and hit dial.

Dove answered on the second ring. "Trent? What—"

"How far away are you?" he asked, cutting her off.

"Truthfully, not far."

"ETA?"

"Six minutes from the gate. Why?"

"Someone's on my property." He kept his voice low, barely above a whisper. "Turn your lights off when you come down the road to my house."

"Pedal to the metal."

He almost smiled. "Gate's open. I'm on foot, east side, near the cypress stand. Find me before you do anything stupid."

"That's my line."

He hung up.

Six minutes. Better than eighteen. But still too long to just wait. And then there was the question of why she was so close with the only answer being that she was on her way to see him. That meant she was breaking their agreement of keeping things in the friend zone.

Again.

He'd deal with that later.

Trent shifted. He'd been walking this property since he could walk at all. Every tree, every dip, every patch of soft ground that would suck at your boots—he knew them all. He circled wide, staying in the shadow of the cypress stand that bordered the eastern edge of the moat, keeping the figures in sight.

They'd stopped near the old dock, the one his father had built for fishing and his mother had used for watching sunsets. The one that Trent couldn't take down or replace, even though he'd built a new one last year.

One of the intruders crouched at the water's edge while the other stood watch, flashlight beam scanning in regular sweeps.

If it was fucking Karl, Trent might toss him in the moat and let him fend off the gators one by one.

Trent found a position behind a thick cypress trunk and settled in to watch.

The figures were talking, voices too low to make out words. The one crouching had something in his hands—a bag, but Trent couldn't be sure. It looked like he was reaching his hand into the bag every so often and bending over, but again, Trent couldn't tell. Maybe they were leaving gator food to keep them occupied, which was the most logical explanation—but they were going about it all wrong.

Four minutes passed. Maybe five.

Then he heard it—the soft squish of footsteps in the wet ground approaching from behind. Moving carefully, but not carefully enough.

Trent didn't turn. "You walk like a city girl, not a combat sniper."

"Yeah, well, when I don't want to get shot by a trigger-happy snake wrangler, I announce myself." Dove materialized out of the darkness beside him, dropping to one knee. Her weapon already drawn. "Jesus, why is the air always so thick out here? Smells like a monkey's ass."

"It's called nature. You've spent too many nights in the jungle not to know the difference."

"Not sure what's worse. That or dry fucking desert."
She peered around the trunk, assessing. "Two of them?"

"That I've seen."

"Armed?"

"Unknown. They haven't drawn on the gators yet, so either they're stupid or they're packing something that makes them confident. One of them is carrying something. It could be gator food, which is really dumb because that could get them killed if they don't know what they're doing."

"I'm surprised you haven't lost a limb," Dove said softly. "Plan?"

"Dawson's maybe twelve minutes out. We wait, let him come in from the road, box them against the water."

"And if they run or do something stupid before he gets here?"

"Then we confront and have a conversation about trespassing."

She cut him a look. "Not a great plan."

"Best I've got on short notice."

In the moat, the water rippled and gently lapped against the grass.

Trent knew the sound before he saw her—the distinctive movement of Dolly cutting through the water, twelve feet of prehistoric murder gliding toward the disturbance at the bank. She'd been living on his land for thirty years after being injured. But she knew the difference between food and not-food, between threat and nuisance.

Tonight, she seemed undecided.

One of the figures noticed the ripple and swung his

flashlight toward the water. The beam caught Dolly's eyes, two orange-red embers floating just above the surface, fixed on the strangers with the patient hunger of fifty million years of evolution.

"Jesus Christ," one of them said loudly.

The other figure grabbed his arm. "I wasn't told there would be so many alligators."

"It's the Everglades. Did you think there'd be bunnies back here?" the other man said.

"That thing's looking at me."

"Then stop looking back. Move."

They continued on the far side of the property, where the tree line thickened and the darkness deepened. Their flashlights danced in the dark. Trent squinted, trying to get a better look at what they were doing with that damn bag, but the night swallowed them.

"I'm losing sight of them. We need to shift position," Trent said.

"Alright." She crawled from behind the tree—breaking from cover, cutting a sharp angle toward the water. Trent quickly followed.

He and Dove moved fast through the underbrush. Her years of training were evident in how she placed her feet and kept low.

The figures were forty yards ahead now, heading for the tree line that angled toward the narrow channel that looped through the back edge of the property and into the freshwater table.

He shifted his gaze toward the dock. A small boat

was tied at the end. Most people didn't dare come down Mallor's Twist, a reservoir of marsh and reptile.

Dove rushed ahead, closing the gap.

All of a sudden, the men stopped moving and leaned over the waterline.

Trent and Dove froze for a moment, crouching down, holding position.

"What the hell are they doing?" Dove whispered.

"No clue." Trent squinted and adjusted to the darkness, but all he saw were shadows.

"Jesus, do you see all those eyes in the water?" one of the men asked.

"Yeah. Let's get the fuck out of here. We did our job, now let's go collect that money before we die."

Both men turned and headed back toward the old dock, which was right between them and Trent and Dove.

"I guess we're going into confrontation mode," Dove whispered. "Stop," she shouted as she stood, legs wide, weapon raised. "Aegis Network. Armed. Don't move."

The figures paused mid-step.

For a frozen heartbeat, everyone stood still—Dove with her gun pointed at the interlopers, Trent coming up behind her with his weapon at the ready, the two strangers caught in the open with the marsh and the moat at their backs. Their boat was tied to the dock in front of them, forty paces away.

Then one of them reached for his waistband.

"Gun." Trent grabbed Dove's arm and yanked her sideways as the night exploded.

The shot cracked past them, close enough that Trent felt the air displacement against his cheek. They hit the ground together, rolling behind a fallen palmetto as a second shot punched into the wood above their heads.

"You okay?" Trent's voice was tight.

"Peachy." Dove was already repositioning, finding a gap in their cover. "You?"

"Ask me later."

A third shot tore through the fronds, inches from Dove's shoulder. She ducked back, cursing.

"They're moving," Trent said. He could hear them—crashing through underbrush, making for the water. "We stay here and they're gone."

"We move—we lose cover."

"I don't think I can just let them walk."

Dove met his eyes in the darkness. "Together," she said. "On three."

"Two's faster."

"One."

They broke cover.

Trent went left, Dove went right, splitting the target zone. Another shot cracked through the night.

The gators were going wild now.

All around the moat, the water churned with their movement—tails slapping, bodies rolling, territorial bellows shaking the air like thunder. The sound was enormous, prehistoric, the kind of noise that reached into your hindbrain and screamed predator.

One of the men stumbled at the water's edge, his flashlight beam swinging wildly. The light caught movement—a gator hauling itself up onto the bank, jaws already open in warning.

Not Dolly. Smaller. Seven feet, maybe eight.

Bonnie.

Trent's heart seized.

Bonnie was young. Curious. She'd wandered into the natural habitat when she'd been barely the size of his arm. The young alligator, unlike many of the others, rarely left the moat. She and Dolly were more domesticated than the others. She didn't have the wariness of wild gators, didn't understand that humans were dangerous. She probably thought the intruders were Trent, coming to feed her.

The man saw the gator coming and panicked. His gun came up, not aimed at Trent or Dove anymore, but at the animal surging toward him with her mouth open wide.

"Don't," Trent shouted.

The first shot was deafening. The second one sounded like thunder. The third one hit the air as if it were coming for Trent's heart. The fourth and fifth ones barely registered.

Bonnie's head snapped back. Her body twisted, a horrible convulsive movement, and then she went still. She slid backward into the water, leaving a dark smear on the mud where she'd been.

For a moment, Trent couldn't move. Couldn't think. Couldn't do anything but stare at Bonnie. At the ripples spreading across the black water as she floated across the water, motionless.

"Trent," Dove's voice was sharp, urgent. "Move."

A bullet whined past his ear and buried itself in a cypress trunk with a wet thunk. He dove behind a mangrove root on instinct alone, his body operating without input from his brain, which was still stuck on the image of Bonnie's head snapping back.

Dove was beside him now, her hand on his arm, her voice low and fierce. "Stay with me. We can't help her now."

He blinked. Focused. The rage came then, cold and clean, burning away the shock.

"On your right," Dove said.

He rolled just as another shot churned up the ground where he'd been lying. The shooter had circled, trying to flank him.

Dove fired. Once. Twice. The shots were precise, controlled—covering fire meant to drive them back, not kill.

Part of Trent wished she'd aimed to kill.

Both figures broke for the tree line, abandoning any pretense of fighting.

Trent scrambled up and ran after them, Dove matching his pace. The ground turned soft, treacherous, sucking at his boots with every step. Ahead, he could hear splashing—they'd reached the water.

An engine roared to life.

By the time Trent burst through the mangroves, the boat was already pulling away from the bank. A flat-bottomed skiff, outboard screaming at full throttle, throwing a wake that slapped against the shore. Two dark figures hunched low in the stern.

Trent raised his pistol. His hand was steady. His aim was true.

He could take the shot. At this range, in this light, he might hit one of them. Might put a bullet in the back of the man who'd killed Bonnie.

Dove's hand closed over his wrist. "Don't."

"He killed her."

"I know." Her grip was firm. "And if you shoot him in the back while he's fleeing, you'll go to prison."

The boat disappeared into the darkness.

Trent stood there, chest heaving, pistol still raised at nothing. The rage had nowhere to go. It sat in his chest like a hot coal, burning with no way out.

"Put the gun down," Dove said softly.

He lowered his arm, but his pulse still soured. "I swear to god, if Karl had anything to do with this, I can't be held responsible for what I might do."

"That's grief talking," Dove whispered. She stood beside him, close enough that he could feel the warmth of her shoulder.

Sirens wailed in the distance, growing closer. Red and blue lights flickered through the trees as Dawson's cruiser came down the drive.

Trent turned as he sucked in a deep breath. Dove pressed her hand against his back and nudged him forward.

Dawson stepped from his vehicle and immediately shone a light. It found the blood first.

It was smeared across the mud at the water's edge, black in the darkness, leading down to where Bonnie's body floated in the shallows. Her eyes were still open, catching the light like dull marbles.

Dawson stood very still for a long moment. Then he turned to look at Trent, and his expression was different than before. Harder. More focused. "Tell me what happened."

Trent did. His voice was flat, mechanical, reciting facts without emotion because emotion was too dangerous right now.

Dove filled in the gaps he missed, her tone professional and precise.

"What do you think happened here?" Dawson asked.

"I think Karl hired someone to pay me a visit—I just don't know what the endgame was because whatever they were doing, it doesn't make sense." Trent let out a long breath and stared out into the river. "I would've expected him to go after one of the gators, or to hit the commercial side of the business. Instead, they were walking the property near the waterline toward the marsh. That part is all protected by the natural habitat. It's useless to anyone."

"I wouldn't go creeping around the habitat or alligator farm alone at night." Dawson shivered. "Even my wife would have reservations about that."

"Are you kidding? Audra loved coming to Mallor's Landing when she was a teenager and she was my hero when I was like six."

Dawson shook his head. "You mentioned they were

carrying a bag but didn't leave with one. Any idea what that was or what happened to it?"

"No, but it wasn't very big and obviously not too heavy." Dove pointed in the direction of where the two men had gone. "We haven't gone down there yet to investigate."

"I'll do that," Dawson said. "Any other enemies I need to know about? People you've pissed off over the years. People who might hold a grudge. Someone may have paid them to hurt you or sabotage your business. Because whoever was at Linda's funeral could've been scoping out all aspects of Mallor's Landing."

"No one's ever threatened me. Karl's the only one who's ever pushed my buttons."

"I paid him a visit after the funeral, and his alibi checked out." Dawson pulled out his phone. "But he doesn't paint a nice picture of you."

"Do I want to know what he said?" Trent shouldn't be surprised that Karl shit-talked him since Karl only cared about Karl.

"Just that he's heard rumors about you doing things that you're not supposed to be doing—again." Dawson arched a brow.

"I've been clean since the last time you had me in your office for questioning during the Ring Finger murders. Swear." Trent held his hands up. "But I can tell you Karl wasn't on my property tonight. If he had anything to do with this, he hired someone." Trent rubbed his neck. "He didn't have that kind of money before, but he did say he had some new potential clients on the hook. People who would pay top dollar. But Karl is usually full of shit."

"I'll check into it," Dawson said. "I'm contacting Chloe. I want her out here to process the scene properly. And I want you—" he pointed at Trent "—to make me a list of anyone else that might want to mess with you. I know you've been on the right side of things for a few years now, but we both know when I first blew into town, you weren't always a law-abiding citizen."

"My mom would take offense to that statement," Trent said. He was grateful that Chloe Fraiser-Bennett would be on the case with Dawson. She was former FBI, which should make him twitchy since she all but accused him of murder once, but it didn't because it was Chloe—the wife of local firefighter Hayes Bennett, and they didn't get any better than him. Or Dawson, for that matter.

Dawson chuckled. "I need to know who might want to come after you besides Karl."

He tapped his fingers on his phone, then paused. "I'm sorry about the gator. I know she meant something to you."

Trent didn't trust himself to respond. He'd been born and raised on Mallor's Landing. It represented three generations of Mallors. Three generations of families who loved and respected the Everglades. He reached into his back pocket and pulled out the flyer that had been burning a hole in his back pocket. "What about Sovereign Resources and their desire to mine limestone near my land? Do you think they could have anything to do with what happened tonight?"

"My wife is losing her shit over this. As is half the town." Dawson glanced at the paper before handing it back. "This morning, a petition showed up at Mitchells Marina, which I signed. But I was surprised to hear that some people support this. All made worse by Stacey Mohawk, local pretend reporter and big-time gossiper, going around interviewing people who support this senator who seems to support mining."

"Garrett Dutton," Trent said. "Former US Marshal, and it concerns me because it will be right next to my property."

Dawson rubbed his chin. "Anything is possible, but I have to ask. Why would Sovereign Resources sneak onto Mallor's Landing? Besides the fact that it's next to where they want to mine, what's here that they'd want?"

"I don't know." Trent shrugged. "But my land is a natural habitat for wild animals. That could mean something."

"It might. Let me check with Fish and Wildlife as well as Parks and Rec," Dawson said. "But right now, I've got little to no reason to be asking anyone from that company questions, and like I've told my wife and Silas Monroe, while I don't want to see a limestone mining company come to this town, they aren't the worst things in the world."

"Tell that to the Everglades and how it will change the ecosystem." Trent kept his emotions in check. He knew all too well how companies like Sovereign Resources would bring jobs and prosperity to a small coastal town. But Calusa Cove was different. It was the bridge between the Gulf and the Glades. Between civilization and nature. Between what once was, and how technology tends to destroy everything in its path. "No one here will want any mining. Hell, we didn't want that damn paper mill years ago. They came, they polluted, and they left."

"I hear you. And I tend to agree," Dawson said. "I'm just saying it's going to be an uphill battle. But I'll ask around."

"Thanks." It was all Trent could ask for.

"The Aegis Network can do some digging," Dove said. "We can do things that law enforcement can't."

"Just don't get in my way or make things difficult for me." Dawson looked between him and Dove. "I'm going to walk the perimeter one more time, see if I can locate what the intruders left behind. Chloe should be here shortly. We'll do what we can tonight, but we'll need to investigate the property again at first light." Dawson turned and his footsteps faded into the darkness, his flashlight beam cutting through the trees as he headed back toward the water's edge.

Silence settled over Trent and Dove.

Trent stared at the moat. He'd lost many gators over the years. He'd had to kill a few, too. But to lose one like that? It broke his heart.

Dove didn't say anything. She just moved closer, until her shoulder pressed against his arm, solid and warm in the humid night air.

"I appreciate you offering to look into things, but money's tight, and—"

"I'll talk to Buddy," Dove said. "I'm sure we can work something out. And if we can't, I'll do it on my own time." She waved her hand toward the moat. "It's not like you need my twenty-four-hour protection. You just need help figuring out who breached your property and why."

"Thanks." He looped his arm around her shoulder and squeezed. "You were on your way here tonight, weren't you?" His voice came out rougher than he intended.

"In a moment of weakness because I was worried about you."

He chuckled. "Right—worried—not something else."

"Maybe a little something else." She turned to face him, and in the dim light filtering from Dawson's vehicle, he could see the mud streaked across her cheek, the loose strands of hair clinging to her neck, the steady calm in her eyes. "I'm not leaving until the cops take off, and I'll decide then if you're really okay—you just had another loss."

"She was just a gator," he said, and hated how hollow the words sounded. "People kill gators all the time. It's—"

"Not to you." Dove's hand found his hand in the darkness, her fingers threading through his. "You raised her. You named her. You loved her. And some asshole shot her because she got in his way." Her grip tightened. "That matters. Your grief matters."

Trent stared at their joined hands. He couldn't remember the last time someone had held his hand and it meant something. Anyone other than Fallon, anyway. "My mom used to say that the measure of a man wasn't how he treated people," he said quietly. "It was how he treated the things that couldn't fight back. Animals. Kids. The land." He swallowed. "Technically, Bonnie could fight back. But, she didn't even know she was supposed to, and she didn't stand a chance against a gun."

Dove stepped closer, rising on her toes, and pressed her lips to his cheek. Soft. Brief. More comfort than kiss. "We're going to find out who did this," she said against his skin. "And when we do, they're going to wish they'd never set foot on your land." She pulled back but didn't let go of his hand. "Come on," she said. "Let's get you inside. I'll pour us a drink. You'll make that list. And tomorrow, we start hunting."

Trent looked back toward the water one last time. He couldn't see Bonnie's body from here, but he knew it was there. Floating in the shallows. But there was nothing he could do for her now.

He let Dove lead him across the bridge toward the house, her hand still wrapped around his.

The night had taken something from him. But it had reminded him of something, too.

He wasn't alone. Even when he wanted to be.

And whoever had come onto his land tonight—whoever had killed Bonnie and disappeared into the dark—they'd made a mistake.

They'd given him another thing to fight for.

Chapter Five

Dove leaned against the doorframe of Trent's kitchen, phone pressed to her ear, watching through the screen door as red and blue lights painted the cypress trees in alternating strokes of color.

It was past midnight, and the swamp had gone quiet except for the occasional splash from the moat and the low murmur of voices carrying across the yard. Trent stood at the edge of the bridge with Dawson and Chloe, his shoulders rigid, his hands shoved in his pockets. Even from here, she could see the tension coiled in his body.

"Start from the beginning," her uncle said.

So she did, using the same tone she'd used for after-action reports in the Army. Facts, not feelings. Feelings could come later, when she wasn't standing in the middle of a house that felt like ghosts lived in it.

It was like a museum to those who were no longer here. It wasn't the pictures that lined the walls. Those were normal things. It was the fact that the first time she set foot in this house, Trent had pointed out everything that had belonged to his father. The chair he made. His favorite fleece blanket that was still tucked under the coffee table. However, what stood out today was that his mother's cardigan was still draped over the back of the couch as if she'd gone to the pub for a night with her friends and forgotten it, like she'd done nearly every time. The faint smell of lavender still lingered in the air.

She watched Trent shake Dawson's hand, watched Chloe squeeze Trent's arm before heading back to her vehicle. Dove straightened against the doorframe. "Tell me about Gulf Coast Energy Partners and Trent's father."

"It was a layered trial. The CEO of the company, Edward Kirk, was indicted on bribery, racketeering, and money laundering, to name a few. Not to mention one of his associates was accused of murder. The DA had them, but then key evidence was burned in a fire. A witness recanted. Another died. Jack's testimony alone wasn't enough, and everyone knew it. While the DA was assessing what to do, Jack and I were T-boned. The case died after that. The DA tried to rebuild. The feds watched the players, the company, and especially Kirk and his associates but could never find anything to bring charges against them."

Through the screen door, Dove watched Dawson's cruiser pull away, followed by Chloe's SUV. The tail-lights faded into the trees, leaving only darkness and the yellow glow from the porch light.

"You've never talked about the case that nearly killed you. Why did you all of a sudden just spill so much?"

"Because you asked, and I can tell it matters to you."

"Bullshit." Dove knew her uncle well enough to know that not only was there more, but she wasn't so sure he was going to tell her the whole truth. "Is Sovereign Resources the real reason you're here?"

"No, my visit was totally social. I wanted to see how my favorite niece was settling in." Slade's voice softened with that sweet timber he had when he'd been there through all the fucked-up missions. "But, since I'm here, and this all feels very familiar, with the mining company, yeah, I want to stick around for that town meeting and see who the players are. But if you'd rather not have me underfoot for that long, I can get a room at Harvey's Cabins."

"You can stay as long as you like, but I honestly don't believe you. And while we're at it, I'd like the names of those who were involved twenty years ago, and I'll do some cross-referencing between the current board of directors and those who were on the Gulf Coast. Same with the directory log of employees."

"I can help you with that while I'm here."

"I won't say no to that offer." Dove rubbed her eyes with her free hand. The adrenaline from earlier had long since faded, leaving behind the bone-deep exhaustion that always followed a firefight. "Why do you want to speak with Trent?"

"I wanted to give him my condolences for his mom, proper like. The bar wasn't the place to do it. And I honestly just wanted to connect with him. Jack wasn't just a job to me. He became my friend."

"Trent might not be too receptive." Dove watched Trent start back toward the house, his boots heavy on the wooden bridge. In the moat below, something large shifted in the water, and she suppressed a shudder. "Seeing you tonight affected him deeply. He's a little on edge with everything that happened, and he's concerned about other things."

"I can only imagine, especially if he's anything like his dad."

Trent was halfway across the bridge. One of the gators—Dolly, probably—let out a low bellow that vibrated through the humid air. Dove watched him pause, turn toward the sound, and say something too quiet for her to hear. The bellowing stopped.

"I just want an hour of his time," her uncle said.

"I'll talk to him."

"Before you go, I want to ask you something."

"I'm afraid to hear this," Dove said.

"Is there something going on between you and Trent?"

Dove resented that she wished there were something real between her and Trent. It was rare for her to care this much for a man. It wasn't that she didn't have relationships. She just didn't do ones that lasted. Ones that required anything other than having a good time, and when they ended, it was no big deal because she hadn't put down roots. The Army moved her from one location to the next, and she'd welcomed the change.

Generally, the Aegis Network kept its operatives in one location, unless a request was made or a new office was opening. This was the first time since high school that she had her feet firmly planted in the ground.

But Trent was supposed to be a fling. When things had started to go sideways even before he'd been shot saving his childhood friend, Fallon, from the assholes who were trying to kidnap and kill her, Dove had to admit, it stung. It still stung. "We're friends."

"Is that all you are?"

"Yes." And, in that moment, it was the truth. Didn't matter that they struggled to keep their boundaries intact because they couldn't keep their hands to themselves. "I've got to go."

"I guess that means I'll see you shortly."

Shit. "Probably not."

"Right. That's what I thought," he said. "For the record, I'm glad you found someone. And if Trent is anything like his father, he's the kind of man I might approve of."

The line went dead before she could respond. Not that she even knew what to say.

Dove stared at her phone for a long moment. Her uncle had always understood her better than anyone—including her parents. Her mom didn't know how to handle a tomboy. Not that her mother didn't love her—she did. But she'd wanted a daughter she could dress up and take to the country club for mother-daughter brunches and fashion shows. That wasn't Dove.

And her dad, well, he hadn't wanted her in the Army.

He hadn't wanted that kind of hard life for his only girl. He'd lived it. Spent eight years in the Army. To him, it was utter hell, nothing more than a means to an end. He got an education and served his time, plus a little extra.

The screen door creaked open, and Trent slipped out of his water-soaked boots before stepping into the kitchen.

His face was drawn, exhaustion carved into every line, but his eyes found hers immediately. "They're gone," he said. "Didn't find anything in the tree line, so no idea what those men had, but if it was feed of any kind, some animal got it by now. Though, that doesn't make any sense, because not all of the gators responded." He moved past her to the sink, turning on the tap and letting the water run over his hands. She watched the mud swirl down the drain, brown fading to gray, fading to clear. "Chloe's going to run the two shell casings she found in the trees through the system," he said. "See if they match anything on file. Dawson's put out feelers with the marine patrol, in case anyone spots the boat."

"That's good."

"It's something." He turned off the water but didn't move, just stood there with his hands braced against the edge of the sink, head bowed. "Probably won't lead anywhere. If Karl hired those guys, he's not stupid enough to use traceable weapons or registered boats."

"He was dumb enough to send a couple of yahoos to a natural habitat in the Everglades without telling them exactly what they were getting into." Dove set her phone on the counter and crossed the kitchen to stand beside him. Close, but not touching. "I want to change the subject for a minute."

"Do you, now." He turned, sporting a familiar grin.

Shit. He was gonna be pissed. "My uncle would like a few minutes of your time."

Trent's shoulders lifted. "I can't imagine why."

"I don't know. Maybe it's twenty years of guilt. Maybe it's something else."

"I take it you believe it's something else." He pushed away from the sink, running a hand through his hair.

"I don't know. But I think it's strange that he showed up. That all this stuff is happening. That an ex-colleague of his is pushing to allow mining next to your property after he knew what happened twenty years ago." Dove let out a long breath. "Will you talk to him? For me?"

"I can do that, just not tonight. I need..."

He trailed off, but his eyes were on her now. Really on her. And the air in the kitchen shifted, thickened with something that had nothing to do with humidity. He closed the distance between them in two steps, his hand coming up to cup her jaw, his thumb tracing the line of her cheekbone. "I wouldn't have turned you away tonight."

She should step back. She should remind him that they'd agreed this was a bad idea, that they were too different, that she couldn't date a man who lived surrounded by things that wanted to eat her.

She didn't step back. "We shouldn't."

"Probably not," he said, his voice rough. "We decided we were better as friends."

"We did."

His forehead dropped to rest against hers. She could feel his breath against her lips, could feel the heat of him through the thin cotton of her tank top. Her heart pounded, which was ridiculous—she'd been shot at tonight without her pulse climbing this high.

"Dove."

"Yeah?"

"I'm going to kiss you now."

"Okay."

His mouth found hers, and for a long moment, the world narrowed to just this—the taste of him, his hands sliding into her hair, the soft sound he made against her lips when she pressed closer.

When they finally broke apart, they were breathing hard.

"That was a bad idea," Dove said.

"Terrible."

"We should stop."

"Definitely."

He kissed her again. Deeper this time, hungrier, his hands finding her waist and pulling her flush against him. She went willingly, her fingers fisting his shirt, every rational thought dissolving like morning mist over the swamp.

"Bedroom?" he murmured against her throat.

"God, yes."

He took her hand and led her down the hallway, past the dozens of photos of his parents hanging on the walls, past the cardigan on the couch and the lavender scent of a woman's absence. Dolly was bellowing again outside, a prehistoric song that should have been terrifying but somehow felt like approval.

The bedroom was dim. The only light came from the moon through warped blinds and the faint glow from the hallway. The air was thick. The fan overhead pushed it in slow, dutiful circles that did nothing to cool her skin. She registered the bed—heavy cypress frame, an old quilt with soft places worn thin—and then Trent's hands found her hips and thought scattered.

He kissed like he'd been holding his breath for hours and finally remembered how to inhale.

She rose into it, into him, into the simple movement of his mouth and hands. Wood creaked. A gator bellowed again, lower and farther off. The noise threaded under the thud of her pulse.

"Tell me to stop," he said, his breath rough against her lips, not really asking.

"I'm not gonna do that," she said, and pulled him back down.

He tasted like cold coffee with a dollop of cream. His stubble scraped the edge of her jaw and sent a tingle sliding beneath her skin. When his fingers slipped under the hem of her tank, she lifted her arms. Cotton skimmed up, and cool air licked the sweat collecting at the base of her throat. She shivered, and his mouth moved there like he'd felt the tremor through his palms.

She knew her body. Knew what worked and what didn't. This—this worked. The weight of him when he pushed her back onto the mattress. The spread of his hands on her ribs, wide and warm. The way he paused when he reached her bra, a half-second of silent question that she answered by arching up so he could get it off.

His mouth closed over her nipple and her spine went taut, the quilt bunching lightly under her shoulder blades as she shifted closer. He was solid between her thighs as she hooked her legs around him.

He kissed a line down her chest, tongue catching in the shallow dip of her belly, and she went liquid in the places that had been locked tight since the gunshots. He worked the button of her jeans, and denim rasped over her thighs, over her knees, and snagged on her heel. He tugged, she kicked, the jeans gave, and she laughed—breathless and a little wild.

He stilled at the sound.

"Hey," she said, reaching down to smooth her palm over his jaw, thumb brushing the corner of his mouth. She wasn't good at being gentle. She tried anyway. "Stay with me."

His exhale touched her wrist. "I haven't gone anywhere." He turned his head and kissed the center of her palm. "That laugh—I just remembered the first time I heard it, and I'm not sure I've heard it since." He dragged the flat of his tongue there. Heat pooled low and insistent. "You need to—we both need to laugh more often."

"We can do that later. Right now, I need you to take off your shirt." She needed fewer layers between them, needed his skin on hers without the barrier of cotton and grief.

The soft whoosh of fabric cleared his shoulders,

followed by the faint thud of it hitting the floor. Moonlight traced the edges of him—broad shoulders, the scar near his ribs. She reached toward him and pressed her mouth to that pale line, tasted salt and old stories, felt him stiffen, then ease.

When she rolled, he went with her, flat on his back, and she straddled him, her knees sinking into the mattress on either side of his hips. He swore, a raw syllable that punched heat into her.

She braced her hands on his chest, the flex of muscle there unspooling the resistance that had been wound too tight inside her for too long. She moved because she couldn't not, a slow grind that let the thick ridge beneath his jeans sit exactly where she wanted it. Pressure, friction, relief that bordered on pain. He clutched her hips and held her there, grounded her in place while she chased the drag of that sensation again.

Cloth was in the way. She reached behind and hooked her thumbs in the waistband of her underwear, dragging them down. He helped, knuckles grazing the curve of her ass. It wasn't neat, but it didn't matter. She sat up, bare and open, and for a beat, the fan's lazy whir sounded like the hush of surf. Ridiculous, with swamp water outside. She couldn't stop the thought. She didn't want to.

"Condoms?" she managed, because she might be suspended over a knife's edge, but she hadn't lost all sense.

"I've got a few, but are we going right to the finish line?" He reached between her legs, teasing and probing.

He'd proven to be an unselfish lover—a lover who paid attention to the wants and needs of his partner. The first time they'd slept together, he joked that he had one simple rule in bed. And that was she comes first. Thing was—with Trent—there wasn't an ounce of falseness to that statement.

"Finish line. I'm desperate."

He chuckled and reached for the nightstand. "I aim to please." The drawer stuck, then gave. A ripped corner of cardboard, the crinkle of foil—the ordinary sounds whispered like a promise. "Take this for a second while I get out of these jeans."

She watched as he shimmied out of his pants and kicked them across the room.

He reached for the condom in her hand.

"I'll do it."

He groaned. "You're the only person I know who's managed to make this part a turn on."

"Are you serious?" She tore the packet with her teeth and tossed the foil to the floor. She cupped him, stroking gently. "Any time my hands and eyes are on this part of your body, you're turned on."

"I'm turned on the moment you enter a room," he said through ragged breaths.

She swallowed—hard—while trying to remind herself it was a line tossed out while she was pleasuring him. It didn't mean anything. It certainly wasn't meant to encourage her to keep expecting this.

His thigh muscles flexed and tightened as she rolled the condom over him.

He reached for her, hands gentle on her thighs, and she sank down in one long, powerful glide. Her body took him in the way that made her teeth catch her lower lip. She exhaled toward the ceiling, and for a moment, she sat still, allowing herself to feel every inch of him inside her.

The moment passed, and she had to move. Slow at first to feel every precise shift, to memorize the way the mattress dipped, and the quilt rasped her knees, the way his thumbs stroked the curve where thigh met hip— a dance that was equal in tenderness and pressure.

Heat gathered—a tide pulling at her in steady increments. She set a rhythm and rode it, chased it, adjusted when his grip tightened and he thrust up to meet her. She leaned forward, planted a hand by his head to keep her balance, and he took that opportunity to mouth her breast again, tongue and teeth teasing the hard point until she swore and rolled her hips harder. He groaned, and the sound flooded her with a fierce, dizzy satisfaction.

The room narrowed to the wild rasp of their breathing. Outside, something splashed. The swamp went about its business. Inside, they created their own weather.

She felt the moment her control started to splinter. It came on fast, a hot coil tightening low and deep. The wrung-out ache tipping toward relief. She chased it shamelessly, angled her hips to catch the pressure exactly where she needed it.

"Look at me," he whispered.

She stared into his warm and kind eyes. This was a man who loved fiercely and deeply. She'd seen that in the way he cared for his mother. Even in the way he treated his friends. Especially his two best friends, Cullen and Fallon. But he was also a man who kept people at a distance. He didn't let many in. But when he did, he was loyal to the bone.

She wasn't quite sure where she fit—perhaps somewhere in the middle of that and she tried to tell herself that was enough.

He lifted his head, wrapped a hand behind her neck, and brought their lips together in a wild and passionate kiss. It didn't last long, but it sent shockwaves across her muscles.

He braced his feet, and drove up into her in hard, sure strokes that punched little sounds out of her throat she couldn't have swallowed if she'd tried.

"Oh, god, yes," she heard herself say, tone unfamiliar and rough.

She broke around him—a relentless, rolling flood that took her apart and put her back together with the edges smoothed down. She held on, nails biting his shoulders, gaze locked with his and rode until her muscles trembled and her breath wouldn't come in even pulls.

She sagged forward, forehead near his, sweat slicking their skin where they touched. He was still thick inside her, still straining. She found the last of her rhythm and kept going, slower now, a steady grind that dragged him after her. She felt his rhythm shudder and then spill. She absorbed it all and she stayed still until the tension bled out of him, leaving them a tangled mess against the old quilt.

The fan ticked. Her heartbeat climbed down out of

her throat and took up residence in her chest again. When she finally eased off him, the realization of how much she cared about this man hit her like a round she hadn't seen fired. She wasn't sure she'd ever cared this much. Wasn't sure she'd even wanted to.

But here she was, falling for a man who was falling apart at the seams.

Silence settled, not awkward, just thick. Her skin cooled in tiny patches where the air hit sweat.

Trent tugged the quilt up enough to cover her hips. His fingers brushed her thigh in the process, a casual stroke that tightened something low in her belly in a softer, slower way. She closed her eyes and let herself float for a minute, the sound of the swamp folding in at the edges of consciousness like a lullaby sung by something with too many teeth.

Tomorrow would come whether she invited it or not. She turned her face into the warm curve of Trent's shoulder and breathed him in—cedar soap mixed with salty air, sunshine, and sawgrass.

"You okay?" he asked, quiet, the words a puff against her hair.

She nodded against him, the movement small. "You even have to ask."

He reached down, laced their fingers under the quilt like he'd done it a hundred times, and held on.

Outside, something splashed again. The gators went silent. She wasn't sure if that was more terrifying than the bellowing. She felt sleep pull at her like a tide she refused to fight. Not tonight. Not here, with his hand warm in hers.

Later, there'd be time for the hard conversations and harder choices. But for now, she'd enjoy this. She'd enjoy him.

She closed her eyes, and the darkness came easy.

Chapter Six

D ove blinked open her eyes, and four things registered immediately.

The gators were making noise. Lots of it.

She was alone in Trent's bed.

It was still dark.

And no coffee had been made.

She lay still for a moment, letting her eyes adjust to the pre-dawn darkness. She turned, and the clock on the nightstand indicated it was only five in the freaking morning. God, why did everyone in this damn town wake so fucking early? She thought when she'd left the Army, her days of having to be out of bed at the butt-ugly hours of the morning were over. But it was like Calusa Cove lit up at four-thirty in the morning just because it could.

She pressed her palm against the sheets where Trent had been. She suspected he'd been up for a bit because he didn't sleep well. Most of that had been because of his mother. But he mentioned he'd always been an early riser and a morning person.

Dove tossed the covers to the side, snagged a pair of Trent's boxers, found her tank top, and padded to the window. She could see him at the edge of the moat, bucket in hand, tossing chicken quarters to the gators who'd made this their permanent home like it was any other morning. Like the world hadn't tilted sideways every day since his mother had died.

Dove watched as one of the small gators eased closer, practically taking the food right from Trent's hands. She shivered. It was amazing that the prehistoric monsters hadn't eaten the man. Or that a python hadn't strangled him. Or that a rattler hadn't bitten him. Oh wait. He *had* been attacked by a few rattlesnakes and had the bite marks on his leg to prove it.

Falling for this man was not a good idea. It was worse than falling for a man in the Special Forces.

She continued to stare at him as he fed his precious gators. He moved with an ease she envied—comfortable in his skin, comfortable on this land, comfortable with creatures that made her want to climb the nearest tree. There was something almost meditative about the way he worked his way around the water's edge, each toss precise, each gator accounted for.

The big one—Dolly—kept surfacing near a spot closer to the bank. Nudging at the water.

Maybe she was looking for Bonnie, who had probably gotten eaten by the other gators because Trent once told her that was a thing.

Dove's chest tightened.

She'd seen a lot of death in her life. Soldiers. Civilians. Targets through a scope who stopped being people the moment her finger touched the trigger. She'd learned to compartmentalize, to pack the grief and guilt into boxes and shove them into corners of her mind where they wouldn't interfere with the mission. It had only taken one bad mission to blow every one of those boxes wide open.

Growing up, she'd been a tough cookie. And the Army had hardened her even more. Her parents tried to understand her, and her father, having been military, did get the importance of separating the job from the person. However, the second that last mission blew up—literally—it nearly destroyed what little humanity she'd had left, and it was difficult for her to face her folks.

The Aegis Network, Buddy, and Sterling had helped put her back together—at least somewhat. Enough that she was no longer a loud-mouthed female who had a death wish and slept with any man willing. Not her finest few months.

Calusa Cove and its good citizens had done something to her soul. Settled it, maybe? It had given her community. Friendships like she'd never experienced before. A sense of belonging that even the Army hadn't provided. However, she still hadn't felt completely whole, and trust didn't come easily or naturally.

But watching Trent feed his gators while one of them mourned—that hit her different. That slipped past the last of the walls she'd built and lodged somewhere soft and unprotected. She hadn't liked the gators. Never pretended she did. But she liked *him*, and the thing about Trent was that you couldn't separate the man from the mud, the Glades, and the creatures he'd built his life around. She was learning to accept that truth about him.

She needed coffee. She also needed to stop staring at a man who was probably already figuring out how to tell her that last night was a mistake. Trent's walls were far higher than hers.

The sound of a cell vibrating on the nightstand caught her attention. She lifted her phone and stared at a text from her uncle.

Aaron: *Breakfast?*

She smacked her palm to her forehead. Sometimes her uncle was worse than her mother when it came to wanting to know the details about her love life.

Dove: *Maybe lunch.*

Aaron: *Still on Army time, I see.*

Dove: *No. Gators come in the house and eat you if you don't feed them early enough.*

Aaron: *That's funny.*

She decided to leave it at that and made her way to the kitchen.

It was clean and quiet, filled with little reminders of Linda. A cross-stitch she'd made that read *Home Sweet Home* hung over the stove. Curtains that Linda had made years ago. Dove understood the need to preserve legacy, and Trent, while a complicated man, wasn't one to go and change anything just because he could.

Dove moved carefully through the space, opening

cabinets until she found the coffee, filters, and mugs—because Trent hadn't moved with the times like everyone else.

The coffee maker gurgled and hissed. Outside, Trent had finished with the gators and was standing at the edge of the moat, staring at the water like it held answers to questions he didn't know how to ask.

Dove poured two mugs and headed for the porch.

He turned toward her when the door opened, and something in her stomach dropped at the look on his face. Guarded. Careful. The expression of a man preparing to have a conversation he didn't want to have. A conversation they'd had before.

"Breakfast of champions," she said, keeping it light and doing her best to act as if nothing mattered as she held up one of the mugs. Acting as if everything were causal. Acting as if she wasn't about to die a little inside when he told her he was sorry, but they were better off as friends.

He crossed the yard toward her, and she tracked his movement the way she'd once tracked targets—noting the tension in his shoulders, the set of his jaw, the way his boots fell heavily on the damp grass. He climbed the porch steps, and when she handed him the mug, their fingers brushed.

She watched him take a sip of coffee, watched him use the motion to avoid her eyes, and felt the last fragile piece of hope crumble that maybe this time things might stick.

"So," she said. "Regrets already."

He peered over his mug with a raised brow. "Why on earth would you assume that?"

"Because we've been here before." She kept her voice steady, like this wasn't a knife sliding between her ribs.

"I don't regret it," he said, and something in his tone made her pause. "I do care about you." He stared into his coffee like it might save him from having to say the next words. From having to let her down easy.

She'd save him the trouble. "It's only been three weeks since your mom passed away," she said. "You're still grieving."

"It's been rough. She was my world, and I'm a little lost without her."

She nodded, leaning against the porch railing. This, at least, she understood. Grief was a sniper's bullet—you didn't see it coming, and by the time you felt the impact, the damage was already done.

"I can tell," she said. "You haven't even moved her sweater from the couch." The words were out before she could stop them.

Trent actually stepped back, coffee sloshing over the rim of his mug, and the look on his face made Dove want to put her fist through the porch railing.

"Shit." She heard her own voice crack. "I'm sorry. That was—I shouldn't have said that."

"It's fine."

"It's not fine. That was cruel, and I didn't mean—"

"It wasn't cruel. It was honest." He set down the mug, and she could see his hands weren't steady. "I was just stunned." He ran a hand through his hair. "I guess I hadn't really noticed that everything is still where she left it. Her toothbrush is still in the sink in her bathroom, where she dropped it. There's a hamper of her dirty clothes. I know I need to take care of it all. I just... can't."

Dove's throat tightened. She knew about objects that couldn't be moved. About spaces that stayed frozen because changing them meant admitting someone was really gone. She had a box in her closet full of letters from a friend who'd died in a training exercise. She hadn't opened it in years. Probably never would.

"Grief doesn't have a timeline," she said quietly.

He rubbed a hand over his face, and she saw the exhaustion underneath the grief, the frustration underneath the exhaustion. "I don't want to end things, but I don't know how to do relationships. Last real one I had was with Fallon. I don't want to hurt you, but I don't know how to tell you to leave because I don't want you to."

"What does that mean?"

He held her gaze. And she suddenly felt terribly exposed—standing on his porch in a form fitting tank top and boxers with her hair a mess and her defenses stripped bare.

"We can't seem to stay away from one another, and that's not something that's ever happened before," he said. "When I've ended things with someone, they've ended. We keep coming together, and honestly... I'm glad."

"I am too," she heard herself say. "But it's not easy for me either. I've spent my entire adult life hiding behind a sniper scope, keeping the world at a safe distance. Literally."

The words kept coming, spilling out of some cracked place she hadn't known existed. She told him about the Aegis Network being her attempt to become human again. About learning to connect instead of observing. About the jury still being out on whether any of it was working.

"I'm not asking you for anything except honesty," she said. "Your friendship means more to me than the sex—although, for the record, the sex was pretty spectacular."

His mouth twitched into a slight smile. Just barely. But she caught it, and her chest loosened.

"Not the only reason I want to be with you, but yeah, the sex is great."

She laughed, and it sounded almost real. "This is usually where I'm the one running out the front door. Ask anyone I've ever dated. I have commitment issues that would make a therapist weep with joy."

He chuckled, leaning against the railing, and placed his hands on the old wood. "As I said, the only real one I had was ten years ago when I lived with Fallon. Which is still just weird because to this day, she's one of my best friends."

Dove rolled her eyes. "You're lucky Buddy hasn't come at you with a gun. He's a jealous man."

"Nothing for him to be jealous of. And while we always joke that we loved each other a little, and maybe we did—do—because I'd kill Buddy with my bare hands if he ever hurt her—it was more about our bond over shared grief and our love for the Everglades." He lowered his chin and grinned. "Do I need to be worried about you being jealous?"

"Of your past relationship with Fallon? God no." And that was the truth. "She and Buddy are so disgustingly in love, I want to vomit. The other day, he opened his lunch, and there was a note from Fallon with cute little hearts all over it. And she put in heart-shaped chocolates, and he was gaga over it."

Trent dropped his head back and laughed. Hard. And the sound vibrated in her chest. She couldn't remember the last time she'd heard him laugh like that. She was grateful that something in this world could bring that out in him.

He cleared his throat. "So, what are we doing?"

"Do we need to define it?" she asked.

"Most people do."

"Most people aren't us." She shrugged, trying for nonchalant and probably missing by a mile. "We're not friends with benefits. And I would be pissed if you were with someone else, so I guess we're a thing."

He held her gaze long enough that her stomach dropped and she was certain he was about to say "sorry, but I can't after all."

Then, he pushed from the railing and sauntered across the porch. He traced her lower lip with his thumb before cupping her chin. He took her mouth in a slow, deliberate kiss.

The sound of tires on gravel cut it way too short.

They both turned toward the driveway, and Dove's

stomach dropped when she recognized the dark govern-ment-looking SUV making its way down the driveway.

Uncle Aaron. Of course. Perfect timing. Not to mention dangerously stupid to show up unannounced.

She felt Trent's muscles go rigid. Watched his jaw tighten. Watched twenty years of grief and resentment surface in the span of a single breath.

"Did you invite him?" he asked, cold and sharp. The voice of a man who felt ambushed. He dropped his hand to his side and took a step back. "Just because I agreed, doesn't give you the right—"

"I didn't ask him to come this morning." She kept her own voice careful, neutral.

"I don't like pushy."

"It can't hurt to hear him out."

"Not this fucking early."

The SUV pulled to a stop on the other side of the moat. One of the gators made itself known, mouth open and ready to strike. Through the windshield, she could see her uncle sitting behind the wheel, waiting. Giving them space—or maybe sizing up the gator. It was the smart play. Slade had always been good at reading rooms, even rooms he wasn't in yet.

"I'm not in the mood for this. Dawson will be here shortly, and I want to prepare for that town meeting in a few days."

"Uncle Aaron is a good man, and he knows Dutton, who's backing that company, and—"

"I mean it. I don't have the capacity to deal with his

guilt this morning." He turned, slamming the screen door behind him before she could respond.

Dove stood on the porch, caught between the man inside and the man in the SUV, wondering how the hell she'd ended up in the middle of this.

She didn't go after Trent. Didn't signal her uncle to leave or come in. Just stood there, watching the gators drift through the moat, waiting for something to break.

The screen door opened, and Trent stepped back onto the porch. "I'm sorry," he said. "For being a jerk, you didn't deserve that."

"I'd be upset, too." She palmed his cheek. "I don't know why my uncle thought it would be okay to show up here unannounced at this hour."

He looked past her, toward the SUV where her uncle waited. "I suppose it must be important to him." He leaned in and kissed her cheek. "Tell him to come on up."

"Thank you."

She started down the porch steps. Behind her, she heard Trent go back inside. She didn't know what he was doing in there. Bracing himself, maybe. Preparing for a conversation he didn't want to have.

Or maybe—just maybe—finally moving his mother's sweater.

Chapter Seven

The kitchen had always been one of Trent's favorite spots in the house. He used to catch his dad sneaking up on his mom while she did the dishes. They'd laugh. They'd dance, right there in front of the window, while the gators made music. Back then, when he'd been all of ten or twelve, Trent dreamed of having a life like his parents filled with love, laughter, and family.

He ran his fingers across the table his father had built thirty years ago—solid oak, hand-sanded, the corners worn smooth by decades of elbows and coffee mugs and family dinners that would never happen again. His mother had loved this table. Said it was the heart of the house. Said you could tell everything about a family by how they gathered around their kitchen table. His mom had moved out, in part because Fallon had moved in, and because she'd wanted him to have his own space. His own life. He was the next generation.

His mom had always wanted to see him settle down, get married, have children. It pained him that he wouldn't—couldn't—ever give that to her. That she'd never had grandchildren sitting around this table in the kitchen she so loved.

Right now, the table held three mugs of coffee that no one was drinking, yesterday's unopened newspaper because even though he'd been born in the digital age, he still preferred to hold a paper in his hands, and enough tension to choke on.

In the back of Trent's mind, his mother's voice echoed in that sweet tone she had, reminding him to be nice. Be a gentleman. To stop being such an ass and grow up. He nearly smiled at the last one. He'd been trying to do that for the last five years.

Slade sat across from him, hands wrapped around his mug, posture relaxed in a way that only made Trent more aware of how strained everything else was. The morning light cut through the window above the sink, painting stripes across the worn linoleum, catching the steam rising in lazy spirals from the coffee.

Dove stood at the counter with her back against the cabinets, arms crossed, positioned like a referee at a boxing match. Ready to intervene if someone threw a punch.

Trent wasn't going to throw a punch.

Probably.

Maybe.

Regardless, he was grateful for her presence. She had

a way of grounding him. Of settling his emotions without even trying.

The silence stretched. Outside, a gator bellowed—probably Dolly, doing her morning rounds, and somewhere in the distance, a boat motor coughed to life on the river. Normal sounds. Familiar sounds. Sounds that belonged to a world where Trent wasn't sitting across from the man who'd failed to protect his father, pretending to be civil.

"You going to tell me why you're here?" Trent finally asked. "Or are we just going to sit here staring at each other until the other one blinks like a couple of middle schoolers?"

Slade's mouth twitched. Not quite a smile. "You have your father's sense of humor."

Trent had a retort, but it would've been sarcastic, not to mention rude, and his mother wouldn't have approved.

Slade set down his mug, the ceramic clicking against the wood with a sound that seemed too loud in the quiet kitchen. "When I learned my niece was moving here, I figured it would be sooner rather than later that I'd pay a visit. I honestly just wanted to pay my respects. I should've said this at the bar. I'm so sorry to hear about your mom. Your father spoke so highly of her."

"They were an amazing couple," Trent agreed. "Thank you." He saw no point in being a jerk. He'd spent half his life pushing boundaries and pissing people off. He was done with that.

"I hadn't planned on showing up this early. Honestly, I was going to call and ask to meet you for coffee, but something happened, and I couldn't wait to speak with you." Slade reached into the inside pocket of his jacket and withdrew a folded piece of paper. He smoothed it flat on the table and slid it across toward Trent. "This is a formal request by my office that was sent to the state trial office for this county."

Trent looked down at the paper but didn't touch it. The header read, *"Department of Justice - U.S. Marshals Service"* in an official-looking font. Below that, a block of text too dense to parse at a glance.

"What is it?" Trent asked.

"Five days ago, a man named Merik Parrish died of pancreatic cancer in a hospice facility in Daytona. He was sixty-seven years old. He had one daughter that he was estranged from," Slade said.

The name meant nothing to Trent.

"Parrish was never charged with anything related to the Gulf Coast case. But he was a known criminal. Hired muscle. Willing to do jobs most people wouldn't touch. Also very good at what he did because he never got caught. He was like a ghost. The feds called him The Janitor."

"I'm confused. What does this have to do with my father and whatever the US Marshals office is requesting?" Trent took a closer look at the document and caught the date. It was sent to the court two days ago.

"When Parrish died, he left his estate to his daughter. She went in and cleaned it out and found what we refer to as a dead man's cache," Slade said.

Trent reached for the coffee mug, brought it to his

lips, and gulped, wishing it had some booze in it. He felt like he'd been dumped in the middle of a mobster movie and hadn't been given the backstory.

"My office, the feds, and local police have been going through documents, photographs, recordings—basically evidence of crimes Parrish committed over the years. None of it was supposed to get into our hands. It was his insurance in case the people who'd hired him tried to screw him, or maybe he blackmailed some of them."

"I'm still not following and wish you'd get to the point."

Slade tapped the document with one finger. "Parrish was hired to take out your father."

"Are you saying that crash wasn't an accident?" Trent asked. His heart lurched upward and landed in his throat.

Dove moved across the kitchen and rested her hands on his shoulders. Normally, he would've shrugged them off because he couldn't stand being touched when he was that agitated. But right now, he needed someone to ground him.

"That's the most bizarre thing about this. Parrish admitted to taking the money, but in all the paperwork we found, he clearly states his plan and that he never executed it. That he sat there and watched a freak accident—one nearly identical to his plan—kill your father and nearly kill me."

Trent stared at the paper. The words on it seemed to blur and shift, refusing to resolve into meaning.

"What exactly are you trying to tell me?"

"I'm saying the Department of Justice is opening an investigation into your father's death."

The words hit Trent like a physical blow. He actually rocked backward in the chair as the air rushed into his lungs, leaving him dizzy.

"They're forming a task force. They want to re-examine what evidence still exists. They want to re-interview anyone who witnessed the crash. The doctors who treated me and pronounced your father dead. The ambulance drivers. Everyone."

Trent's throat had gone dry. "Does this mean they'll reopen the investigation into those involved with the bribery, Gulf Coast, and the murder? Who sold out my father and leaked his name?"

"That all depends on what they find." Slade let out a long breath and leaned back. "Gulf Coast Energy Partners wasn't able to survive the backlash. However, Edward Kirk had other businesses. He survived. The feds tried to nail him on just about everything, including tax fraud, but they couldn't. He retired a wealthy man with money tied up in some questionable places, but no one has proof of anything. I'm sure they'd love to nail his ass."

The kitchen tilted. Trent gripped the edge of the table, the solid oak grounding him, reminding him where he was. His father's table. His father's house. His father's ghost lingered in every corner.

He'd been fourteen years old when he'd seen a man in a suit pass an envelope to a man with a politician's smile. Trent had run home to tell his father because something about it had felt wrong. So wrong.

He'd never told anyone except his parents. His father had made him promise. *Don't ever speak of this again. Not to anyone. You didn't see enough to matter, and if they think you did...*

His father had seen more. His father had dug deeper. His father had witnessed a murder and agreed to testify, but he died in a car crash that everyone said was an accident but wasn't supposed to be. Talk about fucking irony.

"This is all dandy, but it's twenty years too late," Trent mumbled.

"Justice doesn't have an expiration date."

Trent laughed. It came out harsh and broken, scraping against his throat. "That's a nice sentiment. You should put it on a poster."

"My uncle didn't know this was coming. Didn't know a criminal was going to confess to a crime he hadn't had a chance to commit." Dove's voice, soft but firm, cut through the rising tide of his anger.

He reached up and patted the hand she still rested on his shoulder. She was right. She was almost always annoyingly right.

"This brings me to the request my office is making." Slade tapped his finger on the paper. "There are a few requests in this document. One of them being the exhumation of your father's body."

The chair screamed against the linoleum as Trent shoved back from the table. He glanced at Dove, who'd taken two steps back, hands in the air as if to say she'd given up. Or maybe she was just simply okay with him losing his shit because this new information sat in his gut like sour milk.

He was on his feet a second later, his hands balled into fists at his sides, his vision narrowing to a red-edged tunnel with Aaron Slade at the center. "You've got to be kidding."

"I wish I were, but they've made the formal request. It's just a matter of time before the court makes a decision."

"No." The word tore out of him like something with claws, ragged and raw. "You don't get to do that. You don't get to come into my house and drink my coffee and tell me that after twenty years of nothing, after my mother spent two decades waiting for justice that never came, now—now—you want to dig up my father's grave and for what? Confirm that it was an accident? That this hitman didn't do his job because some idiot ran a red light?"

"This isn't my decision," Slade said.

"I don't give a damn whose decision it is." Trent slammed his fist onto the table hard enough to send the coffee mugs jumping. Hot liquid sloshed over the rims, pooling on the oak his father had sanded smooth with his own hands and seeping into yesterday's newspaper that Trent hadn't yet found time to read. "He's dead. He's been dead for twenty years. My mother's dead. Everyone who your justice could have helped is dead." Trent's voice cracked on the words. "Your investigation couldn't solve it. Your justice system couldn't prosecute it. My father burned in that car. Whatever was left of him, we put in a box and put in the ground, and my mother stood there in a black dress and threw dirt on her husband's coffin and didn't stop crying for three months." His chest heaved. His hands shook. Somewhere in the back of his mind, a voice that sounded like his mother was telling him to calm down, to breathe, to remember that anger was just fear wearing a mask.

He couldn't calm down. He couldn't breathe. He couldn't do anything but stand there and shake with a fury so deep it felt like it might crack him open.

"I was fourteen years old," he said, and his voice had gone quieter now, quieter and in that kind of quiet way his mother had always told him was worse than when he shouted. "I watched my mother fall apart. I watched her try to explain to me why Dad wasn't coming home. I watched her stand at that grave every Sunday for twenty years, talking to a headstone as if he could hear her." His eyes burned. He blinked hard, refusing to let the tears fall. "She's been gone three weeks. I haven't even figured out how to move her sweater off the couch, and you're sitting in her kitchen telling me that the government wants to dig up my father."

Dove slowly moved closer.

He wanted to hold up his hand. To push her away. But right now, she was the only person he had to hold on to.

She curled her fingers around his biceps, leaned into him, and suddenly, he could breathe again.

"I don't want to dig up your dad," Slade said softly. "I wanted you prepared for what's coming."

"And I'm supposed to stand here and thank you for that?"

"I want you to know that you can fight this request," Slade said.

"You? A US Marshal is suggesting I take on your office?" Trent's voice steadied. His heart rate slowed to a less painful rate. He raised his hand and placed it over Dove's.

Her presence made everything bearable.

"Why would you do that?" Trent asked.

Slade ran a hand over his face. He glanced toward the ceiling. "I spent two months with your dad. At first, he was just a job. Just another person the marshals service expected me to watch over. But as hours turned into days, and days into weeks, we became friends.

Jesus, Trent didn't want to hear this. It was hard enough listening to Silas Monroe, Cullen's uncle, tell stories about his dad. About the good old days. About when they would sit out in the river, fishing, talking about absolutely nothing, and laughing their asses off over everything. But to hear this from the man who'd been there when his dad died?

Trent wrapped his arm around Dove. He needed her strength. Her energy. Her kindness.

"Jack would tell me all about his wife. About how they met and how three weeks later he found himself at the local church getting married." Slade pressed his hands against the table and stood. "He would talk for hours about Linda and even longer about his slightly out of control teenage son who had a chip on his shoulder, an attitude the size of Texas, and how it was like looking into a mirror of his youth." Slade waved a finger around his face. "You look exactly like him except for the eyes."

"I get that a lot."

"Uncle Aaron," Dove said. "Fighting this is probably a lost cause. Why do you believe he should?"

"I was there. I was driving that car when we got T-Boned. Jack's legs were pinned. He was unconscious. I tried to get him out, but the car was on fire and... and..." Slade turned away and rubbed his temples. "I was lucky. Broken bones. Burns." He sighed and shook his head before turning back. "I'm not sure exhuming your father's body will give my office any answers other than a dead man didn't execute his kill order, but an innocent man died anyway, and I still failed at my job."

"What else does this Parrish guy have that's related to my father's case?" Trent asked.

"Nothing really," Slade said.

"Seems odd to want to exhume Jack's body when the hit wasn't completed," Dove said. "And one of their own is a witness."

"It's all about verifying information." Slade leaned over the table and took a swig of coffee. "I have no idea if you'd win if you fought it, but you could certainly delay it. I'd stand in your corner if you did. I'd give testimony on why we shouldn't exhume the body because I was there when he died. But if you're gonna do it, you need to do it now."

"No offense, but it seems like a waste of time to fight it." Dove patted Trent's arm. "No matter how disturbing it is. And I don't understand why you, of all people, want Trent to spend time and resources doing it."

Slade sighed. "I'm just trying to save him some heartache, considering everything."

"I do appreciate the thought." Trent wished the anger would disappear, but it sat in the center of his gut, boiling. "While I don't want my father's remains disturbed, I don't have the means to fight the government. Not when I've got Sovereign Resources wanting to mine in my backyard, and your ex-colleague doing backflips to make that happen. You want to help me, join that fight."

"I haven't spoken to Dutton in years, I'm happy to do a little digging, though," Slade said. "But I hope you consider at least asking the court to hear why you don't want your dad exhumed." He stretched out his arm.

Trent took his hand and shook. "I'll think about it."

"I'll walk you to the door." Dove squeezed Trent's shoulder.

"Thanks. Those gators are quite the security system."

Trent walked to the window above the sink and stared out at the moat, at the gators drifting through the dark water, at the cypress trees reaching toward a sky that was too blue and too bright for a morning that felt like the end of the world.

Behind him, he heard Slade's footsteps. The creak of the screen door. The click of it closing.

He heard Dove thank her uncle, and adding that next time, he needed to be more tactful and more honest from the get-go. Trent appreciated that. He appreciated every-thing about her. She reminded him of the air. Of the earth. Of the water. Of things that were just always there. Always right. Always what he needed.

And that scared the fucking shit out of him.

He poured himself another cup of coffee, sat down at the table, and snagged the newspaper. He needed to do something normal and reading the paper was just that.

Dove reappeared and leaned against the counter. "I'm sorry," she whispered. "I'm not sure I understand my uncle right now, except that he feels strongly about this."

Trent lifted his mug, took a long, slow sip and did a mental check of his bank account. It was pitiful. Mallor's Landing wasn't cheap to run. The business side made decent money, but he sank much of it into the natural wildlife habitat.

"I think fighting it would cost more than I could ever afford, and for what? I'd probably lose." He grabbed a handful of napkins from the holder in the center of the table and mopped up the coffee he'd spilled earlier. Luck-ily, the newspaper was mostly out of the splash zone. He glanced up at Dove. "As much as I don't want my father's remains disturbed, if it means possibly bringing justice to those who betrayed him and those who he was fighting against, who am I to stop it. Not to mention, what little money I do have, I might need to use to fight Sovereign Resources."

"I'm honestly surprised this is what my uncle wanted to discuss." She strolled across the kitchen, opened the fridge, snagged some strawberries, and sat down next to him. "But I know that car crash changed him. Not just the crash, but the case he was working."

Trent nodded absently at that, his attention snagged on something poking out from between the edges of the paper. Opening it, he stared at an envelope with his name written in curvy handwriting.

He turned it over in his hands and tore it open.

A photograph slid out with a yellow sticky note attached to it.

Mr. Mallor,

We have more where this came from. Sell us the property, or we send everything to the FWC and the police chief. You know what happens after that.

Beau & Emma Henderson

For the second time that morning, Trent slammed his fist on the table hard enough to rattle every mug in the kitchen.

"What the hell?"

He stared at the image of his equipment shed—the one on the main property. Not the processing shed on the alligator farm. The photo had been shot through the side window. The workbench was cluttered with knives and scrapers, and laid out across it, three alligator hides—raw, unprocessed, and not a single FWC tag in sight. Not that it mattered, because for him to keep all his permits, he couldn't skin a gator on this part of his land. It all had to be done on the commercial side.

He brought the image closer. A fourth skin hung

from the ceiling hook. And in the background, barely visible but unmistakable, Trent stood with his back to the camera, skinning knife in hand.

"Fuck." He shoved back from the chair. It scraped across the linoleum and hit the counter. He was on his feet, pacing, hands locked behind his head, chest heaving. "Son of a bitch." He kicked the chair.

"What is it?"

He grabbed the newspaper and hurled it across the room. It hit the wall and exploded into loose pages that floated to the floor.

Dove didn't flinch. She picked up the letter. The photograph. Studied both.

He should have fucking known that a few bad decisions would come back to haunt him. Fallon warned him. Baily had, too. Hell, Silas smacked him on the backside of his head more than once, all while giving him a lecture on what it would do to his mama.

"Is this real?" Dove asked.

He braced both hands on the counter, head down, pulling air into lungs that didn't want it.

His mother's voice echoed in his brain. *Tell the truth. Even when it's ugly. Especially when it's ugly.*

"Yes and no," he said. "I did some shit when I was younger that I'm not proud of. Mostly, I let people do things, and I turned a blind eye." He turned and looked at her. "If that gets out, I could lose my permits. I could lose everything and Fallon—she'd fucking kill me."

"She knows about this?"

He rubbed the back of his neck. "It's part of why she

and I fought like cats and dogs while we were together and all through our friendship. She could tolerate some of the shady things I did because I mostly did good things for the Glades, but she couldn't understand why I allowed Karl to do things I knew were illegal, and if he got caught, it wouldn't matter that it wasn't me doing it— I'd lose everything."

Dove set the photo down. "So, Karl's behind this?"

"It's always fucking Karl. And it's not the first time he's tried to hold it over my head." A few years ago, when Dawson had brought Trent in for questioning during the Ring Finger murder case, Dawson warned him about covering for assholes like Karl, but Trent hadn't listened. "Karl is the only person who knows about this, and I allowed him to use my land to do it himself. But Karl doesn't do favors. He doesn't lift a finger unless there's something in it for him. So I have to ask, what are the Hendersons offering that made it worth handing over ammunition against the one person who could also prove that Karl had his own skeletons he wanted to keep buried?"

"You've got shit on Karl?"

"Nothing that I can prove, but I know some of the things he's done. Only that's a two-way street, I don't think either one of us wants that shit storm."

"This is blackmail and harassment. You need to take this to Dawson." Dove inched closer, but Trent raised his hands.

"I can't. Seriously, if I do that, he's gonna have to call Keaton at Fish and Wildlife, and then there will be an investigation, and Mallor's Landing will shut down. I can't afford for that to happen. Not now."

"You can't let this go."

"I don't plan on it." He let out a long breath. He just wasn't sure what he was going to do, but selling to the Hendersons wasn't the answer.

Chapter Eight

Dove pulled into the crushed shell parking lot at Mitchell's Marina and killed the engine of her truck. She sat there for a long moment, staring out at the sun beating down on the murky water, letting the salt breeze wash through the open window and carry away the stale recycled air from the Aegis office that still clung to her skin like a second shirt.

Eight hours of research. Eight hours staring at screens until her eyes felt like they'd been rolled in sand. Being still had never been a problem. She could lie on her belly, looking through a scope, doing overwatch all damn day. But going down the Google rabbit hole? That was pure hell. But it was what she signed up for, and it was better than some of the other jobs she could've taken when she'd left the military.

She'd started her morning looking into the Hendersons. Looking into employment records. Investments.

Anything on the surface that might ping them as they pretended to be nice in the beginning.

Beau Henderson was a semi-retired real estate investor from Naples with a portfolio of vacation rentals scattered across Southwest Florida. His business history was clean—no lawsuits, no complaints with the Better Business Bureau, no disgruntled former partners crawling out of the woodwork to air grievances. He paid his taxes on time, donated to the local Rotary Club, and had a handicap of twelve at the Naples Grande Golf Club.

What did stick out was that Beau was supporting Garrett Dutton's campaign. There was nothing about how Beau felt about mining, just a quiet nod in the politician's direction. That didn't necessarily mean a damn thing. Lots of people supported Dutton. A few of them resided in Calusa Cove. Didn't mean they wanted to mess with Trent and Mallor's Landing.

Emma Henderson was a former interior designer who now filled her days with charity boards, garden clubs, and a social calendar that required a personal assistant to manage. She'd chaired the Naples Winter Wine Festival's silent auction three years running and had been photographed at enough galas to wallpaper a small mansion.

Their financials were solid—wealthy in an understated way. No debt. No liens. No red flags.

On paper, they were exactly what they claimed to be. A well-off couple in their early fifties looking for a unique property in a charming small town where they could spend their golden years pretending to be country folk while still having access to a decent wine list.

But Mallor's Landing wasn't just any piece of property. It was a commercial alligator farm and a natural habitat. What on earth would they want with a business like that? It didn't make sense.

Made even less sense that they would threaten Trent to get it.

Unless they were tied to Sovereign Resources, and that land represented something that she hadn't figured out yet.

So, she'd dug deeper. Pulled their travel records through a contact who owed her a favor and didn't ask questions. The Hendersons had visited Calusa Cove six times in the past two years—always staying at Harvey's Cabins, always for long weekends, always during seasons when the town was quiet and the tourists were elsewhere. They'd taken Trent's eco tour twice. They'd enjoyed the Everglades Overwatch airboat ride. They'd eaten at Massey's—which was about to formally become Juniper's—at least a dozen times, according to credit card records.

For people who supposedly just wanted a nice retirement property, they'd done an awful lot of reconnaissance.

But recon for what? That was the question Dove couldn't answer. The Hendersons had no obvious connection to Karl Simpson. So, she went down other rabbit holes, because that's what Buddy had taught her. Look at everything, even if the threads weren't the same colors.

The Hendersons had no ties to Sovereign Resources that she could find. No history with Gulf Coast Energy Partners or Jack's case, except for their support of Dutton. They were just... there. Hovering. Wanting.

It made her teeth itch.

And what made her crazier was that Karl Simpson was even harder to pin down.

On paper, he was almost clean. A couple of minor poaching charges years back—fines paid, probation served, nothing that would raise flags outside the local wildlife officer's memory. The kind of stuff that happened when you grew up in the Glades and thought the rules were more like suggestions.

A couple of times, he and Trent were caught doing shit teenagers and young adults weren't supposed to be doing. Underage drinking. Fishing where fishing wasn't allowed or keeping fish that weren't in season or were the wrong size. Nothing too erroneous. Nothing that would make her think he was a total criminal.

But the paper didn't tell the whole story. It never did.

The problem with Karl was that everyone knew he was dirty, but no one could prove it. He was the guy who always seemed to have cash when he shouldn't. The guy whose name came up in whispers at the bait shop but never in official reports. The guy who'd been "questioned" a few times about this or that but always walked away without charges.

The guy who knew enough to bury Trent.

What Dove couldn't figure out was the connection to what was happening now. Karl wanted Trent for his skills —that much was clear, and they had done some shady shit together in the past. But his "clients with deep pockets" remained shadows. No names. No trails. Just money supposedly flowing from somewhere, funding whatever scheme Karl was cooking up, and Trent was part of the recipe, whether he liked it or not.

And that brought her back to the Hendersons. Could they be those deep pockets? But why, and if they wanted Trent's skills, why come after his property before asking him to do the deed?

She rubbed her eyes and stepped out of the SUV, her joints protesting the sudden movement after hours of sitting. It was moments like this when she actually missed the Army.

The marina spread out before her, docks stretching into water that glittered like scattered coins in the late afternoon sun. A pelican sat on a piling near the fuel pump, watching her with the kind of bored judgment that suggested it had seen plenty of humans come and go and found them all equally disappointing.

The air was thick with brine and diesel and sun-warmed wood, underlaid with the faint funk of fish guts and the sweeter note of honeysuckle growing wild along the fence line. A few boats bobbed lazily in their slips, halyards clinking against masts in an almost musical rhythm. Somewhere out on the water, a motor coughed to life, and a flock of ibis lifted off from the mangroves like white paper caught in an updraft.

Dove headed for the main building, hoping to find Cullen somewhere. He wasn't always the easiest man to pin down, but his Uncle Silas mentioned he'd been out on the water helping Keaton Cole, the head of Fish and Wildlife, with a project.

The bell above the door chimed as she stepped inside, and a wall of air conditioning hit her like a welcome slap. Mitchell's Marina was a quaint old place with worn wooden floors that creaked, hand-painted signs advertising bait prices, and a warm, welcoming atmosphere that made it feel more like home than a boat storage.

The walls were covered with faded photographs of past fishing triumphs. Grinning tourists holding up tarpon, local legends posing with record-breaking snook, and one inexplicable shot of what appeared to be Audra, Dawson's wife, wrestling an alligator while wearing a white shirt covered in swamp and a smile that expressed pure joy.

Baily Dane, owner of the marina, stood behind the counter, her dark brown hair escaping its ponytail in about six different directions, and a smear of something that might have been axle grease decorating her left cheekbone. She was ringing up a purchase for Harley, the mangrove trimmer.

"—and I'm just saying," Baily was telling Harley with a grin that could only be described as shit-eating, "that's the third time this week you've managed to be here right when Cullen shows up. That's a hell of a coincidence, don't you think?"

Harley's tan cheeks flushed a shade of pink that clashed magnificently with her faded red ball cap. "I needed gas. My tank was low."

"Uh-huh." Baily's eyes sparkled with the special delight of a woman who'd spent her life in the same small town and had developed an almost supernatural ability to spot romantic entanglements forming. "And yesterday? When you needed gas and your tank was also low?"

"It's a small tank," Harley said.

"It's a twenty-gallon tank. I filled it myself." Bailey leaned her elbows on the counter, settling in like she had nowhere else to be and nothing she'd rather do than watch Harley squirm. "And the day before that, when you came in for... what was it? A new fuel filter?"

"Which I actually needed, by the way. You can ask anyone who's worked with outboards—"

"And the fact that you two made plans to meet up at Juniper's tonight has absolutely nothing to do with any of this."

Dove contemplated making herself known, but honestly, this conversation was too good to pass up, so she decided to hang back for a bit and enjoy. Certainly beat listening to Sterling talk about whether he should have a drink at Junipers, or to Buddy talk about buying a damn engagement ring.

"It's not a date." Harley shoved her credit card slip into her pocket. "We're just friends. He wanted someone to talk to who isn't going to psychoanalyze him every five minutes or ask him how he's feeling about things. I don't need to deal with people's emotions. I talk about boats, mangroves, and whether the mullet are running. It's refreshing, apparently."

"Whatever you say," Baily said.

"It's not—" Harley made a sound of pure frustration. "You're impossible. You know that? Absolutely impossible."

"It's part of my charm. Fletcher says so all the time."

"Your husband also thinks mayonnaise belongs on a hot dog, so I'm not sure his judgment should be trusted."

Dove bit the inside of her cheek to keep from laughing and stepped up to the counter. Both women turned, Harley looking relieved at the interruption and Baily looking like Christmas had come early, bringing a second present.

"Well, well, well." Baily straightened up, her grin somehow widening even further. She glanced between Dove and Harley with an expression of pure, delighted mischief. "Please tell me you're here to talk about your love life, too. I'm on a roll."

"I don't have one of those," Dove said automatically.

"Sure you don't." Baily leaned back against the cigarette display. "And Harley here doesn't have a thing for our local handyman, part-time construction worker and Aegis Network employee with PTSD and cheekbones that could cut glass."

"Believe what you want, but it doesn't make it true," Harley muttered.

"I know I'm right, but I'll drop it for now." Baily

turned her attention back to Dove. "So what brings you in? Don't tell me you need bait. You don't strike me as the fishing type."

"Actually, I was looking for Cullen. His Uncle Silas told me I could find him here."

Harley's expression shifted—not quite guarded, but more careful than it had been a moment ago. "He's down at the dock. Slip eight. Hosing down his boat."

"Thanks." Dove pushed from the counter.

"Mind if I ask what this is all about?" Harley asked.

"Just some weird stuff has been happening around Trent's place, and I'm worried it might have to do with an old buddy of his. A guy by the name of Karl Simpson," Dove said. "They all went to high school together, and I just want to pick Cullen's brain."

"Karl is nothing but trouble," Baily said. "We won't extend him credit at the marina anymore because we've had trouble with him paying. Keaton and Fallon both have had to give him tickets for different things. Karl has been running on smiles and acting like a good person by doing nice things, but people are starting to smarten up."

"I've seen that in action." Harley shook her head. "He's tried to help me out on the river a few times, but then it's all about turning my head when he's doing something he's not supposed to. I've called Keaton about Karl. Not sure if Keaton was able to bust him, though."

"I have no idea why Karl keeps fishing in places he's not supposed to, but he's also doing other shit," Baily said. "Like skirting the rules during the Python challenge. That really gets under my husband's skin."

"I imagine it would." Dove took it all in, filing away the info in various places. It seemed everyone had Karl's number, but he hadn't crossed that line, or hadn't gotten caught, where people would completely turn their backs.

Except for maybe now. But this wasn't her story to repeat, and she'd made a promise that for now, she wouldn't tell anyone about the note.

"I'd better go find Cullen before it gets too late," Dove said.

"Make sure you say hello to Trent." Baily smiled.

Dove groaned as she turned on her heels and strolled across the room. She didn't say another word or glance over her shoulder. No way was she sticking around to have her and Trent's on-and-off whatever-it-was dissected by Baily and Haley.

Dove stepped outside. The docks stretched out over the water like arthritic fingers. Weathered wood that had gone gray from decades of salt and sun. Most of the slips were empty this time of day—the serious fishermen had come and gone with the dawn, and the sunset crowd wouldn't start trickling in for another hour or so. A great blue heron stood motionless at the end of the far pier, its stillness so complete it might have been carved from stone, waiting with infinite patience for something stupid enough to swim within range.

Dove found Cullen standing on the dock next to slip eight with a hose in one hand and a long-handled brush in the other. He worked methodically along the deck of his boat—a twenty-foot skiff that had seen better days but was clearly well-maintained.

He looked up as Dove approached, squinting against the glare off the water. He was the same age as Trent. He was fit but lean, with a weathered build from physical labor and too many years of not eating enough. His dark hair was shaggy, curling over his ears and the back of his neck, and there was a stillness to him that she recognized. The hyperawareness of someone whose nervous system had been rewired by trauma and was still learning how to exist in a world where not everything was a threat.

"Hey Dove." He shut off the hose and straightened, rolling his shoulders in a way that suggested they ached. "What brings you down here?" He tossed the brush into a bucket and wiped his hands on shorts that had probably been blue once upon a time but had faded to something closer to gray. He grabbed a water bottle from the dock and took a long drink, studying her over the rim. "More work from the Aegis Network? Because that would be great. Decker Brown is still doing that big construction project on the West side of the state, and I just can't be that far from my kid now that I get to see him, even if it is supervised visitation."

"Sterling has a new case he needs surveillance for. He'll be in touch. It's straightforward. Local. And I need more than information on this one. Buddy said we can pay you the same as when you protected Fallon."

"That works for me." He sat down on the skiff's bench. "So, what can I help you with?"

Dove leaned against a piling, folding her arms across her chest. The wood was warm against her back, sun-soaked and rough. "I need information about someone you grew up with."

Cullen's expression didn't change. "That's not a long list. Calusa Cove isn't exactly a sprawling metropolis. Who?"

"Karl Simpson."

Cullen shifted his gaze and stared out at the water where the heron had finally speared something and was working on swallowing it whole. "Now there's a name I try not to think about. What's he done now?"

"That's what I'm trying to figure out." Dove lowered herself to the dock, sitting cross-legged, because no way was she going to dangle her feet over gator-infested waters while she contemplated what to tell Cullen. "He came to see Trent about a month ago. Wanted him to get involved in some operation—illegal poaching, from what Trent said. Clients with money. Specific needs. Trent turned him down."

"Sounds like something Karl would get involved in. He was always doing something shady, and unfortunately, back in the day, Trent wasn't too far behind."

"Yeah, well, someone breached Mallor's Landing and killed Bonnie."

"I heard about that." Cullen let out a long breath. "The gators that come and go from the natural habitat on Mallor's Landing are like Trent's kids. I'm sure that hit him hard."

"He's doing well enough."

"He's always been good at pushing things down." Cullen's voice had a bitter edge that surprised her. "Even when he shouldn't have to—and he's done that many times where Karl's concerned. I get Trent has no loyalty to Karl anymore, but he still keeps the past close to his vest."

Boy, did Dove understand that. "I'm trying to figure out if Karl could be connected to whoever was lurking in the shadows at Linda's funeral, or Bonnie, or even if he could have something to do with the couple putting a little pressure on Trent to sell Mallor's Landing. I figured you might have some insight, since you all grew up together."

Cullen laughed—a short, sharp sound. "Grew up in the same town. That's not the same thing as growing up together." He set down the water bottle and stretched out his legs. "Karl and Trent were tight back in the day. Did all kinds of stupid shit together—Python Challenge, gator hunting, whatever scheme Karl had cooked up that week. Me?" He shrugged. "I was on the outside looking in. Different crowd. Different priorities. Different everything, really."

"But you knew them."

"Enough to get into fights with them, sure." A ghost of a smile crossed his face. "Karl had a mouth on him. Liked to run it when he should've kept it shut. He also had a temper with a massive chip on his shoulder." The smile faded. "Trent was a little kinder, but he and I nearly came to blows a few times."

"So you weren't friends."

"Definitely never friends with Karl. Trent and I were close when we were little, but that changed as we became teenagers and more or less just tolerated each other." Cullen leaned forward, bending his legs and resting his elbows on his knees. "I left for the Marines right after graduation. Couldn't wait to get out of this town. Thought I was going to see the world, be somebody, do something that mattered. All that bullshit they sell you at the recruiting office, and for a while it was good, until it wasn't."

Dove didn't say anything. She knew this part of the story, or at least the broad strokes of it. She'd lived her own version.

"Saw the world, alright." Cullen's voice had gone flat—the kind of flat that meant emotions were being held at arm's length because letting them any closer would be dangerous. "Saw things I can't unsee. Did things I can't undo. Lost people I can't get back." He was quiet for a moment, staring at something only he could see. "When I came home, I wasn't right. Wrong in the head. The VA gave me pills and told me to talk about my feelings. My family walked on eggshells, pretending everything was fine. My ex—she tried so hard, but how do you help someone who doesn't know how to be a person anymore?"

"You can't," Dove said quietly. "They have to find their own way back."

Cullen looked at her and nodded. The acknowledgment of someone who'd been to the same dark place and somehow found the exit. "Yeah. That's the thing, isn't it?" He rubbed a hand over his face, stubble rasping. "I spent a while living on the edge. Literally. Out in the Glades, away from people, away from anything that reminded me of what normal was supposed to look like. Lived in a shack, ate what I caught, and waited to either get better or die. Wasn't picky about which."

"What changed?"

"Trent." The name came out soft. "He and Fallon. They kept showing up, kept dragging me back to civilization whether I wanted it or not. Bought food. Bought beer. Brought company that didn't ask me to talk about anything I didn't want to talk about." He shook his head slowly. "I told them to leave me alone. Told them I was fine. Told them some pretty ugly things, actually, hoping they'd give up. They didn't. Just kept coming back—every week, sometimes twice a week. My uncle would join sometimes. Then half the damn town, honestly. This place wouldn't let me disappear."

"Sounds exhausting."

"It was." Cullen laughed, a rough sound. "But it worked. Slow, like growing bone back after a break, but it worked." He met her eyes. "Trent gave me that. He saw something worth saving when I couldn't see anything at all."

The water lapped against the pilings, filling the silence. A mullet jumped somewhere nearby, silver flash and splash, and the heron's head swiveled to track it.

"Now, I'm focused on staying steady," Cullen continued. "Getting my head on straight. Making sure I can see my son, Tyler, regularly." Cullen's face lit up. "He's got my eyes and his mother's good sense, thank God. My ex—she worries. About the PTSD. About whether I'm stable enough, whether something might trigger me when I'm alone with him." He lifted one shoulder. "I don't blame her. She's protecting our kid. That's her job. I just have to keep proving that I'm someone he can count on."

"Sounds like you're doing the work."

"Every damn day. Some days are harder than others." He rubbed his hands up and down his thighs. "But you didn't come here to listen to my sad story. You came to ask about Karl. Specifically whether I think he'd do something to hurt Trent if Trent didn't play along with whatever he wanted."

Dove nodded. "Would he?"

"Outside of taking a few potshots at someone, Karl's not violent. He's the kind of guy who starts fights and lets other people finish them."

"But?"

"I wouldn't put it past him to manipulate. To scheme. To set up a situation where someone else takes the fall." He held Dove's gaze. "Karl's always been about Karl. If Trent's useful to him, he'll be his best friend. The second Trent becomes a problem—or more valuable as a scapegoat than a partner—Karl won't think twice about throwing him under the bus. And the problem is Trent, even when he's being a dick, he's got a heart the size of this country. He's as true as they come, and he tends to see the good in people. All people. Even assholes like Karl."

"Trent told me about the probation."

"That's the kind of person he is." Cullen's voice hardened. "He takes care of people, even when they don't deserve it. And Karl walked away clean. Pissed off Fallon."

"So you think Karl could do it again?"

"In a heartbeat. He doesn't have loyalty—he has interests. If Trent keeps saying no?" Cullen shrugged. "Karl will find a way to make yes the only option. Or he'll find a way to make Trent pay for refusing."

Dove absorbed this, fitting it into the picture she'd been building all day. "Any idea who his clients might be? The ones with deep pockets?"

"No clue. And truthfully, Karl could be bullshitting to get Trent to bite."

Dove pushed to a standing position. "Thanks for the intel. I appreciate it. If you hear anything or happen to see Karl, let me know. We'll be in touch."

"Thanks." Cullen hopped to his feet. "If you need anything else, you know where to find me. And Dove?"

"Yeah?"

"Watch your back. I've never trusted Karl and I trust the people around him less. If someone's targeting Trent —if this is about more than money or petty bullshit—Karl might not think twice about going through anyone standing next to him."

"I can handle myself."

"I know you can. Just saying—be careful." Something in his expression softened. "Trent's already lost enough. His dad. His mom. That gator who made his moat her home. He acts like he can handle anything, but everyone's got a breaking point. Don't let him find his by losing you, too."

The words hit harder than they should have.

"For what it's worth—I'm glad he's got you. He's been alone too long. Not physically, but..." Cullen tapped his chest. "In here. He keeps everyone at arm's length, even the people who love him. If you've gotten past that, you must be something special."

Dove nodded once, not trusting her voice, and turned to head back up the dock, her boots hollow on the weathered wood.

Her phone buzzed before she'd made it halfway back to the marina building.

She pulled it out, half-expecting it to be Buddy with another dead end or her uncle with another complication.

Warmth bloomed behind her ribs when she saw the name on the screen.

Trent: *Dinner at the pub? I'll buy.*

She read it twice, then a third time, a smile tugging at the corner of her mouth.

Trent Mallor. Asking her to dinner. In public. Voluntarily.

This was progress. For both of them, maybe—but mostly for Trent. The man who'd spent three weeks barely able to sit at the local pub without looking like he wanted to bolt. The man who'd been drowning in grief so deep she wasn't sure he'd ever surface.

Dove: *Be there in 20. And I'm paying. You bought last time.*

Trent: *There was no last time. We've never been on a real date before.*

She grinned at the screen.

Dove pocketed the phone and headed for her truck, the setting sun warm on her shoulders, Cullen's words still echoing in her mind.

She wasn't something special. She was just stubborn enough not to give up on someone who'd forgotten they were worth fighting for.

And Trent Mallor, whether he knew it or not, was absolutely worth fighting for.

Chapter Nine

The evening breeze that skimmed across the deck at Juniper's made Trent forget it was Florida in the summer—or at least made him forget long enough to enjoy a cold beer without sweating through his shirt.

Trent leaned back in his chair, one arm draped over the back of Dove's seat, and watched his friends laugh at the tail end of Buddy's proposal story while Harley admired Fallon's engagement ring.

Trent couldn't be happier for his friends.

The big round table they'd commandeered was littered with the aftermath of dinner—empty plates smeared with remoulade, a basket that had once held hush puppies, the balled-up napkins of people who'd eaten well and weren't sorry about it.

Juniper had outdone herself tonight. Blackened grouper that melted on your tongue, fried green tomatoes stacked with pimento cheese, and a key lime pie that

Fallon had declared "almost as good as Linda's." The compliment had hit Trent somewhere soft, but in a good way. His mother would've loved knowing her pie had competition.

"Alright, alright," Cullen said, waving his beer bottle at Trent. "You've been holding out on us all night. Time to tell the boat story."

"Which one?" Trent asked. "Because everything amusing that happened during our childhood happened on a boat." He pointed his finger. "Including the time we were maybe six-years-old, and you thought it was perfectly fine to take an inflatable floaty raft out into the Glades. Damn near gave my father a heart attack when you floated right on by a bunch of hungry gators."

"Yeah, well, I didn't know I was in danger, and your dad just paddled that rowboat out there and scooped me up like it was nothing." Cullen laughed. "But I'm talking about the one where Fallon over there was trying to impress... someone."

Fallon groaned. "Oh, God. Not that one. It totally makes me look like an idiot."

"I think someone else looks like a big doofus, as well." Cullen leaned back and took a swig of his beer.

"Oh, now this sounds interesting," Buddy said, grinning. He pulled Fallon closer against his side. "I mean, she rarely does anything that makes her look foolish, besides the time she dated Trent—which I chalk up to a moment of insanity—"

"Hey, I'm insulted—besides, she's marrying you."

Trent clutched his chest in mock offense, but the truth was, he wasn't. Not even a little.

"I'm the luckiest man in the room," Buddy said. "Now give me some fresh ammunition to tease her with."

"No more chocolates in your lunchbox," Fallon mumbled.

"I doubt that." Buddy kissed her temple.

Dove leaned forward, her chin propped on her hand. "Now, I definitely need to hear this."

Trent took a long pull of his beer, savoring the moment. For months, he'd been a walking zombie while he'd taken care of his mother. All he'd wanted was to cherish her final days. Spend as much time with her as he could, because he'd taken way too much for granted.

After she died, it was like he'd put a foot in the grave with her. But it was time to start living again, and there was no better way to do it than with this group.

Fallon was already turning pink. He'd told this story many times, and it wasn't so much that she was embarrassed by why she'd done it, but more that it happened at all. "So, Fallon here was maybe sixteen—"

"Fifteen," Fallon muttered. "I was fifteen—a child. A silly kid."

"Who thought she was an adult," Trent added. "And there were these boys—twins. Sean and Pat Hamlin. They lived in the next town over but kept their boat at Mitchell's because their dad was friends with Ray, Baily's dad and they were eighteen. Too old for Fallon."

"Technically, they were." Cullen tapped his fingers

on the wooden table. "But everyone that Fallon has ever been interested in was too old for her."

"Do you want to tell this story?" Trent asked.

"No." Cullen lifted his beer. "Proceed."

"Cullen and I were out minding our own business—"

"Trying not to kill each other," Cullen said, interrupting Trent.

"Exactly." Trent chuckled. "Those two boys were maybe thirty feet from us, and here comes Fallon, all by herself in her skiff, decked out in fishing gear. Cullen and I looked at each other and it took everything we had not to laugh because you know, we both liked Fallon, but we couldn't understand what the heck she was doing because she wasn't acting like herself."

"Gee, thanks," Fallon mumbled.

"I assumed she was trying to impress those boys, though I can't imagine why. They were idiots," Trent said.

"I was fifteen," Fallon repeated, like that explained everything. "I was an idiot, but they weren't bad to look at."

"Yeah, no comment." Trent grinned. "So she cruises up to me and Cullen and asks me if I could help her to practice her cast, work on her technique. Very innocent. Very wholesome."

"You're laying this on awfully thick," Fallon said.

"I'm setting the scene. It's called storytelling." Trent winked, enjoying the way his pulse spiked. How his chest rumbled, and how he could picture the day as if it were yesterday. His mom would want him to keep having moments like this. To share his world with his friends. To laugh. To live. To love.

Cullen snorted. "Come on, Fallon, he's not exaggerating."

"Whatever." Fallon lifted her drink and sipped.

"Anyway, I'm helping her, and I'm thinking to myself, she's got this. She doesn't need me to help her get those morons to notice her," Trent continued, "and I tell her that and—"

"Your first mistake," Dove said.

Trent chuckled. "One of many. But now those Hamlin boys are on the move. As a matter of fact, they drove right on past us. I asked her if she needed to go and she glances at her watch and nods." Trent paused for effect. "She stands, and the boat rocks, a little too much, and now I have to stand because it looks like she's about to fall, and I grab her by the hips, and help her back into her boat."

"Fallon, you did not." Buddy jerked his head back and stared at her. "He was how old back then?"

"Twenty-one," Fallon said. "But he didn't know what I was doing."

"Not a clue." Trent smacked his palm to his forehead. "She was just a kid at the time. A family friend."

"What happened next?" Dove asked.

"I thought she was simply trying to impress those twins because she yanked the cord on the two-stroke to restart it, but she pulled too hard, lost her balance, and went ass-over-teakettle right off the side of the boat." Trent mimed the motion with his hand. "Splash. Gone."

Buddy tossed his head back and laughed. "I would've killed to see that. Please tell me there's more."

"Oh, there's more." Cullen grinned. "Fallon hadn't noticed—because she was too busy making eyes at Trent—"

"Hey, Trent didn't notice either." Fallon waved her hand.

"I didn't notice a lot of things that day," Trent said. "You see, we'd drifted right next to Old Moses's favorite sunning spot."

Dove's eyes went wide. "I know you, Mallor, and something tells me that's a name for a gator."

"A thirteen-foot one. Meaner than a stepped-on snake. He'd been living in that stretch of water for as long as I could remember, and he did *not* appreciate being disturbed by a teenage girl cannonballing into his afternoon nap."

"Oh no," Harley said, though she was laughing.

"Oh yes." Trent shook his head. "Fallon comes up sputtering, water in her eyes, still trying to look cool—and Old Moses is about ten feet away, giving her the kind of look that says, 'dinner just arrived.'"

"I didn't see him, at first," Fallon said. "I was disoriented and honestly mortified that my future boyfriend had just seen me make a fool of myself."

"For the record, that boyfriend thing didn't happen for another five years." Trent lifted his beer. "But I distinctly remember her coming up for air and doing her best to smooth down her hair. Like all she cared about was what she looked like, and that was so unlike Fallon."

The table erupted in laughter. Even Fallon was smiling now, the embarrassment giving way to the comfortable nostalgia of a story told too many times to hurt anymore.

"So what happened?" Dove asked.

"I dove in after her." Trent shrugged like it was nothing. "Grabbed her by the back of her shirt and hauled her toward the boat while Moses decided whether we were worth the effort. Lucky for us, he'd already eaten that day. We got back in the boat, and Fallon spent the next few days avoiding me."

"And you couldn't figure out why," Cullen said, barely containing his laughter. He leaned forward, his eyes bright with mischief. "But here's the thing, it took a bit for Trent to understand." He pointed his beer bottle at Fallon. "It wasn't the Hamlin boys she was trying to impress."

Trent rolled his eyes. "I still think she liked one of them."

"Come on, man." Cullen laughed. "She didn't give a damn about those boys. She was trying to get your attention."

"I can't believe you chose to swim in the water with a gator named Old Moses just to get this man's attention." Dove patted Trent's cheek.

"It seemed like a good idea at the time," Fallon said.

Buddy pulled her closer, pressing a kiss to her temple. "I'm glad the gator didn't eat you. For selfish reasons."

"The crush didn't last anyway," Fallon said, waving her hand dismissively. "Living with him killed it pretty quick." She shot Trent a look. "He's a pain in the ass. Leaves his boots everywhere. Talks to the gators more than he talks to people. And don't even get me started on his cooking."

"My cooking is fine." He lowered his chin.

"Your cooking is survival food at best. I gained ten pounds after I moved out just from eating actual meals." Fallon leaned into Buddy, and it warmed Trent's heart that she'd found love.

"She's not wrong," Cullen said. "I've had your chili. It's basically meat-flavored punishment."

"Everyone's a critic." Trent finished his beer and set the empty bottle on the table. But he was smiling. This—the teasing, the laughter, the easy comfort of people who'd known each other long enough to mock each other with love—this was what he'd been missing. What grief had stolen from him for the past few weeks.

It felt good to have it back.

"We should settle up," Buddy said, pulling out his wallet. "Fallon's got an early shift, and I promised I'd make her breakfast."

"Wow, look at you all domesticated." Trent raised an eyebrow.

"Love will do that to a man," Buddy said with a wide grin. "Also, she does this thing where she—"

"Nope." Fallon clamped her hand over his mouth. "We are not sharing that with the table."

"I wasn't going to say anything bad." Buddy kissed her palm.

"You were going to say something that would make

me murder you in your sleep." She removed her hand and kissed him quickly. "Let's go, Romeo. Before you get yourself killed."

They settled the bill liked they'd done a million times. No one argued about who should pay what. It all evened itself out eventually.

Harley pushed back from the table. "Alright, I need to get going. Early morning tomorrow—those mangroves aren't going to trim themselves."

"Right behind you," Cullen said, standing and stretching. "Walk you to your truck?"

"It's fifty feet away."

"Fifty feet of dangerous parking lot. You never know what's lurking."

"Possums, mostly." But Harley smiled as she stood, and she didn't object when Cullen fell into step beside her.

"We're gonna head out the front," Buddy said. "We walked."

"See you later." Trent nodded before taking Dove's hand and guiding her through the maze of people and out to the parking lot.

The night had turned soft and warm, the kind of evening that made Dove want to drive slow with the windows down and nowhere particular to be. Cullen and Harley were already gone, their trucks no longer in the side lot.

"Just us," Dove said, bumping her shoulder against his.

"Just us."

They walked around to the back lot where they'd both parked, the gravel crunching under their boots. Trent reached for her hand, her fingers threading through his like they belonged there.

Her truck was parked under the single light in the lot, a cone of yellow illumination in the darkness. He walked her to the driver's side door and didn't let go of her hand.

"Where's your uncle tonight?" he asked.

"Went to see a friend." She met his eyes. "He asked if you'd been notified about the exhumation?"

"I got the paperwork. But I don't want to talk about that right now." He stepped closer, backing her against the driver's door, his hands finding her hips. She looked up at him, her blue eyes dark in the low light, and didn't resist.

"What do you want to talk about?" she asked, her voice dropping.

"Who said anything about talking?"

He kissed her. Not gentle. Not careful. The kind of kiss that said he'd been thinking about this all through dinner, watching her laugh and talk and fit so perfectly into his life that it scared him. The kind of kiss that said he was done being careful.

She kissed him back with equal intensity, her hands fisting in the front of his shirt, pulling him closer. He pressed her harder against the truck, felt her arch into him, and for a long moment, there was nothing else—no grief, no worry, no ghosts—just her.

When he finally pulled back, they were both breathing hard.

"You gonna follow me home?" he asked, his forehead resting against hers.

She smiled, slow and promising. "I was plan—"

"Well, well. Isn't this cozy."

Trent went rigid.

He knew that voice. Knew the lazy drawl, the undercurrent of mockery, the way it always sounded like the speaker was laughing at a joke no one else understood.

Karl Simpson stepped out of the shadows at the edge of the parking lot, his boots scraping on the pavement, an easy grin plastered across his face like he'd just stopped by to say hello to old friends.

Trent shifted, putting himself between Dove and Karl without thinking about it. His arm wrapped around her waist—protective, possessive.

"Karl." The name came out flat and cold on Trent's tongue.

"Mallor." Karl's grin widened. He looked at Dove, his eyes dragging over her in a way that made Trent's hands curl into fists. "And who is this? I think I've seen you around town. Yeah. With that former FBI guy, right?"

Dove didn't respond. But Trent could feel the tension in her body, the coiled readiness of someone who'd dealt with men like Karl before and knew exactly what they were.

"If you don't mind, we were just headed out," Trent said, not bothering to explain who Dove was.

"I think we need to talk." Karl spread his hands, all innocence. "You never really heard me out the last time, and I'd hate for you to miss an opportunity."

"We don't have anything to talk about," Trent said. "And I don't take too kindly to being threatened."

Karl held up his hands. "When did I do that?"

"Don't play dumb with me." Trent wouldn't come out and mention the Hendersons, or shit that Karl could use to destroy Trent and his business. That would only add fuel to a fire Trent didn't want to ignite.

"I really don't know what you're rambling about." Karl's smile didn't waver, but something shifted in his eyes. Something harder. "I just want to discuss a business opportunity that you're not gonna want to turn down."

"I'm sure it's not for me." Trent kept his voice even, his body still. "But go ahead. Say it. You can speak freely in front of my girlfriend."

Karl chuckled—a low, knowing sound that made Trent want to put his fist through the man's teeth. "Nah. This is a private conversation. The kind that's better had between old friends." He paused. "I'll be in touch."

He gave Dove one more look—measuring, assessing— then turned and walked toward the back entrance of Juniper's, his boots crunching on the gravel until the darkness swallowed him.

The silence he left behind was thick enough to choke on.

"Why didn't you bring up the Hendersons?" Dove's voice was quiet.

"Because if he's behind that, it'll show that I'm running scared." Trent realized his arm was still tight around her waist and forced himself to relax. "Besides, he'll just deny it in front of you, and the point of all this was to see how I'd respond."

"I spoke to Cullen about Karl, but I didn't bring up the note."

He turned to look at her, and whatever she saw in his face made her expression sharpen. "Cullen texted me. And I appreciate you looking into things." Trent glanced toward the door Karl had disappeared through. "Karl is up to something, and it's definitely no good."

"I think this is all connected, and I bet if we dig deep enough, we'll find ties to Sovereign Resources."

"I don't know about that. They're a legit company with more than one mining site."

"Doesn't mean they don't do shady shit or wouldn't do whatever it took to push you off your land. We just need to find the connection," she said. "I know I'm onto something. You need to let me keep digging.'

"Let's sleep on it, and we can talk more about it in the morning."

"If you're not gonna talk to Dawson right away, at least let me read Buddy in on it."

"I'll think about it." He kissed her cheek. "Stay close on the ride home," he said. "I don't trust Karl."

"Okay."

He waited until she was in her truck with the engine running before walking to his own. And all the way home, watching her headlights in his rearview mirror, he couldn't shake the feeling that Karl's visit was more than about some stupid illegal poaching deal he had going.

Karl always had a way of holding the past over Trent's head.

Trent also couldn't shake the idea that the Hendersons and their offer had something to do with it. Worse, that Sovereign Resources and their mining of limestone were somehow connected.

But for the life of him, he couldn't figure out how it was all related.

And soon, his father's body would be dug up, and there wasn't really a damn thing he could do about it.

Chapter Ten

Dove jerked awake, her heart slamming against her ribs before her brain even caught up. Old instincts. The kind that never fully went away, no matter how many years separated her from the battlefield.

Her phone buzzed against the nightstand like an angry wasp, vibrating so hard it threatened to skitter right off the edge.

She reached for the phone, her fingers fumbling against the nightstand.

The room was black. Not the soft gray of approaching dawn, but the thick, velvety darkness that meant the sun was still hours from even thinking about rising. The only light came from the phone screen, a harsh blue-white rectangle that stabbed at her sleep-blurred eyes.

4:10 AM.

Unknown number.

Beside her, Trent stirred. His arm tightened around her waist, pulling her back against the warm wall of his chest. His breath was hot against her shoulder, slow and steady, not quite awake but no longer fully asleep.

"Why's your alarm going off at four in the morning?" His voice was a low rumble, rough with sleep and muffled against her skin.

"It's not."

She stared at the screen, watching the phone vibrate in her palm like something alive. Nothing good ever came from unknown numbers at this hour. That was a universal truth, right up there with death and taxes and the fact that the Everglades would eventually reclaim everything humans tried to build.

She declined the call.

The screen went dark, and she set the phone back on the nightstand, screen down, like that would somehow prevent it from ringing again. Like ignoring a problem ever made it go away.

"Wrong number?" Trent asked.

"Probably."

She turned in his arms, fitting herself against him, her leg sliding between his. His skin was warm, almost hot, the way it always was when he slept. Like he ran a few degrees higher than normal humans. She'd teased him about it once, called him a furnace, and he'd just shrugged and said it came from spending too much time with cold-blooded creatures.

"Well," she said, her fingers tracing up his chest, "since we're awake, we might as well have some fun."

His hand slid down her spine, fingers drawing lazy patterns on her lower back that made her skin tingle. "I'm not opposed to—"

The phone buzzed again—the same angry wasp sound.

She rolled to her side, snagging the cell. Dove's stomach tightened into a cold knot.

Once could be a wrong number. Once could be a drunk dial or a telemarketer with no sense of time zones, or a scammer trying their luck at an hour when people were too groggy to think straight.

Twice was something else.

Twice was intentional.

She tapped the green button and hit speaker. "Hello?"

"Is this Dovelynn Quinn?" The voice filled the dark room—male, professional, carrying a weight that came from years of delivering news nobody wanted to hear. Dove knew that voice. Not the specific person, but the type.

Trent sat up beside her, instantly alert. She felt him go still, felt his attention sharpen in the darkness.

"Speaking."

"Miss Quinn, this is Deputy Director Ethan Corrick with the U.S. Marshals Service. I'm your uncle's supervisor."

The cold knot in her stomach turned to ice.

Trent's hand found her back, warm and solid.

"What's wrong?" she asked.

Silence. One second. Two. Three.

Each one stretched out like taffy, pulled thin and

wrong, the kind of silence that said everything and nothing at the same time. The kind of silence that gave you just enough time to imagine every worst-case scenario before the words came to confirm one of them.

"I'm so sorry to have to tell you this." Corrick's voice softened, and the sound of it—that careful gentleness—made Dove's chest seize. "Your uncle was found a little after midnight. In his vehicle. In a parking lot in Okeechobee."

Trent's hand pressed harder against her back. She could feel the tension coiling through his body, could feel him holding his breath.

"He was murdered. Two gunshot wounds. One to the head. One to the chest."

The words landed like physical blows.

She felt them hit. Felt the impact somewhere deep in her chest, a dull thud that radiated outward like ripples in still water. Her uncle. Aaron Slade. The man who'd taught her to shoot when she was twelve years old, setting up cans on a fence post and patiently correcting her stance until she could hit the center every time. The man who'd shown up at her apartment a month after her team died, when she was drowning in a bottle and didn't care if she ever came up for air, and told her about the Aegis Network. Told her there was still a place in the world for people like them. People who were too broken to go back to normal life but too stubborn to give up entirely.

He was dead.

Murdered.

In a parking lot in Okeechobee, of all goddamn places.

Something inside her shifted. Like a door slamming shut. Like a switch being flipped. One second she was Dove—niece, friend, woman who'd had dinner with him three days ago and laughed at his terrible jokes and promised to call more often. The next second she was someone else. Something else.

Sergeant Quinn. The sniper who could lie perfectly still for eighteen hours waiting for a shot. The soldier who'd watched her team die through a scope and kept breathing anyway. The machine wrapped in skin, running on autopilot because the alternative was falling apart, and falling apart wasn't an option.

It was never an option.

Trent had pulled her against him, his arms wrapping around her from behind, his chin resting on her shoulder. She let him. But she didn't lean into it. Couldn't afford to.

"Do you have any leads?" Her voice came out flat. Controlled. Like it belonged to someone else entirely. "Witnesses?"

"Nothing yet," Corrick said. "The parking lot had minimal security coverage—just one camera at the entrance that caught his vehicle arriving at approximately eleven forty-five PM, but nothing that shows the incident itself. We're canvassing the area, talking to businesses, checking traffic cams on the surrounding streets. But so far..." He trailed off. The silence said what he couldn't.

"Your uncle was two months from retirement," Corrick continued. "He had no major cases on his desk.

Nothing active that would've put a target on his back. Truthfully, we're at a loss. This doesn't fit any pattern we can identify."

Dove's mind was already turning over possibilities, examining them from every angle the way she'd been trained to examine a target zone before taking a shot. Random robbery gone wrong? Possible, but two shots—head and chest—spoke of execution, not panic. Someone from an old case with a grudge? Maybe, but Slade had been careful, always careful, and he'd survived thirty years in the marshals service by knowing which threats were real and which were just noise.

"What about the dead man's cache?" she asked. "The Parrish documents? Jack Mallor's case?"

Behind her, Trent went rigid. His breath caught, and she felt his fingers dig slightly into her arms.

A pause. Longer than it should have been.

"Your uncle shouldn't have mentioned that," Corrick said slowly. "There was nothing active that your uncle was involved in. He was winding down, not ramping up. Transitioning cases to other agents. Clearing his desk." Another pause, a little longer than she thought necessary. "The Mallor case affected Slade. He took that loss personally, and in some ways, he never recovered. Always paranoid about who in our office might have betrayed our witness. Betrayed him. Did your uncle mention something about the case to you?"

"Just that your office requested to exhume Jack Mallor's body." She held her breath for a moment, waiting for Trent to react.

He didn't.

Corrick cleared his throat. "I'm expecting to hear from the judge today, and I also expect that they will allow it."

Trent made a sound—low, wounded, barely audible. His arms tightened around her.

"I don't know if my uncle told you that I'm living and working in Calusa Cove."

"He did," Corrick said.

"My uncle wasn't overly thrilled with the idea of exhuming Jack's body, and he mentioned that to Jack's son. We understand there's new information that needs to be confirmed, but I got the feeling there's more, and I'd just like to be able to give Trent some peace of mind."

Trent brushed his lips across her shoulder, soft and tender.

"You didn't hear this from me, but there are some questions about the validity of the original autopsy and the ME who performed it."

"I don't believe in coincidences," Dove said. "Uncle Aaron said he was in town for a surprise visit, but I don't believe that. He came to Calusa Cove because of whatever is going on with a case that crumbled twenty years ago and now he's dead—murdered—because of it."

"Slade had a few enemies. Anyone of them could've killed him," Corrick said. "Right now, I need you to come to Okeechobee. To make an identification. The local medical examiner is expecting you—you can come anytime, there's no rush. He's..." A heavy breath. "He's not going anywhere."

The words hung there. Obscene in their practicality. Of course, he wasn't going anywhere. He was dead. Dead people didn't go anywhere. They just waited, cold and still, for someone who loved them to come and confirm that yes, this body used to be a person. This shell used to laugh, tell bad jokes, drink bourbon on Sundays, and show up when you needed them most.

"I'll be there as soon as I can," Dove said.

"Take whatever time you need. And Miss Quinn—Aaron was a good man. One of the best I ever worked with. If there's anything I can do—anything at all—please don't hesitate. Day or night."

"Thank you."

"I'm so sorry for your loss."

The line went dead.

The room was silent. The frogs had stopped singing, or maybe she just couldn't hear them anymore. The ceiling fan turned in lazy circles. The darkness pressed in close, thick and heavy, like it was trying to swallow her whole.

Trent's arms were still around her, but she could feel him trembling. Not with cold. With the effort of holding in whatever he was feeling—grief for her, fear about his father's grave, the weight of too much bad news landing all at once.

"Dove." His voice cracked on her name.

She couldn't respond. If she opened her mouth, she didn't know what would come out—words or screams or nothing at all.

She pulled away from him. Gently, but deliberately.

Swung her legs over the side of the bed and reached for her clothes.

"I need to get up." She found her jeans and stepped into them. The denim was rough against her bare legs. Real. Tangible. Something to focus on besides the howling void that had opened up in her chest. "I have to go identify the body."

"Dove—"

"It's procedure." She located her shirt near the window and pulled it over her head. The fabric smelled like Trent's house—cypress and coffee and something green and alive. "Next of kin makes the positive ID. That's my mother or me, and I'm not doing that to my mom."

"You don't have to go right now. It's four in the morning. He said there was no rush."

"I need to do something." She was looking for her boots now, scanning the dark floor, grateful for the task. Grateful for something to do with her hands and her eyes that wasn't thinking about her uncle's body on a slab. "I can't just sit here."

"Dove, stop."

She found one boot near the closet. Where the hell was the other one?

"Just stop for a second."

"I can't." She dropped to her knees, looking under the bed. There. The other boot, kicked halfway to the wall. She grabbed it, shoved her foot inside. "If I stop, I'll think, and if I think—"

"Then think." Trent was beside her now, kneeling on

the floor in the dark, his hands closing over hers. "Feel it. Let it hurt."

"I don't want to."

"You need to."

"You don't understand." She tried to pull her hands free, but he held on. "I can't afford to fall apart. If I start, I won't stop. I know myself. I know how this goes. When my team died, I fell so far down that hole that I almost didn't climb back out. I can't do that again. I won't survive it."

"This is different."

"How?" The word came out sharp. Bitter. "How is this different? Someone I loved is dead. Someone I was supposed to protect—"

"You weren't supposed to protect him. He was a U.S. Marshal. He knew the risks. He'd been doing this job since before you were born."

"And I should have seen this coming." She was shaking now, tremors running through her body that she couldn't control. "I should've known this wasn't just a social visit. It didn't add up. I should've pushed, but I didn't, and now he's—" Her voice broke. Cracked right down the middle like ice too thin to hold weight.

She clamped her mouth shut, jaw tight, teeth grinding together so hard her head ached. The tears were there. They burned behind her eyes, pressing against her lids like water against a dam. But she wouldn't let them fall. Couldn't let them fall. Because if she started crying now, she'd never stop.

"Hey." Trent's hands released hers, and then his

palms cupped her face, warm and rough, tilting her head up until she had no choice but to look at him.

His eyes were dark in the dim room, but she could see the pain in them. For her. With her. The kind of pain that came from watching someone you cared about suffer and not being able to fix it.

"Walking around not dealing with this doesn't make it go away," he said quietly. "Trust me. I know. I spent twenty years not dealing with my father's death, and all it did was turn me into someone I didn't like very much. Angry. Closed off. Pushing away anyone who tried to get close." His thumbs stroked her cheekbones, the touch unbearably gentle. "Don't do that to yourself. Don't do what I did."

"I don't know how to do anything else."

"Then let me help you." He pulled her forward, wrapped his arms around her, tucked her head under his chin. She heard his heartbeat, steady and strong. She could feel the warmth of him seeping into her cold skin. "You don't have to fall apart completely. You don't have to lose yourself. Just... let yourself feel it. For one minute. Let it be real."

She wanted to argue. Wanted to push him away and stand up and keep moving, keep doing, keep functioning like the good little soldier she'd trained herself to be.

But she was so tired.

Tired of being strong. Tired of holding everything together. Tired of pretending fine was even in her vocabulary.

She let out a breath.

And something cracked.

Not all the way. Not completely. But enough. Enough that she stopped fighting his embrace. Enough that she let her forehead drop against his chest. Enough that the tears she'd been holding back spilled over, hot and silent, soaking into his bare skin.

She didn't sob. Didn't make a sound. Just let the tears fall while Trent held her, one hand stroking her hair, the other pressed flat against her back like he could hold her shattered pieces together through sheer force of will.

They stayed like that for a long time. Long enough for the darkness outside the window to soften, the first gray hints of dawn crept toward the horizon. Long enough for the tears to slow, then stop. Long enough for Dove to feel like maybe—maybe—she could breathe again.

Then she pulled back.

Wiped her face with the heels of her hands. "I have to go," she said. "I have to do this."

He studied her for a long moment. Whatever he saw in her face, he didn't argue.

"Okay," he said. "But I'm coming with you."

"You don't have to—"

"I'm coming with you." His voice left no room for debate. "You're not doing this alone."

She could have fought him. Could have insisted she was fine, that she didn't need a babysitter, that she'd been handling her own shit long before Trent Mallor had come into her life.

But the truth was, she didn't want to do this alone.

The thought of walking into that morgue by herself, looking down at her uncle's body with no one beside her —it made the cold knot in her stomach tighten until she could barely breathe.

"Okay," she said quietly.

They drifted through the motions of getting ready in silence. Clothes. Shoes. Teeth brushed, faces washed, and hair pulled back—the small rituals of preparing to face a day that had already broken before it began. Outside the window, the sky had lightened to a pale gray, the sun still hidden below the horizon but making its presence known.

Downstairs, Trent headed for the kitchen. "I'll make coffee. Something to eat for the road. You need to put something in your stomach before we drive an hour and a half."

Dove nodded. Her appetite was nonexistent—the thought of food made her vaguely nauseous—but she knew he was right. Operating on empty never ended well.

"I'll go start the truck," she said, grabbing the keys from the hook by the door.

She stepped out onto the porch, and the humidity wrapped around her like a wet blanket. The air was thick and heavy, the kind that settled into your lungs and stayed there. The moat had come alive with tails thrashing about. Damn things knew it was close to feeding time.

She crossed the bridge as quickly as she could,

ignoring the water rippling beneath her, and headed for her truck parked near the equipment shed.

That's when she saw it.

At first, her brain didn't register what she was looking at. The shape was wrong. Too big. Too twisted. Something massive on the ground near the fence line, on the wrong side of the moat. An area that should have been empty.

She stopped walking.

Squinted through the gray light.

Then it moved.

Coils. Thick as a man's thigh. Mottled brown and tan, patterned like dead leaves, like camouflage designed by something ancient and patient and hungry. The body shifted, muscles rippling beneath the scales, and Dove's stomach dropped as she finally understood what she was seeing.

A python. Massive. Easily fifteen feet, maybe more. A Burmese, from the markings—one of the invasive giants that had been strangling the Everglades for decades, eating everything in their path, breeding faster than wildlife officials could cull them.

And wrapped in its coils, thrashing weakly, desperately, was one of Trent's smaller gators.

Three feet long. Maybe four. Still young. Still vulnerable. Its jaws snapped at the air, tail whipping uselessly, stubby legs scrabbling for purchase that didn't exist. The python's coils tightened with each exhale, patient and relentless, squeezing the life out of its prey one breath at a time.

Dove had seen death before. Had caused it, more times than she could count. But there was something about this—the slow, inexorable crush of it, the way the gator's struggles were growing weaker with each passing second—that made her throat close up.

"Trent!" Her voice cut through the quiet morning like a gunshot. "Get out here, now!"

Chapter Eleven

Trent reached for the coffee filters when Dove's voice split the morning wide open.

Not a scream. Worse than a scream. A command. The kind of sound that came from a woman who'd spent years on battlefields and knew the difference between panic and a problem that needed solving right now.

He flew out the side door, bare feet hitting the porch boards, the screen door banging behind him. The humid air slammed into him like a wall, thick and wet and already warm despite the sun not even hitting the horizon yet.

"What's going on?" he asked.

"Snake. Fucking goddamned snake. Python."

"Where?" His gaze swept the property.

He didn't need Dove to answer. He saw it.

Near the fence line, maybe forty feet from the equipment shed, on the wrong side of the moat. A mass of coils wrapped around one of his younger gators like a fist squeezing the life out of something it had no right to touch. The gator's tail whipped weakly, its jaws snapping at nothing, its stubby legs clawing at dirt that offered no purchase.

His stomach dropped.

"Dove." He kept his voice even. Controlled. The same voice he used when he was working with an agitated animal and couldn't afford to telegraph fear. "Go inside. My handgun is on the top shelf of the bedroom closet. Bring it to the porch. But do not—" He looked at her. "Do not open the screen door."

She stared at him. "What—"

"The gators in the moat are riled. You hear that?"

"I noticed them thrashing about, but they're always active in the morning."

"It's not just that. It's the noises." A chorus of low hisses and guttural bellows echoed across the air. They were the kind of sounds that vibrated in his chest and told him something primal had been triggered. The big ones were agitated, pushing toward the far bank, clawing at the sloped concrete on the side they couldn't normally scale. Normally, being the keyword. A motivated gator could do things that would surprise most people.

"Some of them could get over if they wanted it bad enough," he said. "They smell a fight. Go. Now."

Dove moved. No argument. No hesitation. She disappeared through the side door, the screen slapping shut behind her.

Trent found his boots on the porch and ran toward

the equipment shed. Twenty years on this land had mapped every root, every dip, every patch of ground into his muscle memory.

Inside the shed, he grabbed what he needed. Bolt stunner first—a captive bolt device, humane, designed to render the animal unconscious instantly if placed correctly. Pithing tool next, a metal rod with a sharp point, for the follow-up. An air gun. A snake hook, four feet of aluminum with a curved end. He shoved the smaller tools into a belt and wrapped it around his waist. He slung the air gun over his shoulder.

Then he grabbed a chicken quarter from the bait cooler and dropped it into a bucket.

His hands were steady. That was something confidence and years of being a cocky asshole had brought him. It didn't matter what was going on inside. The fear. The adrenaline. His outsides needed to be calm. It's what had saved his sorry ass many times.

He jogged back toward the fence line, bucket in one hand, hook in the other, the rest of his tools jangling against his hip. The python hadn't moved much. It didn't need to. It was doing exactly what millions of years of evolution had designed it to do—squeeze, wait, squeeze again. Each time the gator exhaled, the coils tightened. Patient. Methodical. Like a machine that ran on hunger and time.

The gator was maybe three and a half feet. Young. Showed up a few months ago. Hurt, bleeding, and would've died if she hadn't found her way to Mallor's Landing.

He'd named her Clarkson, after Kelly Clarkson and the song *Stronger*. And Trent knew it was her based on the pale scar on her left flank.

She was still fighting. Barely. But still.

He set the bucket down about fifteen feet from the tangle, far enough that the smell of raw chicken wouldn't complicate things more than they already were. Then he approached the porch. Dove was standing behind the screen door, his Glock in her right hand, barrel pointed at the ground. Finger off the trigger. Proper form. Because a sniper wouldn't know any other way.

"Here's how this goes," he said, keeping his voice low and steady. "If the snake or the gator comes at me and I can't handle it, I'll tell you to shoot it. If I'm on the ground and something's coming for me, you put it down—but you wait for the signal."

"That won't be a problem."

"I don't want to die today, and I can't wrangle both at the same time." He held her gaze. "But if I tell you not to shoot, you don't. Can you do that?"

"Now, that's asking a lot." She rolled her shoulders, craning her neck side to side. "If teeth come close to breaking skin, I'm gonna shoot." There was no tremor in her voice. No uncertainty. The woman standing on his porch was the trained sniper, not the woman who'd been crying in his arms an hour ago. He was grateful for both versions of her, but right now, he needed the soldier.

"I can live with that."

"That's the plan, Mallor."

He smiled, then turned back to the problem.

The python was massive. Fifteen feet, easy. Maybe pushing sixteen. A Burmese—the invasive bastards that had been decimating the Everglades ecosystem for decades, eating everything from rabbits to deer to the occasional alligator, breeding in numbers that made wildlife officials lose sleep. Trent had caught and killed hundreds of them over the years. Maybe more, if he counted all the Python Challenges and the freelance removals not to mention the times he'd stumbled across one on his property and dealt with it because that's what you did when you lived on the edge of the Glades.

But he'd never dealt with one mid-kill. Not alone.

The snake's head was buried somewhere in the coils, pressed against the gator's midsection, its body a thick rope of muscle that rippled with each constriction. The tail end was loose, draped across the ground like a fat, heavy hose. When the gator thrashed, the tail twitched in response—a warning. A reminder that there was more snake than what you could see.

He gripped the hook and started forward.

Slow. Deliberate. Every step measured, every movement calculated. He'd done this a million times. Approached snakes this size with nothing but his hands and a hook and the quiet confidence that came from understanding these animals in a way most people never would. He respected them. All of them. The pythons included, even though they didn't belong here. They hadn't asked to be released into an ecosystem that couldn't handle them. That was on humans, not the snakes.

But this one was killing one of his gators, and it had to be stopped.

While his body was controlled, his pulse hammered in his throat as adrenaline coursed through his body.

He needed to get behind the head. Pin it with the hook, just long enough to place the bolt stunner against the skull. One clean shot. Instant unconsciousness. Then the pithing tool to finish it. Quick. Humane. The way it should be done.

Ten feet away now. The smell hit him—musk and blood and the raw, earthy stink of reptile stress hormones flooding the air. The gator's eyes were half-closed, its struggles weakening. Running out of time.

Eight feet.

The python's head shifted. Just slightly. A subtle repositioning that said it knew something was there. Something that wasn't prey but might be a threat.

Six feet.

Trent sucked in a slow breath as he raised the hook, angling it behind where the head pressed against the gator's body. A second ticked by. The snake shifted slightly. Simultaneously, Trent blew out the air trapped in his lungs and struck.

The hook caught the snake behind the skull, pressing it down into the dirt. The python's body reacted instantly —coils loosening from the gator, muscles surging with an almost electric power. The gator's jaws flew open, a hiss exploding from deep inside its body, raw and ragged—the sound of something that had been seconds from death and had suddenly found air.

The snake's tail whipped around like a bat, thick as Trent's thigh, catching him across both shins with a force that buckled his knees. The world tilted. He went down hard, his shoulder hitting the ground, the hook ripping free from the snake's neck as his grip failed. "Fuck," he mumbled.

"I have the shot." Dove's voice from the porch. Sharp. Ready.

"Don't. Not yet." He rolled, trying to get his feet under him, but the tail was already wrapping around his left leg, coiling with a speed that defied the animal's size. Thick muscle cinched against his calf, his knee, tightening with that same patient, relentless pressure he'd watched it use on the gator.

His heart hammered. Not panic—he didn't do panic, not with reptiles, not after thirty-plus years of living alongside them—but a healthy, urgent awareness that he had about ten seconds before this got significantly worse.

He grabbed the air gun from his shoulder, fingers finding the grip with the ease of a tool he'd used many times. The snake's head was free now, risen off the ground, weaving in a defensive posture, tongue flicking, trying to locate the threat. If it struck, it would hit him in the face or chest from this distance. Burmese pythons weren't venomous, but a mouth full of rear-facing teeth sinking into flesh wasn't something you walked away from without a trip to the ER or worse—being placed in a coffin.

He shifted his body, ignoring the squeeze on his leg, the pressure building toward pain. Angled the air gun upward. The snake's head swayed. He needed a shot at the top of the skull, behind the eyes. The sweet spot where a single pneumatic bolt would do its job and the animal wouldn't feel a thing.

The head dipped.

He fired.

The bolt connected. A sound like a muffled punch, and the snake's body went slack. Not dead—unconscious. The coils around his leg loosened like a rope coming undone, the massive body sagging against the ground in a boneless heap.

Trent was on his feet in an instant. He ripped the remaining coils from his leg, the scales rough against his skin, and grabbed the pithing tool from his belt—one quick, precise thrust into the brain stem.

The snake was gone.

No suffering. No drawn-out death. Just a switch flipped off, the way nature didn't do it, but humans owed it to the animals they'd displaced.

But the gator was still tangled.

Three and a half feet of panicked, oxygen-deprived alligator with jaws that could snap off a man's hand at the wrist. Its eyes were open now—wide, wild, pupils blown. It hissed again, a wet, guttural sound, its tail slapping weakly against the dead snake's body. Disoriented. Scared. And likely to bite whatever came close.

"It's okay, Clarkson. You're gonna be just fine," he whispered. "I'll be right back." He grabbed the bucket and brought it closer. He lifted the chicken quarter with the hook, threading it onto the curved end so it dangled like bait on a line. With his free hand, he carefully peeled the dead snake's coils away from the gator's body, working quickly, keeping his fingers well clear of those jaws.

The gator snapped at the air. Once. Twice. Testing. Looking for something to fight.

"Easy," Trent murmured. "Easy, Clarkson. Nobody's gonna hurt you."

He held the chicken quarter out on the hook, low to the ground, letting the smell do the work. The gator's nostrils flared. Its head tracked the meat, instinct overriding panic. Hunger was a hell of a motivator, even when a gator had nearly been crushed to death.

Slowly, carefully, Trent guided the hook toward the moat, step by step, the chicken quarter swinging gently. The gator followed, its gait unsteady, weaving slightly like a drunk navigating a parking lot. But it followed. Because it was a gator, and gators followed food the way rivers followed current. It was just what they did.

At the moat's edge, Trent swung the chicken quarter out over the water. The gator lunged, snapping the meat off the hook with a crack that echoed across the property, and slid into the dark water with a splash. The steep concrete on this side would keep it from climbing back up. Safe. Contained.

Trent exhaled. His mind and body finally registered the kind of danger he'd been in, like it always did after he'd encountered something that wasn't considered a routine pithing or gator confrontation. His pulse hitched. His breath caught in his throat. His hands even trembled. He shook them and blew out a long breath.

He lifted his leg, which throbbed where the python had squeezed, a dull ache that would probably turn into a spectacular bruise by afternoon. He rolled his foot, giving it a good stretch before putting it back on solid ground. His shoulder hurt from the fall.

He looked up at the porch.

Dove stood behind the screen door, the Glock still in her hand, still at her side, her face pale but composed. The morning light caught her blond hair, turning it almost white, and for a second she looked less like a woman and more like a ghost—something caught between this world and the next, not quite committed to either.

"You can come down now," he called.

"No, thank you. I'm good right here."

He laughed. He couldn't help it. After everything—the phone call, the news about Slade, the tears on the bedroom floor, a fifteen-foot python trying to make a meal of his gator and squeezing his leg—the woman who could drop a target at a thousand yards was standing on his porch refusing to come down because there might be reptiles.

"It's not funny," Dove said. But there was something in her voice. Not humor, exactly. More like the echo of humor. The memory of what laughing felt like, preserved somewhere beneath all the grief and shock and exhaustion.

"It's a little funny."

"You almost died."

"I did not almost die."

"The snake was wrapped around your leg," she said.

"I had it under control."

"You were on the ground."

"Temporarily. Part of the process."

She stared at him through the screen, her expression balanced and unreadable. "I don't know if I want to strangle you or kiss you."

"I'd prefer the kiss, and I'll be up in a second to get it." He figured that was about right for the two of them on any given day. He turned back to the dead python, pulling a breath of thick morning air into his lungs, tasting the musk and blood and the green of the Everglades waking up around him. The bruise on his leg pulsed in time with his heartbeat. Normal morning at Mallor's Landing. Just another...shit.

Slight movement near the tree line, low to the ground, where the tall grass met the fence.

His eyes narrowed, tracking the motion. A ripple through the grass. Then another. Different direction. Then a third, further down the fence, sliding along the base of a cypress trunk.

More snakes.

Not as big as the one he'd just killed. Eight, maybe ten feet. But unmistakable—that distinctive lateral undulation, the mottled pattern catching the early light as they moved through the undergrowth. He counted them, his jaw tightening with each one.

One near the fence post. Another along the drainage ditch. A third coiled at the base of the equipment shed. A fourth disappeared into the grass near the south bank.

Four. At least four.

His blood went cold.

He hadn't seen a python on his property in years. He was constantly looking for them. Looking for nests nearby. Clearing them out when he found them. But the last time he saw one slithering on his land was about six years ago.

Something was wrong for this many to be gathering.

He collected the bolt stunner, the pithing tool, and the air gun, leaving the dead python where it lay. He'd feed it to the gators later once things settled down. He walked back toward the porch with a calm he didn't entirely feel, his gaze scanning the perimeter, counting threats, calculating distances between the snakes and the moat.

"We've got a problem," he said, setting the tools on the porch step.

Dove's eyes sharpened. "Worse than the one you just handled?"

"More pythons. At least four that I can see. Maybe more I can't." He ran a hand through his hair. "I need to call Fish and Wildlife. Actually, I'll call Fallon directly, and she'll call her boss, Keaton Cole. I can't deal with this many on my own, and if even one of them gets into the moat..." He shook his head. "A python that size could easily take one of my smaller gators. And if they get into the breeding area, it'll be a massacre. But the bigger gators could easily deal with the pythons, but it would be an all-out battlefield and a messy one."

Dove straightened. "Okay. You deal with this. I'll go to Okeechobee and—"

"No."

"I can't sit around here. I have to go identify my uncle's body."

"And you will. With me. Not alone." He closed the gap between them. "I just need to wait for Fish and Wildlife to get here and get set up. Once they're on the property doing their thing, I'll go with you."

"That could take hours."

"Then it takes hours."

"I'm not going to fall apart driving to Okeechobee by myself."

"I know you won't." He kept his voice low. Gentle but immovable. "But I also know what it's like to walk into a room and look at someone you love on a table and have nobody standing next to you. My mother took her last breath with me sitting next to her. Alone. Then I sat there, alone, waiting for them to take her. Then I sat here for hours because I couldn't move. I couldn't breathe. All alone."

Her eyes glossed over.

"You're not doing that by yourself," he said. "I won't let you. So we wait."

She opened her mouth. Closed it. He could see the war playing out across her face—the part of her that needed to move, to act, to do something before the grief caught up with her, fighting against the part that knew he was right. That recognized the truth in what he'd said because she'd seen her own version of that utter sense of aloneness.

He took the Glock from her hands, gently, and set it on the end table by the old sofa. "I care about you." He cupped her face, his thumbs tracing the dark circles under her eyes, the tear tracks that had dried on her cheeks.

She looked up at him. Those blue eyes, rimmed in red now, bloodshot from holding back the tears and filled with something that wasn't quite fear and wasn't quite grief but lived in the space between them. The morning light was soft on her face, washing out the edges, making her look young and exhausted and so far from the woman who'd walked into his life like she was built for war that it broke his heart.

"I'm not okay," she whispered.

"I know."

"I don't know how to do this."

"Nobody does." He pressed his forehead against hers. "But you don't have to figure it out by yourself. That's the whole point of this. Of us. Whatever we are."

She let out a shaky breath. Her hands came up to grip his wrists, holding on like he was the only solid thing in a world that had gone liquid and uncertain.

"Okay," she said quietly. "I'll wait."

"Good decision because if you had said no, I would've had to tie you down, and that's not how I wanted that to go, if you know what I mean."

"Now you're being a pig."

"I'm a man."

She chuckled as she pulled back and wiped her eyes with the back of her hand. Then she straightened her shoulders—a deliberate thing, like someone putting on armor one piece at a time. "I'm going to make muffins."

Trent narrowed his stare. "Muffins?"

"I need to do something with my hands, and if I can't shoot something or punch something, baking is the next best option." She moved toward the door, then stopped and looked back at him. "You have flour, right?"

"I have flour."

"Eggs? Butter? Sugar?"

"I think so."

"Blueberries?"

"Fresh ones that you bought the other day."

"Then I'm making muffins." She pushed through the door into the kitchen, and he heard her opening cabinets, the familiar sounds of someone looking for mixing bowls in a kitchen they didn't know well enough to navigate without searching.

Trent stood on the porch and watched the morning settle over his property. The gators in the moat had calmed, their bellows fading to the occasional grumble. Somewhere in the grass, a python he couldn't see was making its way toward a place it had no business being. His leg ached. His shoulder throbbed. Inside, a woman he was falling for was making muffins because it was the only thing standing between her and a grief so big it could swallow her whole.

He pulled out his phone and called Fallon.

It rang twice before she answered, her voice thick

with sleep. "Trent? It's not even six. Someone better be dead or dying."

His chest tightened. "I need you and Keaton and maybe one or two other FWC officers out at Mallor's Landing. As soon as possible."

"What's going on?"

"I've got a python problem—at least five, including a fifteen-footer I already put down. The rest are spread across the property, making their way toward the moat. I've never seen this many on my land. Not even close." He watched the grass near the fence line, tracking a subtle movement that could have been wind but wasn't. "Something's not right."

"Getting out of bed now," Fallon said. "I'll call it in and make it official."

"Thank you."

He hung up and leaned against the porch railing, listening to the clink of a mixing bowl being set on the counter and the soft thud of the fridge being closed. It was the sounds of someone building something small and good in the middle of something terrible.

His leg throbbed.

The snakes were still out there.

And somewhere in Okeechobee, Dove's uncle was lying on a cold steel table waiting for someone who loved him to come and say his name.

Chapter Twelve

The medical examiner had used the word "peaceful." Odd word choice to describe a man who'd been murdered.

"You doing okay?" Trent asked.

"Hanging tough." Dove watched the highway unspooling through the windshield of Trent's truck, the flat stretch of Florida sliding past in a blur of sawgrass and sky. She couldn't stop hearing that word. Peaceful. Like her uncle had drifted off to sleep. Like two bullets hadn't ripped through him in a parking lot while he sat alone in his car.

The ME had cleaned up her uncle and closed the wounds. Folded his hands across his chest. Made him look like a man resting instead of a man snuffed out by God only knew who. And Dove had stood there under the fluorescent lights that buzzed like the ones in every military facility she'd ever set foot in, staring at a face she'd known her whole life—the thick jaw, the crooked nose he'd broken twice, the deep lines around his mouth from decades of either laughing or clenching his teeth through things no one should have to see—and confirmed that yes, this was Aaron Slade.

She'd kept it together. She'd nodded when the ME spoke, signed where they told her to, answered the questions in a voice so flat and controlled it could've been a recording. Trent had stood behind her the whole time, close enough that she could feel his presence like a hand on her back, even though he wasn't touching her. Just there. Solid and warm in a room full of cold steel and antiseptic.

She hadn't cried. Not in the room. Not in the hallway. Not in the parking lot where Trent had opened the truck door for her and waited while she climbed in and buckled her seatbelt with hands that didn't shake because she wouldn't let them.

But now, forty minutes into the drive south toward Fort Lauderdale, the numbness was wearing off. And what was underneath it wasn't grief. Grief was a luxury she couldn't afford yet. What was underneath the numbness was something hotter. Something with teeth.

Rage.

It smoldered in her chest like a coal, white-hot and glowing, radiating heat through her ribs and into her throat until she could taste it—metallic, bitter, the flavor of blood after she'd bitten the inside of her cheek too hard.

This wasn't random violence. This wasn't a mugging gone wrong. This was an execution. And executions meant planning. Surveillance. Intent. Someone had decided Aaron Slade needed to die, and they'd made it happen with the kind of precision that said they'd done this before.

Dove was going to find them. And when she did—

She stopped that thought. Packed it into a box. Shoved it into a corner. Not because she was afraid of it, but because she needed to think clearly, and fantasies about retribution didn't help with that.

She turned her head and looked at Trent.

He drove the way he did everything—steady, unhurried, one hand on the wheel and the other resting on the center console. His jaw set, eyes fixed on the road, she could tell by the way his thumb tapped against the steering wheel that his mind churned.

"You don't have to do this," she said.

He glanced at her. Just a flick of his eyes before they returned to the road. "What?"

"I can rent a car when we get there," she continued. "You've got enough on your plate between the pythons, the hearing, and—"

"Don't be ridiculous."

"I'm serious. I know you need to get back. Not to mention now more than ever, I think you need to talk to Buddy and Dawson about what the Hendersons are holding over your head."

"I don't disagree with you about the latter." He

reached across the cab and took her hand. His palm was rough. Calloused from years of handling animals and tools and everything this land demanded of a man who'd chosen to live on the edge of it. He lifted her hand to his mouth and pressed his lips against her knuckles. Warm. Firm. The kind of kiss that wasn't about romance but about something sturdier. "But for now, I'm not going anywhere," he said. "We check your uncle's place, we see what we see, and we head back. It's not that far. One thing at a time."

"The hearing—"

"Isn't until tomorrow night. We have time." He set her hand down on the console but didn't let go. His thumb traced a slow circle on the inside of her wrist, right over the pulse point, and she wondered if he could feel how fast her heart was beating. How hard the rage pushed against the walls she'd built around it.

She turned back to the window and watched the landscape change. The Everglades gave way to suburbs, the sawgrass replaced by strip malls, gas stations, and housing developments that all looked the same—stucco boxes in shades of beige and salmon, red-tile roofs baking under a sun that didn't care about grief or murder or the fact that the world was supposed to stop when someone she loved was taken from it.

The world never stopped. That was one of the first things the Army had taught her. People died, and the world kept spinning. The sun kept rising, and somewhere, someone was eating breakfast and laughing at something stupid on their phone while her whole life burned down around her.

Slade's condo was in a quiet development off Federal Highway—a two-story townhouse with a small yard and a one-car garage, the kind of place a single man with a government salary and simple tastes would choose. Nothing flashy. Nothing drew attention. He'd always been like that. Understated. Practical. A man who'd kept his head down and his eyes open and survived thirty years in federal law enforcement by never making himself a target.

Until someone made him one anyway.

Trent pulled into the driveway and killed the engine.

The front entrance was visible from the driveway—a simple wooden door, painted dark blue, with a brass knocker shaped like an anchor that Slade had thought was hilarious for reasons he'd never adequately explained.

"Shit. The door's ajar," she said softly.

Not open, not closed. Just slightly off—a half-inch gap between the door and the frame that might have looked like carelessness to someone who didn't know Aaron Slade.

The uncle she knew locked every door, checked every window, and set the alarm before he left the house to check the mail. Thirty years of protecting people who were being hunted had made security reflexive—something his body did without his brain having to give the order, the same way Dove's body still cleared corners and checked sight lines every time she walked into a room.

Trent lifted his center console and pulled out his Glock.

She lifted hers from its ankle holster and shifted. The grief and the rage and the exhaustion—all of it got shoved into a compartment and sealed shut. What replaced it was clean. Sharp. The focus of a woman who'd spent years looking through a scope at a world reduced to distances and angles.

"Stay behind me," she said. "Do exactly what I say. Clear?"

"Would it be in poor taste to say you talking to me like that turns me on?"

"Such a pig."

"Again, I'm a man." But Trent didn't argue. Didn't posture. Didn't remind her that he was capable and armed and had been handling dangerous situations since before she'd finished basic training. He just fell in behind her, and she loved him a little for that. For knowing when to lead and when to follow. For understanding that this was her world, the same way the moat and the gators and the pythons were his.

They moved to the door. Weapon up, Dove pressed her back against the wall beside the frame and nudged open the door with her boot. The door swung inward on silent hinges. The gap between door and frame widened, revealing a sliver of hallway, then a wall, then—destruction.

Sucking in a deep, controlled breath, she ignored her racing pulse. She entered fast, weapon sweeping left, right, up. Trent shadowed her, his footsteps light for a man his size. They began to move through the house the way she'd been trained to clear a structure—room by room, corner by corner, each space checked and declared before moving to the next.

Living room. Clear. But the couch had been flipped onto its back, cushions slashed, stuffing spilling across the floor like foam guts. The coffee table was upside down, and one leg snapped off. Books were pulled from the shelves and scattered—a lamp shattered on the hardwood.

Kitchen. Clear. Drawers were yanked out and dumped. Canisters of flour and sugar swept off the counter and cracked open on the tile. The contents of the refrigerator were untouched—whoever had done this wasn't looking for anything that would be hidden in a jar of pickles.

Guest bedroom. Clear. Mattress pulled off the frame, box spring sliced open. Closet emptied, clothes in a heap.

Bathroom. Clear. Medicine cabinet open, contents on the floor, but nothing taken, as far as she could tell.

Master bedroom. Clear. Same treatment—mattress gutted, closet ransacked, dresser drawers turned out.

They reached the office last. The door was open, and Dove stepped through the doorway, her weapon lowering as the tactical part of her brain yielded to the investigative part.

The room looked like a paper bomb had gone off. File cabinet drawers pulled out and upended, their contents scattered across every surface. Manila folders everywhere —on the desk, the floor, the chair, draped over the computer monitor like tan flags of surrender. Papers fanned out in overlapping layers so thick you couldn't see the carpet beneath them.

"I wonder what they were looking for," Trent asked from behind her. His voice was low, careful.

"Your guess is as good as mine." Dove scanned the chaos—systematic, grid-pattern, cataloging details without dwelling on any single one. The file cabinet had four drawers. All four had been emptied. The desk drawers, too—three of them, all pulled out and dumped. The bookshelf above the desk had been swept clean, with reference manuals, binders, and loose papers cascading down like an avalanche frozen mid-fall.

But it was the folders that drew her attention.

Some were closed. Some were open. And some were open and empty.

She stepped closer, careful not to touch anything, and read the labels on the folders nearest to her feet. Case numbers. Names she didn't recognize. Dates going back years, decades. Her uncle's career distilled into paper and ink and the quiet bureaucratic language of law enforcement.

Then she saw it.

A manila folder lay on the floor near the overturned desk chair, splayed open like a book. The label, written in her uncle's precise block letters, read: MALLOR, JACK —GULF COAST ENERGY PARTNERS.

Empty.

"Jesus," Trent whispered behind her. "Looks like whoever trashed this place got what they wanted."

She crouched down, hands on her knees, and stared at the folder. The tab was creased, the edges soft from handling, the kind of wear that said this file had been opened and closed many times. But whatever had been inside it was gone. Every page. Every document. Every note her uncle had kept about a case that was twenty years old and supposedly dead.

"Unless he took the contents to protect them, which is what I would've done." She straightened and looked around the office again, counting. Three other folders she could see were also open and empty. Different labels but related to Jack's case. "The other files all have to do with Gulf Coast Energy Partners and Armond Jackson."

Trent inched closer and bent down.

She grabbed his arm. "We can't touch anything," she said, pulling her phone from her pocket. "This is a crime scene."

She pulled out her cell phone and called Corrick.

He answered on the second ring, his voice carrying the strained patience of a man who hadn't slept and was running on caffeine and duty. "Miss Quinn."

"We're at my uncle's place in Fort Lauderdale. The front door was kicked in. The house has been tossed. Every room."

"Are you safe? Is the location secure?" Corrick asked.

"We cleared the house. No one's here. But his office is destroyed. Files everywhere."

"I'll contact Fort Lauderdale PD. I'm getting in my vehicle. Ten minutes out," he said.

"See you when you get here." She hung up and

looked at Trent. He was standing over his father's empty folder, arms crossed, with an expression she couldn't quite read. Not anger. Not fear. Something older. Something that lived in the place where a fourteen-year-old boy had watched his father drive away for the last time, never understanding why.

"Come on," she said. "We should wait outside."

They stepped onto the front stoop, and Dove didn't bother shutting the door. The street was quiet. Modest homes with neat lawns and cars in driveways and the distant sound of a lawnmower somewhere down the block. Normal. Suburban. The kind of neighborhood where people waved at each other and complained about HOA fees and assumed the worst thing that would ever happen was someone parking in the wrong spot.

She sat on the top step. Trent lowered himself beside her, close enough that their shoulders touched. The afternoon sun was brutal, pressing down on them like a hand, and the concrete was hot through her jeans. She didn't care. The heat felt good. Real. Something to focus on besides the inside of that house. She pressed her palms against her knees, fingers splayed and stared at the pavement. "He didn't talk to me about his work. And I couldn't talk to him about my work. It was all classified, compartmentalized."

"I understand that," Trent said. "What bothers me are all the coincidences. All the ways this just falls into place. Add in the weird shit that's been happening. The person at my mom's funeral. The snakes. The Hendersons and their threat. Fucking Karl. It all has to be connected somehow. But I can't for the life of me figure it out."

"There's a thread there, and it all comes back to what someone might want Mallor's Landing for."

"Karl's an opportunistic asshole. If he sees a paycheck, he'll do almost anything," Trent said. "Mallor's Landing is unique because of the two distinct aspects—commercial and natural habitat. But it's not easy to run. Fish and Wildlife has to inspect both properties to make sure they don't mix. There's licensing for the business, permits for both sides. In some ways, it's a logistical nightmare, and I nearly destroyed it all when I was being a young, angry jerk." He ran a hand over his face. "I still might have, considering what the Hendersons have. But I can't imagine anyone wants both the business and the habitat. If it weren't for my father and grandfather's long-lasting relationship with this community, and my ability to turn my shit around, it wouldn't work at all."

She snapped her head toward him. "Doesn't mean Karl, the Hendersons, and whoever else is involved won't have plans."

A dark sedan turned onto the street and pulled up behind Trent's truck. Corrick stepped out—tall, lean, early sixties, wearing a suit that looked like it had been slept in and a face that confirmed it. He carried himself like a man who'd spent his career in rooms where the stakes were life and death, and he'd long ago stopped being surprised by either.

"Miss Quinn."

"You can call me Dove," she said. "This is Trent Mallor."

He shook both their hands. His grip was firm but brief, the handshake of someone who understood that formalities mattered even when everything was falling apart. "I came straight from the office. Fort Lauderdale PD is five minutes behind me."

He looked at the door. At the gap. At the splintered wood near the lock, where someone had put a boot or a shoulder through it. His jaw tightened, and Dove saw something flash behind his eyes—not just professional concern, but something personal. Slade had been his agent. His colleague. Maybe even his friend.

"Walk me through what you found," he said.

They did. Room by room, in the same order they'd cleared it. Corrick listened without interrupting, his hands clasped behind his back, his expression schooling itself into the careful neutrality of a man who was cataloging every detail for later.

When they reached the part about the office—the files, the empty folders, Jack Mallor's name—Corrick inhaled slowly through his nose. It was the only crack in his composure.

"I won't lie to you," he said, turning to face them. "I have no idea who would do this or what they were after. Slade's last few active cases were straightforward. Witness protection check-ins, administrative closures, nothing that would warrant this kind of..." He gestured toward the house. "Aggression."

"What about enemies?" Dove asked. "Thirty years in the marshals. He had to have made a few."

"Slade was meticulous. He didn't cut corners. He built cases by the book, protected his witnesses, and kept his head down." Corrick's voice carried the weight of someone defending a man who could no longer defend himself. "All that said, he could also be antagonistic, and he knew when and how to bend rules. While he was well-liked in the marshals' office, there were a few who didn't particularly care for him, and he definitely made a few enemies among the criminals."

"What about regarding my father's case?" Trent asked. "About there being a mole." Trent glanced at Dove. His brow scrunched and the muscles in his face were tight. "He told me that he didn't see the point in exhuming my father's body. That he'd help me fight that if I wanted to. And for some reason, that doesn't make sense to me."

Dove understood the comment because she agreed. However, she didn't like the implication that her uncle was hiding something, even if she believed deep down in her bones that he had been.

Corrick folded his arms. He blew out a puff of air from his nose like an agitated bull. "I shouldn't be surprised that Slade came to you and suggested that. The only problem is he didn't have a decent enough argument as to why we shouldn't, and I told him that." He adjusted his stance. The kind of subtle shift that told Dove the next thing out of his mouth was going to be uncomfortable. "Did Slade tell you that the medical examiner who performed your father's autopsy twenty years ago—Dr. Raymond Weiss was brought up on charges eighteen months ago? Falsifying records. Taking bribes to alter findings on several cases." Corrick's voice had an edge. "Dr. Weiss has agreed to testify against the person inside the justice department who asked him to falsify records."

"You've got to be kidding me," Dove said as her pulse picked up speed.

"He's adamant your father's case was clean. But given the scope of his misconduct and the person involved, the DOJ is compelled to verify the integrity of every autopsy he performed during the relevant period. Your father's included."

The words settled between them like stones dropped into still water. Dove watched Trent's face. The muscle jumping in his jaw. The way his hands curled into fists at his sides, then slowly, deliberately, uncurled.

"There is no reason to believe there was any tampering with your father's autopsy," Corrick added quietly. "There was more than one witness to the accident. But one other witness died. Evidence burned. And now this dead man's cache. We need to cover our bases."

Trent was quiet for a long time. Long enough that the sound of approaching sirens began to thread through the neighborhood—thin and distant, growing closer. "I won't fight it," Trent said.

Dove stared at him, unable to say anything because the change in his opinion shocked her.

"I don't like it," he continued. His voice was rough, the words dragged out of somewhere deep and reluctant.

"I hate it, actually. The idea of someone digging up my father's grave makes me want to put my fist through a wall." He held Corrick's gaze. "But if there's even a chance that it leads to whoever did this to Slade—gives Dove some answers—I won't stand in the way."

"I appreciate that. More than you know." He pulled a card from his jacket pocket and handed it to Dove. "I'm going to keep you in the loop—both of you. Whatever we find—in this house, in the investigation, in the exhumation—you'll know. That's a promise."

The sirens were close, now—two Fort Lauderdale PD cruisers turning onto the street, light bars washing color across the pale stucco of the neighboring houses.

Corrick straightened his jacket. "Excuse me. I need to brief the responding officers." He took a step, then turned back. "Your uncle was one of the finest marshals I ever had the privilege to serve with. I don't say that lightly, and I don't say it just because he's gone. I mean it. And I *will* find out who did this." He walked toward the cruisers, his stride purposeful, his shoulders squared against whatever came next.

Dove's throat ached. "He was going to retire," she said. The words came out small. Fragile. Nothing like the the professional voice she'd used in the medical examiner's office. "Two months. He had a place picked out in Jupiter. He loved scuba diving and fishing and said that place was the best for both. He sent me pictures." She pressed her fingers against her eyes. "He was going to get a dog. A lab. He always wanted a lab but said his schedule wasn't fair to a dog. He was finally going to get one."

Trent didn't say anything. He just put his arm around her and pulled her against his side, and she let him. Let herself lean into the warmth of him, the solid, sunbaked weight of a man who smelled like the Everglades and coffee and the faint musk of python that still clung to his clothes from this morning.

"I'm going to find who did this," she said. "And whoever's coming after you."

"I know you are."

"And when I do—"

"We'll figure all that out together."

She looked up at him. His face was half in shadow, the afternoon sun cutting a line across his jaw, his eyes darker than usual, holding something that wasn't pity and wasn't sympathy but was more useful than both. Understanding. The bone-deep, hard-won understanding of a man who'd lost people, lived with the weight of it, and had come out the other side still standing.

"Together," she repeated.

"That's what I said."

She almost smiled. Didn't quite get there, but something moved in the right direction. A muscle in her cheek. The smallest acknowledgment that even in the middle of this, something was holding her up that hadn't been there before.

A cruiser door slammed. Radios crackled. Corrick's voice carried across the lawn, calm and authoritative, directing officers toward the house.

Dove straightened. Wiped her face. Put the armor back on, piece by piece, the way she always did.

But she didn't pull away from Trent's arm. Not yet. She gave herself ten more seconds of leaning into him, of letting someone else hold the weight, of breathing in the smell of cypress and swamp and the stubborn, complicated man who'd driven two hours without being asked and hadn't once suggested she didn't need him there.

Chapter Thirteen

The gators were restless this morning.

Trent could tell by the way they surfaced —not the lazy, drifting emergence of animals at ease, but the sharp, angled rise of heads breaking water with purpose. Eyes scanning. Nostrils flaring. Something had shifted in the moat overnight, and every cold-blooded creature in it knew it.

He tossed the last chicken quarter to Dolly, who snapped it out of the air with a crack that sent a heron flapping off the dock in protest. She'd been extra possessive of the south bank since the python incident, patrolling the waterline like a twelve-foot security guard, her tail sweeping slow arcs through the shallows.

Clarkson was sunning herself on the flat rock near the east bank, moving more slowly than she should. Favoring her left side, where the coils had done the most damage, and her breathing had a slight wheeze that Trent didn't love. But she was eating. She'd taken two chicken pieces this morning without hesitation, snapping them down with the single-minded determination of an animal that had stared death in the face and decided it was hungry anyway.

New gators floated in, and some of the regulars had made their way back out into the wild. It's how the habitat worked. But a few made this their home, and Trent made them his family.

He crouched at the moat's edge for a long moment, watching Clarkson breathe. If the wheeze got worse, he'd monitor more closely and hope he wouldn't have to put the creature down. If it got better, he'd call it a miracle and move on. That was the deal when you lived alongside animals that had been around since the dinosaurs. You did what you could. You accepted what you couldn't.

He rinsed his hands in the bucket by the feeding station, dried them on his jeans, and then headed toward the house.

The sky was shifting from black to gray, the sun still crouched below the tree line but throwing its first hints of color—pale pink and amber threading through the clouds like veins of ore in dark rock. The air was heavy with dew and the distinct green scent the Everglades exhaled every morning, as if something alive were drawing its first breath.

Inside, the house was quiet. Not the terrible quiet of those first weeks after his mother died—the absence that had weight and teeth and lived in every corner—but a different kind. The quiet of something that had been through the worst and was still standing.

He started the coffee, leaning against the counter while the machine gurgled and hissed. The kitchen still smelled faintly of blueberry muffins. Two batches yesterday. The first had come out golden and perfect and she'd stared at them like she couldn't remember making them. The second she'd burned because she'd been crying at the table and forgot the timer. He'd scraped the blackened bottoms without a word and they'd eaten them anyway.

The machine beeped. He poured two mugs, added a splash of cream to hers, and carried them upstairs.

The bedroom was dim, curtains filtering the early light into a soft gray wash. Dove was on her side, facing the window, the quilt pulled to her chin, her blond hair fanned across the pillow in a tangle that said she'd slept hard or at least tried. Twice in the night, she'd jerked awake, gasping, her body going rigid beside him, before she remembered where she was and allowed herself to settle back down.

He set her mug on the nightstand and sat on the edge of the bed.

She rolled toward him, eyes opening slowly, bloodshot, heavy with the kind of exhaustion that sleep hadn't come close to fixing.

"Hey," she murmured.

"Hey, yourself." He nodded toward the mug. "Coffee."

She pushed herself up to a sitting position, reached for it, and wrapped both hands around the ceramic like it was the only warm thing in the world. She took a sip and her eyes closed. A small sound escaped her—gratitude and pain tangled up together.

"How are the gators?" she asked.

"Good. Dolly's standing guard, like she's waiting for something else to happen and Clarkson's acting like she didn't almost die yesterday. Tough little cookie, that one."

"She gets that from her dad."

Trent chuckled. Even wrecked, even running on no sleep and grief that could swallow a person whole, she could still make him laugh—he loved her a little for that.

"How are you?" she asked, peering over the rim.

"I should be asking you that question."

"I got there first."

"I know, but you asked because you don't want to talk about yourself, and you need to." He took a sip of his coffee. "How are you feeling? And don't say fine."

Her facial muscles grew tight. Not a wall going up—more like one threatening to. She held his gaze for a beat, then looked down into her mug. "I'm feeling like I want to burn the world down, and I can't because I don't have any fire."

He understood that. The fury that had no target. The kind that ate you alive because there was nowhere to put it. He'd carried that for years after his father died, and it had turned him into someone he hadn't liked very much.

"What can I do?" he asked. "With funeral plans. Arrangements. Whatever you need—I'm here." He wasn't sure when his feelings for Dove had shifted, probably before his mother had died. Maybe before she'd been diagnosed. Caring so intensely for her scared the crap out of him, and he knew it was why he'd pushed her away after he'd been shot.

He'd only loved once, but he hadn't loved Fallon the way she deserved. Certainly not in a forever kind of way. And honestly, Fallon had one foot out the front door the second she moved in. They'd helped each other during a moment in time, and he was grateful they'd always been able to remain friends.

Now, he was treading in waters he had no idea how to navigate but was no longer willing to swim to shore and get out.

Dove shifted against the headboard, pulling the quilt around her waist. "My mom's handling everything. She called last night while you were in the shower." Dove paused, and her eyes lightened as her face relaxed. Not quite a smile, but close. "He'd already laid it all out. Exactly what he wanted. Cremated. Wait a month so people have time to process. Then throw a big ass party and celebrate his life. But he also suggested that they have it wherever it was convenient for them. That the few true friends he had would travel. My mom's a little confused as to where to have it now, but she said she'd follow her brother's wishes." A breath of laughter escaped her—thin, fragile, but real. "Because Aaron hated funerals."

"Smart man."

"He said funerals were for the living and the living should be doing something better with their time than crying over someone who couldn't hear them anyway."

Trent chuckled. "My mom was the opposite. She

wanted the whole thing. Church service. Calling hours. The reception afterward with casseroles and people telling stories. She planned every detail." He stared into his coffee. "But it wasn't for her or for people to mourn her. She did it for me. She wanted to make sure I was fed properly, and I wasn't alone."

Dove laughed. Quiet. A little broken. "And then you spent a good five days after she died alone anyway."

It wasn't an accusation. It was recognition. The kind that came from someone who understood the difference between what people wanted for you and what you were actually capable of accepting.

"I did," he admitted. "Sat right here in this house with the doors locked and the phone off and convinced myself I was handling it."

"You were a wreck when you finally let me in." She set her mug down on the nightstand. The click of ceramic on wood was loud in the quiet room. She turned to face him fully, her legs folding beneath her, the oversized t-shirt—his, faded, and three sizes too big—slipping off one shoulder.

Her eyes were different now. The exhaustion was still there, the bloodshot redness, the dark circles that makeup couldn't touch. But underneath all of that, something had surfaced. Something raw and urgent and wide open, like a wound that had stopped pretending it wasn't bleeding.

"I don't want to be alone," she said.

The words were simple. But the way she said them—with her voice stripped down to nothing, no armor, no deflection, no Sergeant Quinn standing guard—made his chest crack open.

"You're not," he said.

"I need you." Her hand came up and pressed flat against his chest, right over his heart. Her fingers curled into the fabric of his shirt. "Selfish of me. But right now, all I want to feel is you. All I want is your arms around my body. I want to lose myself in you."

He opened his mouth to say something—he didn't know what, something careful, something that acknowledged the grief driving this and the fact that she was hurting and he didn't want to be something she regretted later—but she didn't give him the chance.

She kissed him.

Not soft. Not tentative. Not the careful, measured kiss of two people figuring each other out. This was a collision. Her mouth found his with a force that rocked him backward, her hand fisting his shirt, pulling him toward her like she was drowning and he was the only solid thing in the water. Her teeth caught his lower lip and the sharp sting of it sent electricity down his spine.

He tasted salt. Tears. Coffee. The raw, desperate flavor of a woman who was using his mouth to keep from screaming.

His hands found her waist, steadying her, steadying himself, because the intensity of it had knocked something loose inside him, too. This was just her burying the pain. It wasn't lust. It wasn't what he referred to as a little bit of love.

It was real and gut-wrenchingly honest.

She pulled back, her forehead pressed against his, her breath coming fast and ragged against his lips. Her eyes were open, inches from his, and what he saw in them wasn't just desire. It wasn't just need. It was the bone-deep, soul-level connection that had nothing to do with sex and everything to do with the one thing they both had been running from their entire adult lives—and she was still avoiding love.

"I think we need to—"

"Don't think," she whispered. "Don't be careful. Don't ask me if I'm sure." Her fingers released his shirt and slid up his neck, into his hair, gripping hard enough to hurt. "We can think later. Talk about why I need this—later. Right now, just be here. With me."

He could have stopped it. Could have been the steady one, the one who said maybe we should wait until you've had more than three hours of sleep and aren't running on adrenaline and grief. He could have held her instead. Could have stroked her hair, told her it was going to be okay, and been the kind of man who said those three little words that had never left his mouth before. And that she'd probably never heard.

However, love meant knowing, and he knew Dove. Saying those words now would only push her right out the door. Hell, just thinking them were making his heart race and making him wonder if he shouldn't backpedal.

Dove wasn't asking to be held. She wasn't asking to be comforted or soothed or managed. She was asking for someone she trusted to help her feel something other than pain. To be reminded that she was alive, that her body could do more than carry grief, that there was still something in this world worth reaching for.

And Trent understood that. God, he understood that. Because in the weeks after his mother died, the only thing that had made him feel anything at all was the weight of Dove's hand on his arm and the sound of her voice cutting through the silence. She'd been his reminder. His proof that the world still had texture and warmth, and that someone in it gave a damn whether he lived or died.

He hadn't recognized that as love. Not until recently.

But now it was his turn to give her what she needed.

He kissed her back.

Not gentle. Not careful. He gave her what she was asking for—all of it, everything, his hands and his mouth and the full weight of whatever he was feeling. She arched into him, a sound catching in her throat that was half sob and half something else entirely, and he swallowed it. Took it in. Held it for her so she didn't have to.

Her hands were everywhere. Pulling at his shirt, pushing at his shoulders, dragging him down onto the bed with an urgency that bordered on desperate. She was relentless. Demanding. Moving against him with the focused intensity of a woman who'd spent her adult life channeling every emotion into action because sitting still with feeling was the one thing she'd never learned to do.

He let her lead. Let her set the pace and the pressure and the rhythm of it, because this wasn't about him. This was about giving her whatever she needed to get through the next hour, the next minute, the next breath. If she needed fire, he'd burn. If she needed tenderness, he'd be soft.

The quilt his mother had made ended up on the floor. His shirt was somewhere near the window. Her hands found the scar on his ribs where a gator had caught him when he was nineteen, and she pressed her mouth against it like she could heal old wounds with new ones.

He watched her tongue trace that old line of raised skin, and the heat of it shot through him. He slid his palm up under the hem of the shirt she still wore and found warm skin.

"Dove," he said, or maybe he just breathed it. Her name tasted like honey and whiskey and the morning. He gathered the shirt in his fists and pulled it up. She lifted her arms without hesitation, hair catching on the fabric, and then she was bare in the gray light, every inch of her goose pimpled from the blast of air and the kind of need that didn't care about temperature.

He set his mouth on the slope of her shoulder where the shirt had slipped before, then lower, tasting skin that still held the faint blueberry sugar of yesterday. She arched and gripped his head like she intended to keep him there.

He had other plans.

He kissed his way across her neck as he cupped her perfect breasts. He licked one nipple and then sucked it into his mouth, hard, demanding, and unforgiving.

A half gasp mixed with a deep guttural groan escaped her mouth.

Easing off the bed, he shed his jeans and tugged her

to the edge. Curling his fingers in the elastic of her panties, he yanked them to her ankles, and tossed them across the room. For a moment, he held his breath and just stared at her, sprawled out in his bed like she belonged there. Like she was home. He reached out and twisted one nipple while he slipped a finger inside her, rubbing his thumb across her clit.

She arched into his hand, spreading her legs wider, rolling her hips, as if begging for more. He stroked her with one finger, then two. She clutched the sheets in her fist and bit down on her lower lip as she moaned softly.

He could do this all day long and be satisfied.

But right now, she needed more. He leaned over and pressed his tongue where his thumb had been, his fingers still gliding in and out.

"Oh god." She clutched his head, her fingers threading through his hair, and her hips rolling with the rhythm of his tongue. "Yes, Trent. Yes..."

He draped both legs over his shoulders and drove his tongue deep inside. If sunshine were a flavor, that's what she tasted like, and he couldn't get enough. He reached up and toyed with both nipples, plucking, twisting, and pulling. Not too hard, but hard enough that he was meeting her demands. He lapped at her clit, circling and sucking, before diving inside, and then repeating the motion while her fingers dug relentlessly into his scalp.

Her breath came in quick pants. Warm liquid spilled from her like a fountain as her body bucked and jerked.

"Oh, yes, yes," she managed. Her legs tightened around the sides of his face. Her back arched. Her muscles continued to twitch, and soft moans rose from her lips and landed on his ears like sweet music.

Carefully, he pushed her legs apart and kissed his way up her belly, across her breasts, to her lips. She shoved him to his back, her hand gliding down his chest.

He grabbed her wrist. "I won't last if you do that. Not today."

"That's fine." She smiled, climbing him, thighs bracketing his hips, heat searing between them. She reached for him and guided him in with a surety that knocked the wind out of him. He had a last flash of the world—curtains breathing with the morning, the smell of damp earth finding its way through the screens—and then it narrowed to the tight, yielding slide of her around him.

His body knew what to do. He tried to take inventory —steady her, let her set the pace, don't get lost and leave her alone in this—and then she moved, and thinking fell away like useless equipment tossed overboard. She rocked hard, head tipped back, throat bare. He set his hands on her hips, gripping tight, holding on for dear life as she controlled everything.

She made sounds that hit him low, not pretty, not composed—broken pieces that told him she was right there with him, and that was all he needed. He bit the inside of his cheek and kept his eyes open, watching her face change as the rhythm found them. Sweat slid down his temple. The mattress complained.

"More," she said, rough as gravel.

He gave it. He sat up and wrapped an arm around

her back, pulled her tight against him, chest to chest, her heartbeat knocking against his. He filled his palm with the curve of her, thumb drawing a line that made her gasp and clench. He swore under his breath and did it again because that sound lit him up like a match in dry grass.

He kissed her mouth, her jaw, the damp hollow below her ear where her pulse hammered. She caught his earlobe in her teeth, and he almost came from that alone, that small, mean sweetness, the way she claimed him without asking permission.

He shifted his angle and felt the change hit her. Her fingers dug into his shoulders hard enough to bruise. She rode him like the motion itself could scratch grief out of bone. He held on, pushed up into her, gave her that angle until her breath broke on a sound that went straight through him and scattered everything that wasn't this.

She tightened around him, sudden and hot and insistent, and he felt the surge take her. She shuddered, body clamping down, forehead thudding into his with a soft curse that might have been his name. He didn't close his eyes. He watched the way her mouth parted, the way her eyelids fluttered, the tear that slid down her cheek because even pleasure couldn't outrun everything.

It undid him. He thrust again, and then he was gone, muscles snapping taut, heat ripping through him in a way that felt like surrender and relief and something he wanted to say, but it wasn't the right time. Not yet.

He held her while it took him apart. He held her after, both of them shaking a little, breath sawing the quiet to pieces.

They stayed tangled like that. Her weight settled warm and heavy on him, skin damp, the room smelling like sweat and coffee and the humid green of the morning. His heart pounded against her palm where it still rested, as if it had been waiting there for her hand the whole time.

He smoothed his palm up and down her spine in slow passes. Her shuddering eased by degrees. He felt the small, involuntary after-twitches inside her and swallowed hard, wanting to say something stupid and reckless. Instead, he kissed her temple.

Outside, a bird called once, sharp and distant. The house clicked as it adjusted to the day. She made a low sound that he felt more than heard and tucked her face into his neck, breath damp and warm.

"I've got you," he said, quietly. He could at least promise that much without scaring either of them. He eased them down onto the mattress fully, still joined, unwilling to let the world slide back in just yet. He reached for the edge of the quilt with his foot and dragged it up awkwardly until it covered her back.

Her shoulders rose and fell. Another minute, maybe two, and the rigid line between them softened. He let himself memorize the weight of her, the heat, the way her hair stuck to his cheek. If there were a way to keep this exact version of time, he would have figured it out. He didn't know how. He only knew he would stay.

Outside, the sun broke the tree line. Light spilled through the gap in the curtains, cutting a warm stripe across the bed, across them, turning the gray room gold.

The gators bellowed in the moat. A mockingbird started its morning repertoire from the cypress stand—cycling through stolen songs, one after another, like it couldn't decide which one to keep.

His breath caught in his throat. He hadn't reached for the nightstand. He hadn't grabbed a condom. As much as he hated the damn things, they were necessary since Dove wasn't taking any birth control. Something about having an IUD removed sometime after she'd left the military, but hadn't gone about getting on the pill yet. Something she kept meaning to do and never did.

He was about to say something, but then Dove's hands found his face. Held him there. Made him look at her while the world narrowed down to the space between them, and all thoughts that weren't Dove drifted away. There was nothing left but heat and her skin and the sound of her breathing and the way her eyes, even wrecked, even swollen and red-rimmed and exhausted, were the most alive thing he'd ever seen.

The conversation could wait a moment or two.

"Do you have to leave for your meeting with Keaton and Fallon soon?" she asked.

"About a half hour, but you can come if you want to. Actually, I'd feel better if you did. No reason for you to be alone."

"I'm not staying in this reptile-infested house by myself."

He chuckled. "You know, since we're a thing, you kind of need to get used to that."

"Not sure that's possible." She shivered, tossing her arm and leg over his body."

He kissed her nose. "After the meeting, I want to come back here because they're exhuming my father's body, and then I need to get ready for the town meeting."

She propped herself up on his chest. "So far, I haven't been able to make a connection between Sovereign Resources and the Hendersons, but I'm going to dig deeper."

"My land wouldn't necessarily help Sovereign. They can access the water reservoir where the limestone is without setting foot on Mallor's Landing," he said. "But Fallon and Keaton gave me some paperwork about how their blasting could upset the natural habitat that Mallor's Landing has provided for three generations. Not to mention the eco tours and educational programs run through the commercial side."

"Do they believe you could stop them from mining?"

"Neither one of them can be completely sure, but they do think I have the power to make Sovereign's life a little bit miserable in gaining permits and whatnot. But they could also be prepared for the likes of me. They could already have answers to all the questions I'd ask. Could have a plan in place to protect the wildlife here. It's not like companies like that aren't aware they're gonna disrupt communities."

"What about the Hendersons and their threat to expose you if you don't sell and how that might play into all this?" She arched a brow. "You can't just ignore that and think it will go away."

"I'm not going to and I'll talk with Keaton, Fallon, and Dawson." He tucked her into his side. "But I don't want to think about any of that right now. I want to take ten minutes of silence before the world gets loud again."

And for a moment, there was nothing else. Just the two of them, tangled together in a bed that smelled like coffee and cypress and something new. Something that he was ready to admit to himself but wasn't sure either one of them was brave enough to embrace what it meant. He'd deal with the lack of a condom when he wasn't too scared to discuss the implications.

Chapter Fourteen

Dove leaned against the counter, mug in hand, and watched as Trent made eggs.

It was such a normal thing to do—cracking shells against the rim of a cast-iron skillet, the butter sizzling, the smell of coffee filling the kitchen alongside the early morning light—that Dove almost forgot they were living inside a disaster. Almost forgot that her uncle was dead. That someone had planted pythons on this property. That a blackmail note was sitting in an upstairs drawer. And the man standing barefoot at the stove had just had sex with her like the world was ending.

She moved to the table, sat with her legs pulled up beneath her, wearing his shirt again, her hands wrapped around a mug that was too hot, but she didn't care. The heat felt good. Everything about this kitchen felt good—the old linoleum, the gurgling coffee maker, the way the light came through the window above the sink and caught the steam rising from the skillet in slow, lazy curls.

Trent slid a plate in front of her. Scrambled eggs, toast, and a handful of strawberries. He sat across from her with his own plate, fresh coffee, and for a few minutes, they ate in the kind of silence that didn't need filling. Forks scraping. Mugs lifted and set down. The gators grumbling in the moat outside like a low, constant engine that never shut off.

Then Trent set his fork down. "We need to talk about something."

She looked up. He was staring at his coffee, his thumb tracing the rim of the mug, and there was something on his face she didn't see often—uncertainty. This man walked into gator-infested water without flinching, but whatever he was about to say had him fidgeting like a kid called to the principal's office.

"This morning," he said. "I didn't use a condom. I didn't even think about it. I should've, and I'm sorry."

Her heart dropped to the bottom of her toes and then flew back to her throat. "I didn't realize that until just now." She lifted her gaze, catching his, and the conversation that needed to happen—the one about timing and responsibility and what it meant and what they were going to do about it—hovered between them like something fragile balanced on an edge.

Dove opened her mouth to say something—anything —but out of the corner of her eye, she noticed something outside.

Movement. Through the kitchen window, past the

moat, near the equipment shed. A figure, low and fast, slipping out through the side door. Then a second figure behind the first. He closed the shed door and moved swiftly across the property toward the mangrove near the waterline.

She jumped to her feet. "We've got company, and not the good kind."

He pushed his chair back, turning his head. "Motherfucker." His bare feet hit the linoleum, and he crossed the kitchen in three strides. He grabbed his Glock from the top of the refrigerator and racked the slide.

Dove was right behind him, snagging her weapon, which she'd placed on the counter by the door when she'd come downstairs this morning. She had it in her hand and her feet in her boots in seconds.

"Out the back," he said. "They're moving toward the south dock." Trent didn't bother with boots, which she thought was crazy, but she wasn't about to argue. Not now.

They went through the screen door fast. Dove's gaze locked on the two figures now visible between the cypress trees. They'd cleared the large trees and were making for the waterline where a flat-bottom boat was tied to the old dock—the one Trent's father had built.

The boat looked new. Clean. Shiney. Like this was its maiden voyage.

The morning air was thick and hot—tasted like mud mixed with cypress bark. The gators in the moat sensed the commotion—heads turning, bodies repositioning, Dolly letting out a low bellow that vibrated in Dove's sternum. She ignored all of it. Her focus narrowed the way it always did when the switch flipped—peripheral noise gone, vision sharp, every detail registering and cataloging in real time.

The two figures reached the dock. One of them jumped into the boat while the other untied the line. Both were dressed in dark clothing with long sleeves, hats pulled low, and gloves. No faces visible from this distance.

"I'm not letting them get away this time." Trent veered toward his airboat, tied on the south side of the dock where the water opened into the river. "Come on."

She scurried down the wooden planks, through the tall weeds, and raced up to the other dock.

Trent hopped into his boat, hit the blower, and the big fan roared to life with a sound that scattered every bird within a hundred yards. Dove quickly untied the lines from the cleats and landed in the seat beside him, one hand on the rail, the other holding her weapon against her thigh.

The intruders pulled away from the old dock, its outboard churning white water as it swung south into the channel.

Trent dropped the throttle and the airboat surged forward, skimming across the shallow water with a force that pressed Dove back in her seat. Wind ripped at her hair, her shirt—his shirt—and she had to squint against the spray. The sawgrass blurred on both sides, a green wall rushing past, and ahead of them, the flat-bottom picked up speed.

She pulled her phone from the pocket of Trent's shorts—the only thing she'd managed to grab besides the gun—and shot Buddy a quick text about what had transpired.

Seconds later, he responded that he was en route.

The channel widened. The flat-bottom had maybe two hundred yards on them, but the airboat was faster in the shallows and Trent knew these waterways the way she knew a rifle—by instinct, by memory, by the kind of intimacy that came from a lifetime of paying attention. He cut through a gap in the sawgrass that shaved fifty yards off the distance, the hull skimming over water so shallow she could see the mud bottom flashing beneath them.

A hundred yards. She could make out details now—the boat was a center console skiff, clean lines, the outboard gleaming. Not the kind of vessel that belonged to poachers or local troublemakers who'd lifted it from a dock.

Eighty yards and closing.

The flat-bottom cut hard to the left.

"Shit," Trent muttered as the skiff whipped around, engine howling, and the passenger rose from behind the console with something long and black braced against his shoulder.

"Down!" Trent wrenched the airboat right, the hull tilting as the fan screamed at full power.

The first shot cracked across the water like a whip. It punched through the fiberglass hull of the airboat two feet to Dove's left, leaving a hole the size of a quarter and sending splinters spraying across her bare legs.

A second shot split the air where Dove's head had been a half second earlier, and she felt the heat of it pass —or imagined she did, which was close enough.

Flattening herself against the seat, she brought her weapon up. The flat-bottom was broadside to them now, maybe sixty yards out, the shooter repositioning for another attempt. She could see the rifle—semi-automatic, scoped, the kind of hardware a person didn't buy at a sporting goods store.

She fired twice. Controlled. Center mass on the shooter's position. The shots hit the console, and she saw fiberglass explode, but the shooter ducked. She couldn't tell if she'd tagged him.

A third round came back at them. This one hit the fan cage, the metallic clang ringing through the boat like a bell. Trent swore and cranked them left, driving the airboat into a stand of mangroves that swallowed them in green darkness. Branches scraped the hull. Leaves whipped across her face. The fan choked on vegetation and Trent eased off the throttle, letting them drift into cover.

"You hit?" he asked. Breathing hard. Eyes scanning the water through the gaps in the mangroves.

"No. You?"

"No." He wiped spray from his face. "But my boat's got a hole in it."

Through the mangroves, she could hear the flat-bottom's engine—still running, still close, the sound echoing off the water in a way that made distance hard to judge. She held her weapon up, sighting through the branches, waiting.

"They've got real firepower," she said. "That's not a hunting rifle."

"I noticed."

Another burst of engine noise. But it was moving away now—south, deeper into the channel, the sound thinning as distance opened between them. They were running. Not circling back for another pass.

Trent eased the airboat forward, pushing through the mangroves until they had a line of sight down the channel. The flat-bottom was a quarter mile out now, growing smaller, cutting through the water at full speed.

Dove lowered her weapon. "No registration numbers."

"A lot of boats around here that don't have them." Trent shielded his eyes against the morning glare, watching the boat shrink into the distance. "That was a fifteen-foot Mako Pro Skiff. Brand new, and it wasn't the same one from the other night—I'd bet my life on it."

"Any chance that could be Karl's?"

"He prefers a Carolina Skiff, but anything's possible."

They sat in the damaged airboat, drifting in the shallow water at the edge of the mangrove stand, listening to the flat-bottom's engine fade into nothing. The morning was bright and hot and absurdly beautiful—the sky a deep, cloudless blue, the water glittering, a great blue heron standing motionless on the far bank like none of this was its problem.

Dove's hands shook. Not from fear—from the adrenaline dump, the chemical crash that came after the shooting stopped and her body realized it wasn't dead. She'd lived through this cycle enough times to know it would pass. She holstered her weapon and pressed her palms flat against her thighs until the tremor eased.

Trent turned the airboat around and headed back.

The ride to Mallor's Landing was quiet except for the fan and the wind and the ugly sucking sound the hull made where the bullet had punched through. The hole was above the waterline, but barely. Trent kept their speed even and their course straight and didn't say a word the entire way back.

She could feel him thinking. Could feel the anger building in the set of his shoulders and the way he gripped the controls.

They pulled up to the dock and Dove saw two vehicles in the driveway—Buddy's truck and the black SUV that Sterling had backed into the driveway, nose out, ready to move, like he was still running CIA agency operations.

Buddy met them at the waterline, already assessing—the hole in the hull, the fiberglass splinters, the weapons in their hands. He didn't ask if they were okay. He looked at Dove, looked at Trent, and saw that they were standing, and that was enough for now.

"I take it they got away," Buddy said.

"They were a little more prepared," Dove said, stepping onto the dock. "Opened fire with a semi-automatic rifle. We didn't feel like dying today."

"Direction?"

"South through the main channel. They're long gone."

"Maybe, but worth calling our contacts at the sheriff's office. They can have whoever's on patrol look out near the main access point." Buddy turned, lifted his phone to his ear, and informed their contact of the situation.

Sterling appeared from behind Buddy's truck, moving toward them across the bridge with the careful, high-stepping gait of a man who was absolutely certain something with teeth was about to lunge at him from the water. His hand rested on his sidearm and his eyes darted between the moat and the dock and the moat again, like the gators were the bigger threat than whoever had just shot at his colleagues.

Dolly surfaced six feet from the bridge. Opened her mouth wide—that prehistoric display of teeth that said I see you, and I haven't decided if I like you yet—and Sterling stopped dead.

"She's not going to eat you," Dove said.

"You don't know that."

"I've crossed that moat a dozen times, and I still have all my limbs. You'll be fine."

"That ditch might as well be loaded with C4." Sterling skirted the far edge of the bridge, giving Dolly the widest berth the narrow crossing allowed, and Dove stifled a laugh.

The four of them regrouped on the path between the house and the equipment shed. Buddy examined the shed—door closed, no visible damage, no sign of forced entry from the outside.

"I saw them come out of the shed," Dove said.

"And you didn't go inside?" Buddy asked.

"I wasn't letting another intruder get away," Trent said. "I still don't know what they were doing on my property the last time, so maybe we'll find a clue this time." He reached for the handle.

Buddy and Sterling flanked him, weapons drawn. Dove took a position to the right, covering the tree line out of habit.

Trent's fingers closed around the handle.

Gravel crunched behind them. All four of them turned.

Dawson's cruiser rolled down the driveway, lights off. He parked behind Buddy's truck and stepped out, one hand on his belt, his gaze sweeping the property like he did every time he walked into a scene, whether he was on duty or not.

"Don't open that door," he called across the yard. His voice carried the authority of a man who wasn't making a suggestion. He walked toward them at a brisk pace. "Nobody goes in there without me."

Trent's hand hovered on the handle. "You're twenty feet away. What's the big deal?

"I'm not going to say it again," Dawson said, closing the distance.

"Someone came on my property again." Trent stepped back.

Dawson reached them and positioned himself in front of the shed door. "I got a call about something happening here at Mallor's Landing, and it didn't have anything to do with intruders," Dawson said.

"What the hell are you talking about?" Trent asked.

"We'll get to that in a second. For now, everyone is going to back up and let me do my job. Got it?"

Trent nodded.

Dove didn't like it. Something about this didn't settle right. Not after what had just happened. She inched closer to Trent. She had no choice but to let Dawson take over.

Chapter Fifteen

Trent grabbed Dove's hand like it was his only lifeline. His only connection to anything real and safe. "Dawson." He kept his voice as level as he could. "What do you mean you got a call?"

Dawson's expression didn't shift. The man had one of those faces built for poker—wide, flat, unreadable when he wanted it to be. Right now, Trent suspected Dawson wanted it to be exactly the same way it had been a few years ago when he'd questioned him during a murder investigation.

That had not only been terrifying on so many levels, but Trent had learned that Dawson could be one scary ass cop.

"I'll tell you after I look inside," Dawson said.

"That's my shed, and while I'm not going be any trouble or try to stop you because someone just trespassed—*again*—on my property. I think I have the right to know why." Trent squeezed Dove's hand.

"Let me do my job." Dawson turned back to the door. Not unkindly, but with the kind of finality that said the conversation was over until he decided it wasn't.

Trent looked at Dove, who gave him the weakest of smiles.

Sterling and Buddy had moved further from the door. Buddy was tapping away on his cell, and Sterling had his to his ear.

Dawson pulled the door open and stepped inside.

The smell hit Trent first. He knew that scent. Had lived it his entire life. Fresh blood and fat and the sharp, faintly sweet odor of green meat—that particular combination that had lived in Trent's bones from a lifetime of processing it. It was mostly associated with the commercial side of this land and business. The unglamorous reality of what it took to keep Mallor's Landing funded and breathing. It was a smell that, if he were on the other side of the property, would've been normal.

But not coming from this shed.

He leaned past Dawson's shoulder and his stomach dropped straight through the floor. Tears burned his eyes.

Two gators. Laid out on his workbench. Decent-sized animals—eight, maybe nine feet—already skinned, the hides peeled clean and hanging from the ceiling, the meat broken down and portioned with the kind of efficiency that took years to develop. No FWC tags. No paperwork. Nothing but the raw evidence of a transaction that hadn't happened yet.

He'd killed many alligators over the course of his life. It was part of his job. Part of his business. He raised gators specifically for this reason—skins and meat to be sold. But there was a difference between wild gators and farm-raised ones.

His gaze stayed on the skins, moving from one to the next, and his pulse damn near stopped at the second skin.

He knew that animal.

Not by name—because that one never stayed long enough for him to get to know and contrary to popular belief, these creatures did have personalities.

But he had the markings. The slight broadening at the base of the skull, the particular distribution of the scute rows down the back, the old scar along the left flank that had been there since the gator had first sunned himself near the waterline.

This gator had been coming to the bay since Trent was in high school, drifting in and out of Mallor's Landing the way certain animals did when a place felt safe—taking nothing, threatening no one, just existing in the water with the permanence of something that had decided this patch of the Everglades suited him just fine.

He'd eaten more than a few of Trent's chicken quarters over the years—not by hand, but the ones that Trent laid out for the gators who found their way to this sanctuary and looked as though they could use a good meal.

"Those aren't mine." The words came out quieter than he intended. Not defensive. Just true. "I didn't do this. I swear this wasn't me."

Dawson turned to look at him. He studied Trent's face for a moment—long enough that he felt the weight of it, and that made him more than nervous. Dawson had come to town a few years ago—an ex-Navy SEAL and good friend of Fletcher Dane, Baily's husband. At first, Dawson made Trent nervous. Then again, anyone who carried a badge made Trent twitch.

But Dawson had grown on Trent.

"I believe you." Dawson placed his hands on his hips and sighed. "But I can't ignore what my eyes are seeing."

"The people who just shot at us. They came out of this shed," Dove screeched.

"I know that, too." Dawson nodded.

"How can you know that?" Trent's hands curled at his sides. He stared at the second hide—at the scar along the flank—and tried to swallow the thing climbing up the back of his throat. Grief, yes. But under the grief, quieter and more insidious, something that felt too much like rage. The kind of rage that could destroy him if he wasn't careful.

"I got an anonymous tip about the same time Buddy texted me that you and Dove were being shot at," Dawson said.

Gravel crunched in the driveway.

Trent glanced out the window. A Fish and Wildlife truck pulled up and parked at the edge of the yard, and Keaton Cole stepped out—all six feet of him. He had a military bearing that twenty years in the field couldn't be shaken no matter how long he'd been out. He scanned the scene before his door was fully closed. He hadn't grown up in the Glades, but he'd come to Calusa Cove the same way Dawson had—with Fletcher. And Keaton had made this place his home in more ways than one.

"Let's step outside." Dawson waved his hand toward the door.

Dove rested her hand on Trent's elbow as she gently guided him through the door.

He glanced down as his feet squished into the grass. He was still barefoot.

"Good morning." Keaton looped his fingers in his belt.

"What brings you here?" Dove asked. Trent was grateful because his mouth was so dry he couldn't form words.

"Someone called the FWC hotline claiming you're dealing gator skins and meat out on Mallor's Landing." Keaton tilted his head. "I'm sorry, but I had to check it out.

"I find it interesting that Dawson got a similar tip the same morning two assholes were lurking around on my property and then shot at Dove and me." Trent looped a protective arm around Dove, pulling her tight to his side. "I've got a bullet hole in my boat to prove it."

"That doesn't change the fact that there are two gators skinned and chopped in that shed," Dawson said. "With no tags."

"This is bullshit," Dove muttered. "Trent didn't do anything wrong. I've been with him for the last few days. Twenty-four-seven. What's in that shed is fresh. No way could he have done that."

"I'm not standing here accusing either of you of

anything. I'm telling you what brought me to this property," Dawson said.

"You've got cameras, right?" Keaton asked

"I do." Trent pulled out his phone. Opened the security app. The feed was there—the equipment shed camera, live, showing the empty interior. He scrolled back through the motion log. "App didn't go off. No alerts." He turned the screen toward Keaton. "Someone disabled it. Or knew how to move without triggering it." Which meant someone who'd done homework. Someone who'd been here before or had information about the property layout. The thought settled into him like cold water, spreading through his chest, finding every hollow place it could reach.

He felt a hand close around his elbow.

Dove turned him slightly away from the group, her voice dropping to somewhere between his ear and the morning air. "You need to tell them everything. The Hendersons. The photo. All of it."

He stared into her eyes. Her face was calm in the way it got when she was holding something back, managing the situation from the inside out.

"If you don't control this narrative right now," she said quietly, "someone else will. Someone like Stacey Mohawk."

Dove was right. She was always right—especially at the moments he least wanted her to be.

He turned back, keeping his eyes level and said what he should have said the moment that envelope fell out of the newspaper. He told them about the past. Not all of it, not every gray edge and justification he'd built around his younger choices, but the relevant bones—the animals he'd let Karl process on his land when he should have turned him away, the permits he'd put at risk, the years he'd spent putting distance between himself and those choices because he'd thought if he walked straight long enough, the crooked parts would no longer matter.

He told them about the Henderson's letter. The photograph. The threat.

Keaton planted his hands on his hips, looked down at the ground, and shook his head. Dawson crossed his arms, widened his stance, and just stared at Trent, gaze burning.

Trent swallowed. Hard. He'd been a cocky kid, and that cockiness had been born out of anger and grief. He'd carried it into adulthood. Fallon had come close to getting him to shake it. And he'd gotten rid of most of it the day he'd told Karl to fuck off.

Only, Trent had always been a loyal soul—still was to a certain extent. And Karl was a manipulator who'd used that to get what he wanted.

"Do you still have the letter from the Hendersons and the photo?" Dawson asked.

Trent nodded, his throat to dry to form words.

"Both are in the house," Dove said. "I can get them for you, but we'd like copies."

Dawson was quiet for a moment. He looked at Keaton. Some kind of conversation passed between them. They'd served together in the military and had nearly died together more than once. They had the kind of bond that didn't require words half the time.

"Alright," Dawson said finally. "I need you to understand—" He gestured toward the shed. "What's in that shed requires a report. There's no version of this where Keaton and I don't document it."

"Does that mean you're going to arrest me?" In his youth, Trent hadn't ever been frightened of spending a night, or two, in the town lock-up. But now? It was utterly terrifying. Not because he was afraid of closed spaces. Or because he couldn't hack a night in jail. But because he knew deep down he was better than that. And damn it, he didn't want to disappoint his parents. It didn't matter that they were no longer among the living, but what they would've thought of him and his life choices mattered more now than ever.

"No," Dawson said quickly and definitely. "We have an eyewitness that someone was on your property this morning. You were shot at. Add in all the other strange happenings and some other matters we'll get into once my office has looked into a few things, I don't believe that's necessary right now." Dawson raised his hand when Trent opened his mouth. "I don't want you saying one word about what went on here this morning." Dawson turned to Keaton. "You good with that?"

"I can delay filing anything for a day. Maybe two." Keaton nodded. "But if someone called this in, we have to be prepared that someone also tipped off Stacey Mohawk."

Trent groaned. "That woman is a menace. And she

never checks her sources. Thanks to her, I was a suspect in a murder case."

"That didn't last very long," Dawson said.

"Not an easy thing to forget," Trent said softly. "Everything that's happening has to be connected. Karl. The Hendersons. Slade's death. The limestone mining. The fact that the government wants to dig up my dad's body. Maybe even this Dutton guy. I just don't know how or why."

Buddy moved up beside Trent. "I've put Cullen on the payroll until we figure this out."

"I've got some old contacts looking into it," Sterling said. "Background checks on everyone. I'm even going to dive deeper into Dutton to see if his interests in limestone mining are something outside of campaign promises."

"Someone in law enforcement leaked my dad's name. Maybe it could've been this Dutton guy." Trent looked at his boat. The hole in the fiberglass. His father's dock, where strangers had tied off a brand-new skiff and calmly walked onto his property and killed two animals that had done nothing wrong except exist in a place someone wanted to use against him.

"Give us a little time to do our jobs," Dawson said.

"What about the meeting?" he asked.

"We'll meet this afternoon," Keaton said. "After we get a chance to process this shed."

Which put it somewhere between the exhumation and the town meeting tonight, wedged into a day that was already running out of road. Trent nodded because there was nothing else to do.

Dawson gestured toward the yard. "I need everyone to step out and let us work."

They filed out into the bright, punishing morning. Buddy and Sterling said their goodbyes with the clipped efficiency of people who had things to do and would do them without being asked twice. Keaton and Dawson disappeared into the shed with their phones out.

Trent walked toward the house, and Dove fell into step beside him.

The screen door creaked the way it had since he was a kid. Inside, the kitchen smelled like eggs and coffee and the ordinary morning they'd had about forty-five minutes ago, before the world had another go at him. He stood in the middle of the kitchen floor, his hands at his sides. "I don't know how much more of this I can take," he said. "They used a gator I knew." He stared at the floor. "He's been coming here since I was a teenager. He's never bothered anyone." His voice didn't crack. He wouldn't let it. "He came here because I made it safe." He felt the failure of that in places words couldn't reach.

"Don't do that to yourself. This isn't your fault."

"Maybe not. But I seem to be the center of it, and it's not just gators that are being killed. It's people." He held up his hand before she could say a word. "I'm sorry about your uncle." He lifted his gaze. "I know he didn't tell us everything. But whatever it was that he was trying to do, he didn't deserve to be murdered. He didn't deserve to be gunned down in a parking lot, and over what?"

"I don't know, but whatever it was, my uncle was willing to risk his life for it." She leaned against the counter and crossed her arms, her eyes steady on his. "He came here to warn you, or help you, or maybe to stop something." She paused. "Which means there's a thread here somewhere. And when we find it and pull it, the whole thing comes undone."

He looked at her—this woman who hated gators and showed up anyway, who'd watched her team die and got back up, who was standing in his kitchen less than a day after identifying her uncle's body and talking about threads instead of falling apart.

He loved her. God, he loved her. He knew that the way he knew the moat—every depth, every current, every cold-blooded creature that called it home. He knew it without needing to say it out loud and without being ready to, which was the quiet cruelty of being a man who'd spent most of his adult life keeping his mouth shut about the things that mattered most.

He pulled out a chair and sat down. He was a coward and she deserved better.

Pushing off the counter, she poured him a fresh cup of coffee and set it in front of him, then sat across the table in his father's chair.

Outside, the gators moved in the moat. A tail slapped the water, sharp and authoritative—a way of announcing that one of them was watching.

He wrapped his hands around the mug.

Find the loose stone.

Okay. He could do that. He'd pulled twelve-foot snakes off struggling animals with his bare hands. He'd held this property together through his father's death and his mother's slow disappearance and every bad decision he'd made in between.

He could find a loose stone. And he'd find the threat and neutralize it.

And once it was all over, he had to find a way to tell Dove how much he loved her. How he couldn't see his future anymore without her in it.

Chapter Sixteen

Trent pulled into the Aegis Network office parking lot and cut the engine. Stepping out of the truck, his heart was still in his throat. He'd just watched the backhoe dig up his father's grave. He watched them lift the casket out of the earth and move it into a large tent. He'd stood there with Dove, staring at that tent for what seemed like hours, but was actually maybe forty minutes before the ME exited, with his father's remains in a new container.

Gently and respectfully, they put that container into a hearse and drove away.

Trent was told it would take one to three days for confirmation that the remains were indeed his father's. But the rest of the information the feds wanted could take weeks to obtain.

He did his best to shake the image of his dad's empty grave from his head and focus on... well, everything that had turned to shit.

Dove came around from the passenger side, and they fell into step together, crossing the lot toward the low-slung building that sat just outside of town. Decker Brown owned it—his construction company office down the hall from the Aegis space—and there was nothing on the exterior that would tell you what happened inside. No signage. No indication. That was the point.

"Are you okay?" Dove asked.

He had no idea how to answer that question. Worse, she was going through it too with the death of her uncle, and yet, here she was, holding his hand. He should be the one being strong for her, instead of this shell of a man who could barely complete a whole thought.

"Are you upset because I asked Cullen to follow Karl?"

Trent paused in the middle of the parking lot. "I wish you had told me, but I'm not mad. You're trying to help, and I appreciate it."

She stopped beside him, hands in her back pockets, chin up—ready for whatever came next. "Are you worried about this meeting?"

"Very," he admitted. "I took the heat for Karl eight years ago because I believed in loyalty, even though I knew he was an asshole and I was distancing myself. As time went on, he started to threaten me with exposure for what he'd done on my land. It worried me, and I'll admit, sometimes I helped him with stupid stuff. Nothing that would get me more than a ticket or a fine. Karl's been more bark than bite, and I realized he'd have to own his criminal activity, and he'd never do that. Then a few years ago, he asked me if he could use Mallor's Landing after he learned I helped out another buddy. One who was actually a friend. Someone who just did a stupid thing for the right reasons." Trent ran his fingers through his hair and stared at the building. It was just something for his eyes to focus on. Nothing really registered. Just something to occupy his body with while he let his emotions curl around his chest like a python.

"I called Karl's bluff, and nothing happened. He went away. I barely saw him. It wasn't until that day, a few weeks before my mother died, that he showed up at my house, telling me he had the opportunity of a lifetime. It was the same day my mom told me about the Hendersons' offer." Trent shifted his gaze, catching Dove's blue eyes as the sun's rays sparkled in the electric color. He cupped her face.

His mother used to tell him that the best kind of love —the love that lasts a lifetime—was the kind that snuck up on you and seeped into your bones like a warm summer day. Or a nice shot of tequila.

"If Dawson and Keaton can't prove that someone tried to frame me for those gator skins and meat, I'm not only going to lose all my permits and possibly my land, I could go to—"

She covered his mouth with her palm. "You didn't do anything wrong."

He curled his fingers around her wrist and kissed her hand. "Not this time, but that doesn't mean they can turn a blind eye to what I've done in the past."

"It's gonna be okay."

He wished he could believe that. He stood there for a beat, then started walking again. "Alright," he said. "Let's find out what everyone has."

Inside, Buddy was behind his desk, sleeves rolled to his elbows. Sterling sat across the room at his own desk, boots crossed at the ankles, something on his laptop holding his attention.

"Afternoon." Buddy looked up and waved a hand over his head. "Everyone's down the hall waiting. Sterling and I have more research to do. Cullen has everything Sterling and I know, but I'll join you in a bit."

"Before you head into the conference room," Sterling said. "I heard back from my contact at the CIA. He said the information the marshals and the feds have on Parrish is locked up tight, and they've kept that circle real small. The only thing I learned is that there's some information in that cache that's damaging to some powerful players. Until they sort through it, they aren't giving anything up." Sterling raised his hand when Trent opened his mouth. "I asked about your dad's case, and I got a beat of silence. That tells me there's a connection. Not sure what it is, but I'll keep digging."

"I don't know how to repay you for doing all this," Trent said.

"It's what we do for family." Buddy pointed toward the hallway. "They're waiting for you."

Dove took Trent by the hand and led him down the hall towards the conference room.

It was a modest space with a rectangular table, eight chairs, and a credenza along the wall with a coffee station. A box of doughnuts sat in the center of the table beside a plate of muffins that had Fallon written all over them.

Keaton sat on the far side, patient and still, the way a man got after spending years in the military.

Fallon was beside him, notebook open. She glanced up, tilted her head, and pursed her lips like she always did when she was disappointed.

Trent couldn't blame her for that. He was disappointed in himself.

Cullen was next to her with his arms crossed and a manila envelope in front of him. He'd gotten another haircut, and he'd been keeping his facial hair respectable. He looked good. Not like the broken man who'd come home a few years ago and jumped at the sound of an engine backfiring.

At the head of the table was Dawson, who offered him a smile, but it didn't stop Trent from feeling like he was back in the interrogation room at the police station. On the table in front of Dawson was a closed folder.

Dove poured two cups of coffee from the credenza, handed one to Trent, and they took their seats across from Cullen, Fallon, and Keaton.

"We've had a busy day since we left Mallor's Landing, so let's get started." Dawson wasn't the kind of man who liked to waste time. "Keaton. Fallon. Go."

"We found seven pythons on the property," Keaton said. "Total, including the one Trent put down. All Burmese. All healthy. All wild."

"Also all male," Fallon added. She looked at Trent,

and her features softened just a little. "Not a single female in the bunch."

The number sat in the room like something alive. "Males don't congregate like that," Trent said. "Not without a reason. And the only thing that draws that many into one area is a breeding female. Or female pheromones."

Dawson reached beneath the table and held up a clear evidence bag. Inside was a mesh bag, darkened with residue, about the size of a grapefruit. "Keaton found this floating in the reeds, tucked up good. It was down on the very southern tip of your land. The substance tested positive for female Burmese python pheromones."

So there it was.

Not migration. Not nature doing something unpredictable. Someone had walked his land—his family's land, the land his father had bled for, the land his mother had watched the sun set over from the old dock every evening of her life—and turned it into a killing field.

"We only found the one bag, and that might have been all it took depending on how they contaminated the land," Keaton said. "The distribution pattern of where we located the snakes suggests there were likely more lure points across the property."

"I walked the rest of the acreage right after the incident," Trent said. "No signs of any bags or more snakes. But I'll keep at it."

Dawson set the evidence bag on the table. "We'll get this processed, but you mentioned the night you had intruders, they were carrying something. Do you remember the size?"

"It was dark. And it did look like they were dropping stuff. But it wasn't very big," Trent said. "They could've easily been dropping smaller bags like that one with sponges containing pheromones." He let out a long breath and ran a hand over his face. "I'm not proud of this, but back in the day, when I used to do stupid shit, that's how I'd lure pythons. My sole purpose was to kill them, and I did so humanely, but it's not legal."

"Nope, it's not. At least, not for you," Keaton said. "But that was before my time."

"Wasn't before mine," Fallon muttered. "Imagine what it was like for me when I learned the man I was living with was doing that when I was an FWC officer." Her eyes narrowed. "But I could let that go. Those snakes are a menace. What the hell were you thinking, letting Karl use Mallor's Landing? Please tell me it wasn't when we were living together?" Fallon crossed her arms. "I could've lost my job."

"I would've gone to jail before I let that happen and no, it was after," he said softly. "And it's not like I offered the shed to him. Or even let him do it. He just did, and I was stuck covering it up."

"You should've let him go to jail." Fallon let out a long breath.

"He saved my life." Trent held her stare. "Back then, I just couldn't forget about that."

"Ever think he saw that other snake and let it attack, waiting for the right moment to come in and be a hero?"

Cullen asked. "Because that's what it looked like to me from where I was sitting that day."

"I suppose that could be true." Trent had never wanted to believe that. Karl was a lot of things, but to risk his friend's life? Oh, hell, they weren't friends. They never really had been because Karl only cared about himself.

Cullen picked up the manila envelope. "My turn." He opened the flap, slid a photograph out, and pushed it across the table.

Trent picked it up. Slightly grainy, taken at a distance, phone camera pushed to its limits, but clear enough. Two men in a parking lot. One was Karl Simpson. Unmistakable, even blurred. The bulk. The sun-ruined skin. The posture of a man who'd spent his whole life believing he was the smartest person in any room and being wrong every single time.

The other man was clean-cut and well-dressed. The kind of polish that didn't grow in the Everglades. But he also had an edge. It was the way he stood. Wide stance. Arms crossed. Shoulders square.

"Why is Karl Simpson talking to Garrett Dutton?" Trent set the photo down. "The man's running for state senate."

""He's also a former U.S. Marshal. Twenty-one-year career. Southern District of Florida," Dawson said.

"I'm well aware of what he used to be," Trent said. "He also was on my father's protection detail with Slade."

Dawson shifted his gaze to Dove. "I believe your

uncle might have been keeping things from you and from Trent."

"I don't doubt it," Dove said. "Whatever he knew, someone killed him for it."

"I've asked Buddy and Sterling to do some digging where I can't," Dawson said. "But I've learned something quite disturbing."

Trent ran a hand across his face. "I can't imagine anything more unsettling than watching your father's casket come out of the ground."

"I'm sorry you had to deal with that today," Dawson said, leaning forward. "But one of the reasons Slade might have shown up here is because Dutton is romantically involved with Courtney Kirk." Dawson tapped his fingers on the table. "As in the daughter of Edward Kirk, who was the CEO of Gulf Coast Energy Partners."

"You've got to be fucking kidding me," Trent mumbled.

"It gets worse." Dawson reached for his coffee and took a long sip, as if this were a great time to pause. "She's a criminal attorney. Has done some white-collar stuff but also has some shady clients that have been associated with mobsters."

"Fucking wonderful." Trent stared at the photograph on the table. Karl's stupid, smug face next to a man in a tailored jacket. Two people who had no business knowing each other, standing three feet apart, talking like it was the most natural thing in the world. He thought about spiderwebs—how you could stare at individual strands for hours and never see the design until you stepped back far enough.

He was stepping back now. And he didn't like how the present looked a lot like the past.

"My theory is that Karl can provide key information on you and Mallor's Landing," Dawson said.

Trent turned to Dawson. "Why is my property important to any of these people?"

Dawson flipped open the folder. "On a hunch, based on the odd happenings at your place, Slade's death, and especially this morning, Buddy looked more closely into Sovereign Resources." Dawson pushed a few pages across the table.

"What am I looking at?" Trent asked as Dove leaned over his shoulder.

"Official complaints from residents who live near one of their mining sites." Dawson leaned back.

Trent lifted one of the pages. "It says here that not only do the residents believe they are mining irresponsibly, but that there is strange activity at all hours of the night."

"I'll take over here." Buddy had stepped into the room holding a few pieces of paper in his hands. "A couple of residents who live the closest and never wanted the company there in the first place, hired a private investigator." Buddy set the papers on the table and sat on the edge. "The PI is still investigating and can't prove anything yet, but he's pretty sure that Sovereign Resources is using their mining sites to bury evidence for Courtney's clients."

"Her clientele is quite eccentric," Dawson said. "Her roster reads like a list of people you don't want to meet anywhere, let alone a dark alley. Mob-adjacent. Organized. Violent. The kind of people who keep attorneys on retainer the way normal people keep dentists—not because they might need one, but because they know they will." He looked around the table. "Chloe is reaching out to FBI contacts to pull whatever she can on Courtney's background and client history. Sterling's working his CIA channels to do the same. If there's something to find, they'll find it."

Trent set down the paper and rubbed his temples. "I don't understand any of this."

"From what I can tell, Sovereign Resources acts as an evidence laundering service, and Courtney is at the center of it," Buddy said. "Her clients need evidence buried, she offers them a service, and she takes care of it. They need someone to disappear—she helps them with that. And what better place to do that than the Everglades."

"And Dutton, Courtney's boyfriend, is all about the mining," Cullen said.

"Not to mention that buried in all the LLCs that own Sovereign Resources is Courtney's name, along with her father." Buddy tapped the papers. "They want Mallor's Landing because it gives them water access. Allows them to come and go without being noticed."

"Jesus," Dove muttered, grabbing Trent's hand under the table.

He took it. And squeezed. Hard. "And the Hendersons?"

"Big campaign backers of Dutton." Buddy stood. "But also, I found Emma's name—her maiden name—on an LLC filing for one of the holdings for Sovereign Recourses."

Trent pushed his chair back but couldn't bring himself to stand. He didn't trust his legs would hold his weight. "This is similar to what my father went up against. Slimy politicians. Criminal activity." He closed his eyes, sucked in a deep breath, and let it out slowly before blinking open his eyes. "I bet Dutton was the agent who leaked my father's name."

"Probably destroyed evidence too," Buddy said. "I have a lot more digging to do for tonight's town hall. So, I'd better have at it." He turned and strolled out of the conference room.

Dawson straightened. "One more thing. I received word this morning that Dutton plans to attend the town hall meeting." He let that settle across the table. "My entire team will be on duty tonight, and Buddy and Sterling agreed to help. But I want everyone in this room to be on their best behavior and act like you don't know shit about any of this and do not engage." Dawson shifted his gaze between Trent and Dove. "Do I make myself clear?"

"I'll keep him in check," Dove said.

"She won't have to." Trent rolled his neck. "I have no desire to get into it with any of these people. I know what it cost my father. I'll let you do your job," he said. "But if Karl's there, he'll come for me."

"Just don't do anything stupid," Keaton said.

"I'm working on an angle with Karl." Cullen had a calm, settled expression that he didn't always carry. He might have come a long way from the man who lived in the shadows waiting to die, but he was still a man who struggled with daily life.

"I thought I'd reach out," Cullen continued. "See if he wants to grab drinks either before or after the meeting. A couple of guys from Calusa Cove haven't caught up in a while. Keep it easy. See what he says when he thinks he's talking to an old friend."

"You were never friends." Something cold moved through Trent's chest. Not fear for himself—he'd long ago made peace with the risks that came with living the way he'd lived. But the idea of Cullen walking toward something dangerous, wearing a friendly smile as camouflage, landed differently now. Loss had sharpened his awareness of what he still had, and the people sitting around this table were most of it.

"We weren't either, and look at us now." Cullen smiled. "Uncle Silas calls what we have a bromance."

Dawson chuckled. "I say that about Hayes and Keaton."

"You're just jealous," Keaton said.

"You all can make light of this if you want, but you don't know Karl like I do, and you don't know the shit he put Cullen through when we were kids. I don't like it," Trent said.

"I know you don't. But you don't have to." Cullen

cocked his head. "There's a lot at stake here, and let's not forget the marshal's office dug up your dad's body. They did that for a reason, and something tells me it wasn't just to check information."

"Agreed." Dawson nodded. "Either they believe the dead man's cache is bogus, or they're lying to us, or something else entirely is going on. Whatever it is, I'm sure it's making Dutton nervous."

"That doesn't make me feel better about Cullen—"

"I appreciate the concern," Cullen said, interrupting Trent. "I'm doing great, and if I weren't, I'd step back. You need to trust that."

"Okay." Trent nodded.

The meeting broke up after that. Chairs pushed back. A last reach for doughnuts. Coffee cups refilled or abandoned.

"I need to go speak with Buddy," Dove said.

"I'll be out in a minute." Trent held her gaze.

She leaned up, kissed his cheek, and disappeared into the hallway.

Dawson shook Trent's hand on the way out. Keaton followed. Fallon paused long enough to catch Trent's eye and give him the look she'd been giving him since he was twenty-one and had pulled her out of a river—the one that said everything without speaking a word.

No matter what, she was still his best friend. That meant more than words.

Then it was just him and Cullen.

The conference room held the kind of quiet that

lived between two men who'd known each other since childhood—since before the fights and the grudges and the slow, stubborn work of building something real from the wreckage of being young and angry and convinced they didn't need anyone. The kind of quiet where you could say something that mattered or say nothing at all, and both were fine.

Cullen leaned back, watching Trent with the unhurried patience of a man who had no intention of leaving until the conversation he came for actually happened. "How are you doing?" he asked. "Not the snakes. Not the mining. Not whatever the hell is going on with Karl and Dutton. I'm asking about you."

Trent turned his coffee cup in a slow circle on the table. The mug was empty. He kept turning it anyway, because his hands needed something to do while his mouth figured out how to say what his chest already knew.

"I'm actually doing ok. But I'm worried about Dove," he said. "She's running on fumes. Didn't sleep but a few hours last night. She's pouring everything into movement, into staying busy—because the second she stops, the grief catches up. And she'd rather run herself into the ground than let that happen."

"Sounds familiar."

"Yeah." No point denying it. "It does."

Cullen didn't push. He just sat there—patient in a way that people who didn't know him mistook for indifference but was actually the opposite. Cullen watched. Cullen listened. He just didn't make a show of it.

"I'm falling hard," Trent said.

He hadn't planned to say it. The words just came up from somewhere deep and unguarded, the place he'd spent most of his adult life keeping bricked over because it was safer to feel nothing than to feel something and lose it. But the bricks had been coming loose for weeks now. Since before his mother died. Maybe since the first time Dove had crossed his bridge with a careful smile and looked at his gators like they might eat her alive.

"Harder than I've ever fallen for anyone. And I don't know what I'd do if I lost her." His voice roughened on the last part. Cullen had earned the right to hear him sound less than steady. "And it terrifies me."

"Does she know this?" Cullen asked.

"I can't say we've had a deep conversation about our relationship. Too many other things are happening in our lives right now.

"That's the perfect time to stop sitting on the sidelines," Cullen said, his voice low and steady. The voice of a man who'd learned the hard way what happened when you let the important things pass you by because you were too proud or too scared or too convinced you didn't deserve them. "Fight for her. Not the way you're used to fighting—not fists and stubbornness and that thick skull God gave you. Fight for her by letting her in." He tapped his fingers on the table. "You both have some pretty tall walls. Knock yours down already, and then start chiseling through hers."

Trent looked at him. "I'm afraid if I push too hard—if I tell her how I really feel—she'll run."

"She's a tough woman. And right now, that wall is keeping the grief out. And maybe it's keeping you out, too." Cullen leaned forward, elbows on the table. "You want in—really in—you gotta be willing to risk your heart. And maybe she's been waiting for you to figure it out because your walls have been bigger than hers."

Trent thought about that a moment. His friend might be right. "Since when did you get so wise?"

"Not wise. But I'm a man who lost everything. My wife left me and took my son. I had nothing but walls." He tapped his finger on the table. "And then some asshole from my past kept showing up, trying to tell me I wasn't a waste of time."

Trent thought about this morning—the gray light in the bedroom. The way Dove had looked at him with her defenses down and her voice stripped bare. The way she said, "I need you" like the words had cost her something she wasn't sure she could afford. The way she'd kissed him like she was trying to outrun something that was gaining on her. And then, afterward—the walls went back up, one by one, and the talk turned to meetings and case files and keeping busy was grief's only language she understood—and he'd allowed it all because he was too afraid to admit that he loved her.

There it was. The word. Still inside his head, still unspoken, but so close to the surface now, it pressed against his teeth every time he opened his mouth.

Cullen stood and pushed in his chair. He clapped Trent on the shoulder as he passed. "You got this, Mallor. Don't overthink it."

He left. And Trent sat alone in the conference room, hand over his chest. He loved Dove, no question about that. He should be terrified that they hadn't used birth control. But the only thing that frightened him was the idea that she might not be ready to love him back.

Chapter Seventeen

ove had noticed the SUV two blocks from the Aegis office.

Dark. Small. Tinted windows deep enough that the driver was nothing but a shape behind smoked glass. It pulled out from a side street as they cleared the parking lot—no signal, no hesitation—and settled three car lengths back with the practiced patience of something that didn't need to rush because the driver already knew exactly where they were going.

She didn't say anything yet. Just watched it in the passenger mirror, tracking without turning her head. The vehicle matched every speed change. It held the distance like a precise, deliberate measurement.

"We're being followed," she said.

"I just noticed that." Trent's hands shifted on the wheel.

She pulled her phone, kept it below the window line,

and fired off a text to Buddy and Dawson. Four words and her location. *Dark SUV. Following us.*

Buddy responded in three seconds that he was on it.

Dawson responded right after that, his ETA was twelve minutes.

She mapped the route to her rental in her head, the way she'd been trained to map everything—exits, choke points, sight lines. Two miles to the town limits. After that, the road opened up and narrowed down at the same time, the buildings dropping away and the Everglades closing in on both sides, no intersections, no cover, no one close enough to see or hear anything that happened out there.

She unholstered her weapon and held it low against her thigh, muzzle toward the floor. Out the window, Calusa Cove slipped past in pieces—the diner with its hand-lettered specials board, the hardware store, the bait shop with the pelican sign so faded you could barely read it. All of it slow and sunbaked and ordinary. A woman pushing a stroller. A kid on a bicycle. A man loading bags into the back of a minivan.

All of them obliviously to the situation.

The last stoplight in town turned yellow. Trent didn't slow down. He glided through the light.

So did the SUV.

The sign thanking people for coming to Calusa Cove appeared in the mirror. Then shrank. Then disappeared. And just like that, the town was gone—the buildings swallowed by sawgrass, the road narrowing, the sky opening up overhead in a way that always made Dove feel exposed, like a moving target on an empty table.

The bridge now only a few miles away.

The SUV sped up.

"Shit, they're closing in," she said.

"What do you want me to do, because if we don't turn soon, we're gonna be stuck on this road for a while."

One car length. Half a car length. The dark grille filling her mirror, details emerging as it closed the gap—a rental plate, she caught that much, and a crack in the lower left corner of the windshield, and then she didn't have time for details anymore.

"Brace yourself," she managed.

The impact exploded through the truck like a detonation.

Metal shrieked. The world lurched sideways. Her shoulder slammed into the door so hard she felt it in her teeth, her head snapping back against the headrest, her weapon hand pressing down hard on the dash to keep the muzzle pointed safe. The truck fishtailed—tires screaming, rear end swinging right—and for one nauseating second, she was looking at the shoulder of the road and the drainage ditch beyond it and the sky tilting at an angle it shouldn't be.

Then Trent's hands moved, and the truck straightened.

She pushed off the dash and got herself upright. The mirror showed the SUV dropping back, recalibrating, the driver steering it back to center after the ram.

"They're not done," she said.

"I didn't think they were, but we've got to do—"

"Duck!" She put her head between her legs and swallowed her breath.

A shot cracked from behind them.

Not a pop—a crack, the deep, flat percussion of a rifle, and the back window exploded inward. Safety glass cascaded over her shoulders and into her lap, tiny cubes of it, some sharp enough to sting. She felt two or three hit the back of her neck, felt the bright, quick pain of them, and registered it and filed it away because it wasn't important yet.

She had her window down before the glass finished falling.

The wind hit her like a wall—hot and wet and tasting of sawgrass and road heat. Behind them, the SUV was accelerating again, the engine note climbing, and she could see the passenger window down now and an arm extended.

"They're gaining. What do you want me to do?" Trent asked with a voice too calm for the situation.

"Don't swerve yet." She grabbed the door frame with her left hand, leaned into the wind, found the SUV in her sights. "Keep it steady. Thirty miles an hour. Whatever you do, don't touch the brake."

"There's a curve—"

"Take it. Then a straight line. I need a platform. Steady speed, straight road."

He took the curve. The truck leaned and she leaned with it, knuckles white on the door frame, everything in her body fighting the centrifugal pull while she kept the weapon up and the muzzle tracking. They came out of the curve and the road opened ahead of them—flat and empty, a quarter mile of nothing but cracked asphalt and the heat shimmer rising off it.

Two shots came in fast succession from the SUV. One punched through the tailgate—she heard the hollow bang, felt the truck shudder. The second caught the trailer hitch with a sound like a hammer striking an anvil and the whole rear of the truck vibrated with the impact.

"I need you to breathe," she said. Her own voice surprised her—flat, almost conversational, the voice she used when the world was on fire and conversation was the only thing that kept it from getting worse.

"Working on it."

"Closer." She adjusted her grip, squared her shoulders against the wind. "Close the gap just a little. Ten feet. Can you do that?"

"You want me to slow down while they're shooting at us?"

"Yes."

"And you think me living with gators is nuts." He lifted off the throttle, and the SUV rushed forward in the mirror, filling it, thirty feet and then twenty and she could see the shooter more clearly now—passenger seat, upper body out the window, rifle braced on the door frame. Experienced. Anchored. Taking his time because he thought he had it.

He didn't have it.

She breathed out.

Found the left rear tire—not the center, not the inner

edge, the sweet spot just behind the valve stem where the sidewall met the tread and the rubber was thinnest—and fired twice.

The first round clipped the sidewall. The second punched through dead center.

The tire didn't slowly deflate. It detonated—a sound like a second gunshot, and then the SUV lurched hard left, dropping onto the rim, the back end swerving and fishtailing and dragging along the shoulder in a rooster tail of sparks and shredded rubber. The shooter disappeared inside. The rifle dropped out of frame.

"Move to the right, give me the angle," she said.

"They're still—"

"Move right."

Trent drifted the truck toward the centerline. The SUV wrestled itself back to the road—two-wheel drive on a flat rim, still doing forty, the driver working hard to keep it from spinning out. She'd give him credit. He was good.

Not good enough.

"Lift off again," she said. "Just for two seconds."

"Are you serious?"

"Two. Seconds."

He came off the gas.

She breathed in. Breathed out. The wind tried to drag the barrel left, and she compensated without thinking, the same micro-adjustment she'd made a thousand times from overwatch positions in places that didn't exist on maps. The right rear tire filled her sight picture. The truck's motion. The SUV's motion. The wind variable, twelve miles an hour out of the southwest—

She fired.

The right tire exploded.

The SUV dropped hard on both rear corners simultaneously, the chassis slamming down onto two bare rims, and the sound of it was catastrophic—metal on asphalt, shrieking and grinding, a fountain of sparks that lit up the shoulder like something burning. The vehicle slewed sideways across both lanes, tires gone, momentum carrying it in a long, ugly arc, and then it scraped to a stop half on the road and half in the shoulder with the driver's door crumpled against the guardrail and both rear quarters torn open.

Still.

Smoke rising from the wheel wells.

For one second, nothing moved.

"Go," she said. "Straight to my place."

Trent floored it.

The truck surged forward and the wrecked SUV shrank in what was left of the rearview mirror—two doors cracked open now, figures moving inside but moving slow, moving hurt, not following. In the distance, faint but growing, the sound of sirens. Dawson, vectoring in from the south.

She pulled herself back through the window. Slumped into the seat. Her shoulder was going to bruise where she'd hit the door—she could feel it already, a deep ache spreading outward from the joint. Glass fell from her hair onto her lap. She pressed the back of her hand against her neck and felt the sting of three or four small cuts, nothing deep, nothing that needed more than a few minutes and some antiseptic.

She texted Dawson. Informed him of the SUV's current location and warned him that the perps were armed.

She looked at Trent. His knuckles were white on the wheel, jaw set, eyes forward, a thin line of blood at his hairline where a piece of glass had caught him.

Close. Too close.

She reached up and touched the cut. "You're bleeding."

"I'm fine." His gaze went from the road to the side mirror, to the rear mirror, back to the road, before repeating.

Physically, maybe he was fine. But he wasn't any better than she'd been during the fifteen minutes she watched him deal with a gator and a snake. Two dangerous worlds that neither one quite understood and, in the matter of days, got to experience firsthand.

They drove in silence for a moment. The adrenaline still moved through her—she could feel it in the edges of her vision, in the slight tremor starting in her hands now that the shooting had stopped. She pressed her palms flat on her thighs and let it run its course. This was just chemistry. This was just her body finishing what the threat had started.

"Buddy always told me you were a good shot." Trent reached across the cab and took her hand.

"Don't sound so surprised."

Something crossed his face that wasn't quite a smile

and wasn't quite not one. "I'm not. I just—" He exhaled. "I've never watched anyone do that. While being shot at. It's terrifying and impressive at the same time."

"So is watching a man untangle a python from a gator."

That won her a chuckle. "I suppose it is."

She looked at the road ahead. Her rental was four minutes out—but she knew—even before they turned the corner. It was particular knowledge that lived below thinking, below language, in whatever part of her had been paying attention to the world long enough to start understanding its grammar.

Holding her breath, she glanced between the clock on the dash, and the house coming into view. That unsettling feeling filled her gut. The same one she'd had before she knew she'd have to pull the trigger.

Trent slowed his truck as it approached the house. It wasn't much to look at. An old stucco Florida modular home that looked like it had seen better days.

Shit. The front door was open.

Not open like someone had forgotten to close it. Open like it had been argued with and lost—the frame splintered around the deadbolt, the door itself hanging inward at an angle that made her back teeth ache, wood pulp scattered across the concrete step like something that used to be solid and wasn't anymore.

Trent pulled the truck to the curb and cut the engine. "I think we should text Dawson."

"On it.

Dawson's response came back immediately—*officer en route in 8 minutes.*

She held up her weapon and slipped from the vehicle. "We do this the same way we did my uncle's place. Got it?" She glanced over her shoulder.

Trent was a step behind, Glock drawn, moving to her left to take the flank. "I'll follow your lead, but I'm not asking for permission to shoot anything or anyone that comes at us."

"Just don't shoot me." She went in slow and low, pivoting right off the doorframe, sweeping the entry.

The living room was a disaster.

Couch overturned, cushions slashed. The bookshelf knocked forward, her paperbacks and one framed photo —her team, taken three months before they died, eight people smiling in the Kandahar sun—face down in a scatter of pages and broken glass. Every drawer in the end table pulled out and was thrown. The abstract print she'd actually liked, the one she'd driven forty minutes to a consignment shop to find because something about the colors felt like the water here, lay face down on the floor with the backing torn off and the frame snapped in two.

"Clear," she called out of habit.

They moved through the space in sequence, covering each other's blind spots—she took point, Trent covered her six, both of them in the operational silence that operating in a cleared space required. Not the silence of calm. The silence of listening hard for breath, for movement, for the sound of weight shifting on a floorboard.

She was impressed by the way Trent instinctively

knew what to do. Perhaps from years of sneaking up on prehistoric creatures.

She pushed herself against the wall near the opening of the kitchen. Trent was on the opposite side. "Ready," she said softly.

He nodded.

Easing into the room, she scanned every inch with her heart in her throat. She'd done this a million times, but it had never been this personal.

Every cabinet open. The contents swept from the shelves and onto the floor—canned goods rolled to the baseboards, the box of pasta she'd bought last week split open and spilled across the linoleum. The coffee maker on its side, the carafe cracked. The bourbon she kept above the refrigerator—the good bottle, the one she'd been nursing for six months—was shattered against the baseboard, and the smell of it filled the room, sharp and sweet and wrong, mixing with the damp heat coming through the open door.

"Clear," she managed with a thick lump in her throat. "My bedroom next." She inched down the small hallway, one foot in front of the other, placed softly on the floor as not to make a noise. She held her breath as she pivoted and the room crossed her line of sight. "Fuck," she muttered.

The mattress was dragged off the frame and left at an angle, the box spring exposed. Closet emptied, her clothes in a pile on the hardwood, hangers bent and broken. Every box she'd stored on the closet shelf torn open—winter gear, tax documents, an old go-bag she'd never gotten around to tossing—contents spread across the floor in a forensics pattern that told her exactly how systematic this had been. Methodical. Room by room. Not rage. Purpose.

Her go-bag—the current one, the operational one she kept loaded and ready—unzipped and dumped against the far wall. Spare magazine, medical kit, backup phone, the folded emergency cash she'd carried since her second year in the Army. All of it scattered.

She catalogued the violations with the part of her brain that did that, and she let the rest of her feel absolutely nothing about it. There would be time to feel later.

This time she didn't bother saying clear. There was no point. No one was in the house. If they were, they would've come at them or bolted. But she remained at the ready because the one thing she'd learned over the years was to be prepared for the unexpected.

With her heart hammering in her chest, she turned her attention to the guest bedroom across the hall.

Stood in the doorway, tears threatening to break free. She'd handed her uncle a cup of coffee right here in this hallway. She'd laughed at one of his stupid jokes, and she'd blushed just a little when he'd made a comment about Trent and her spending the night the morning she'd come back to get a change of clothes, and her uncle had left to visit a friend.

That was the day he'd been murdered. The last time she'd seen him.

Trent came up behind her, resting a gentle hand around her waist, thumb rubbing softly on her hip.

They'd gotten off to a really bad start months ago. She wasn't in the right headspace to be anything other than a good time, and he used his alligators as a form of female repellent.

Damn, things were growing on her.

She sucked in a breath and focused on what the job called for and she needed to treat this as a job. She could fall apart later.

"This room is worse than the others," Trent said.

The mattress hadn't just been dragged off the bed—it had been slashed across the middle in two long cuts, the foam batting pulled out in handfuls and scattered. The pillow her uncle had slept on, still in the case she'd washed after he left because she hadn't been able to bring herself to launder it before he died, was torn open, stuffing pulled loose and dropped on the floor without ceremony.

The nightstand drawers were gone. Not emptied—gone, ripped from the housing and taken entirely, or thrown hard enough that they'd broken apart and she couldn't find the pieces in the mess.

The desk had been upended, its underside examined and discarded. The closet rod was yanked from the wall. The baseboards on the left side had been pried away from the wall—she could see the tool marks, the raw wood beneath the paint—and shoved back imperfectly, not quite sitting flush anymore.

Someone had taken this room apart with the focused, systematic intensity of a person who knew what they were looking for and had searched every place it could be hiding.

She looked at the mattress her uncle had slept on, which had been slashed. The pillow torn and the stuffing littered on the floor. She gave it one full second. Let it hit her the way it needed to. The violation. The hands on his things. Someone had stood in this room—the room that still smelled faintly of Old Spice and coffee—and had torn it apart looking for what he'd tried to protect.

"What the hell was he hiding?" she whispered the question. "Why couldn't he have trusted me?"

"I get the feeling he didn't trust anyone with it." Trent rested his hand on her shoulder. "But whatever they were looking for, it had to do with the empty folder with my father's name that we saw at your uncle's townhouse."

She holstered her weapon.

"The question is, do they have it?" She turned and held Trent's gaze. "Or did my uncle hide it somewhere else, and now it's up to us to find it?"

Chapter Eighteen

The parking lot outside the town hall smelled like exhaust, cut grass, and the charged tension that settled over a crowd when nobody wanted to be the first one to go home.

People stood in clusters under the lights, voices low, most of them still holding whatever printed materials the Sovereign Resources team had handed out. Glossy. Professional. The kind of thing that took money to produce. The kind of thing this town wasn't used to.

Trent had folded his into quarters and shoved it in his back pocket, and every time he shifted his weight, he could feel the sharp edge of it pressing into him. A reminder of the past. And a kick in the ass about what he needed to fight for in the present in order to save the future.

He stood with Dove, Cullen, and Silas near the edge of the lot, far enough from the nearest cluster to talk without being overheard. Cullen had a doughnut from the refreshment table inside—he'd palmed it on the way out and was eating it with the calm focus of a man who'd learned to find food wherever he could and to savor every last bite.

"They were prepared," Silas said. "I'll give them that." He held the folded brochure between two fingers and turned it over without looking at it. "Every question someone asked, they had an answer ready. Charts. Studies. That gentleman in the gray suit—"

"The environmental consultant," Dove said.

"He had a real smooth way of saying nothing for fifteen minutes and making it sound like information." Silas tucked the brochure into his shirt pocket. "And Dutton." He shook his head. "That man could sell you a screen door for a submarine, and you'd thank him for it."

Cullen finished the doughnut. "The jobs argument landed with some people."

"In a town like this, that one always lands," Trent said. He looked out at the crowd. He knew almost everyone here—people he'd known since grade school, people who'd been at his mother's funeral three weeks ago, people who kept boats at Mitchell's Marina and ate breakfast at the diner on Saturdays. Some of them had pushed back hard. Some hadn't pushed back at all, and he understood why. A person couldn't pay their power bills with principle. "Half this town's been hurting for years. You dangle steady work in front of somebody who needs it—"

"It changes the math," Cullen said. "I know. I'm there. I'm hustling every day to make money so I can be a good dad for my kid. But I'm not sure I could take a job that requires me to sell out the Glades. Not after living out there for a while. And certainly not after growing up here."

"But you understand how something like this will change the town," Silas said. "And not in the way they're promising. I've seen this before." He looked out at the same faces Trent stared at, and his expression settled into the weight having watched this happen before. "They come in talking about partnership. About investment. About how nothing will really change, they'll just be part of the community, too. And then one morning you wake up, and the water's different, and the birds are gone, and the people you grew up with have moved on because there's no reason left to stay." He was quiet for a moment. "This isn't just land. It's a community. You mine the land, you mine everything built on top of it."

Nobody argued with that because Silas was right. It was the price of that kind of progress.

"I best be going," Silas said. "Before my wife agrees to drinks with someone I don't want to spend time with." He patted Cullen on the shoulder. "See you Sunday for dinner?"

"Absolutely." Cullen smiled. "I might be a little later than usual. Tyler's coming for a visit. Just a couple of hours, but his mom agreed to a boat ride and fishing. And it turns out, the social worker enjoys the water."

"You know, you can always have visits at our place. We love seeing that boy," Silas said.

"If there's time, we'll stop by." Cullen slapped his uncle on the shoulder.

Silas turned and strolled away, waving to half the town.

Trent looked across the parking lot and his gaze landed on the Hendersons. His stomach pitched and rolled. When the couple started walking toward him, bile lurched into his throat.

"Here comes trouble," Dove whispered.

"Let's go." Trent took her hand, but before they could take even two steps, the Hendersons caught up.

"Leaving so soon?" Beau stopped a few feet out, hands easy at his sides, the smile he wore the way other men wore cologne.

"Meeting's over," Trent said. "No reason to stick around any longer."

"I suppose." Beau nodded. "But I'd like to have a quick word with you. Just the two of us?"

"Anything you have to say to me, you can say in front of my girlfriend and Cullen."

Beau's smile didn't waver. His eyes moved across Dove and Cullen and came back to Trent. "This matter is better handled privately."

"If you've got something to say, say it. Otherwise, we need to get going." Trent really didn't want to stick around and listen to this asshole, and he figured if he refused to chat alone, Beau Henderson and his wife would go away and make their threats behind paper and pen.

"Have it your way." He rubbed his hands together

like an excited little boy. "We've heard there has been some..." he looked to the sky and rubbed his chin. "... Some activity on your property." He shifted his gaze back to Trent. "Something about a visit from the police. From Fish and Wildlife. That you were going to be charged with a crime and could lose your permits."

The words settled into Trent's chest like congestion that wouldn't come up.

Dawson and Keaton had promised to keep things quiet and hadn't filed a single piece of paperwork yet due to extenuating circumstances. Nobody outside that shed this morning should know a thing.

He breathed in. Breathed out. Let his mother's voice remind him, for the thousandth time, that the hothead version of him never won anything— except a cell in the Calusa Cove lockup for a night.

"You're misinformed," Trent said. "Nothing like that has happened." He kept his voice easy. Conversational. Like the man in front of him was telling him something mildly interesting about the weather. "I'd be careful about repeating rumors. They tend to come back and bite you in the ass." His mother might not like that comment, but it felt fucking good to say something.

Beau's smile tightened at the corners. Just slightly. "I only want you to consider your position."

"I'd be more worried about your own."

"I think it would be wise for a man in your predicament to consider my offer."

"Only thing I'm considering is whether or not I want

chocolate or vanilla ice cream tonight." Trent held his gaze. "My answer will always be no."

"Don't say I didn't warn you." He took his wife's hand, turned, and walked toward the main parking lot.

"That man has balls," Cullen said, almost admiringly. "He just strolled over here and basically threatened you in a parking lot full of people."

Dove lifted her cell. "Look at this."

Trent took her phone and stared at Buddy's text. *Dawson just leaked a little information to the Hendersons. Consider this your heads up.*

Trent shook his head. "That came over a minute too late."

"It's a good play, though," Cullen said as he pulled his phone from his back pocket. "I got a text from Buddy. Time to chat with Karl before he leaves." He looked up. "You good?"

"Go."

Cullen peeled off, and Trent and Dove stood alone in the gap he left. The lot moved around them. Two women near the steps talking too fast. A man on the phone with his back turned. The Sovereign Resources executives loading into an SUV. Dutton shaking hands near the corner of the building, working the crowd the way men like that always worked crowds—like they were depositing something into each person they touched with a plan to collect the interest later.

Trent watched him.

He'd spent twenty years wondering what the face

looked like. The face of the person who'd traded his father's life for...something—a career, money, protection, whatever it was that made one man decide that another man's life was an acceptable currency. He didn't know for certain that face belonged to Dutton. Not yet anyway. He forced himself to look away.

"Come on." He took Dove's hand and guided her toward his Jeep. "Let's get out of here."

"I just can't get it out of my head that my uncle was lying to me the second he set foot into Calusa Cove." Dove curled her fingers around the handle of the passenger side door and paused. "All these people who have a connection to your father. Dutton. His girlfriend Courtney Kirk, who happens to be Edward's daughter. Who was the CEO of the company your father was fighting against. And now they're all swinging back into town, and my uncle gets murdered, and your father's body gets exhumed because a dead man said he was hired to kill your dad, but didn't, along with an ME who was paid to change autopsies, but didn't change your dad's?"

"You still don't buy that." Trent rested his palm against the hood.

"Do you?"

"Not really, but no one will tell us anything, and not even Buddy or Sterling can get any information."

"Whatever's going on here goes back twenty years, and my uncle was knee deep in shit." She pulled open the door and climbed in.

Trent wasn't about to argue or defend her uncle

because, for the last twelve hours, all he could think about was how Slade had rolled into town, and strange things had started to happen. He didn't blame Slade. Didn't believe it was Slade's fault. But he did believe, without a shadow of a doubt, that Slade hadn't been honest about things both past and present.

Trent climbed up into the truck, pressed the ignition button, and eased out of the parking spot. Mentally, he groaned as he pulled past the local news van, with Stacey Mohawk standing there, all dolled up, mic in hand, reporting on god only knew what, because it was never the actual news.

He glanced toward Dove as he pulled out onto the main drag and noticed she had her Glock resting on her thigh.

He didn't say anything because it didn't surprise him. And considering the events of the day, he was happy she was ready for anything.

So was he. He checked the mirrors, and every set of headlights that appeared behind them was looked at hard until they turned off or fell back far enough not to matter. The blown-out rear window let the hot night air pour through—loud, relentless—and every time it gusted, he felt it like a reminder he didn't need.

A vehicle came up behind them on the two-lane. Too close and too fast.

His hands tightened on the wheel.

"Slow down, let's see what he does," Dove said, raising her weapon a little higher.

"You scare me sometimes." He eased off the gas. The car behind them slowed too, held for a long moment, then swung left down a side road and disappeared.

He breathed.

She rested the gun on her leg again, but her fingers remained on the trigger.

They drove in silence for a while. The kind that had weight to it. The kind that carried more than one problem. More than one issue.

"We never did really get to finish talking about our lack of birth control," he said.

"You want to chat about that, now?"

"Ignoring it won't make it go away."

"Never said that, but we have other things to deal with right now." Her foot rattled the floorboard, and her free hand went right for her face, as she shoved her index finger in her mouth and chewed on her nail.

He didn't blame her for being nervous. The idea put him a little on edge. But he worried it wasn't for the same reasons, and that was something he needed to address. Not wanting to see her reaction, he kept his eyes on the road, and said, "I'm not scared of it, and that surprises me." He exhaled slow through his nose, like he was checking himself for damage after a fall. Nothing broken. Nothing that felt like he should take it back. He stole a glance in her direction.

She pulled her finger from her mouth and tucked a piece of hair behind her ear. Her thumb moved in a slow arc against the grip of the Glock. But otherwise, her face remained basically expressionless. "I keep waiting to feel like I can't breathe. That overwhelming desire to run that I always get, but then I keep throwing myself at you," she said softly.

"I wouldn't go that far."

"I pushed us into being a thing, and that's not what I do." She glanced at him. "I come in like a wild woman, create a storm, and then walk away, leaving nothing but wreckage behind. I should be terrified of how I feel about you, because I've never felt this way before."

"Can't say I have either."

"You've at least had a real relationship. All I've had is a cold view from my sniper rifle and frozen dinners."

"Don't forget chicken and rice soup."

She poked his arm. "I'm being serious here."

"I know. I'm sorry." He reached across the cab and squeezed her thigh.

"I haven't lived anywhere that felt like home since I was a kid, and Calusa Cove has wormed into my bloodstream like a good drug." She shifted her gaze from the side mirror to him. "I've never wanted to be in a relationship where someone cares where I am and what I'm doing, but it matters with you. And I've never been irresponsible when it comes to birth control, and yet, I hadn't even given it a second thought."

She'd just handed him everything. Home. Her. The carelessness of someone who'd stopped calculating the cost. She no longer kept one foot out every door she'd ever walked through, had just admitted she wasn't looking for the exit anymore.

He had those three words right behind his teeth. He

opened his mouth to let them pour out, but headlights blinded him as he approached the gate to Mallor's Landing. "Who the fuck is that?"

"No idea. I don't recognize the truck." Dove leaned forward, resting her weapon on her thigh while she pulled out her cell. "Texting Buddy and Sterling the license plate and asking for backup."

Two men leaned against the hood, arms loose at their sides, faces turning toward the incoming lights. They wore jeans, dark button-down shirts, boots, and cowboy hats, which weren't unheard of in Florida but also weren't the norm.

Trent stopped the vehicle at a safe distance. "What do you want to do?"

"Buddy, Cullen, and Sterling are ten minutes away." She tucked her phone in her back pocket. "Let's go see what they have to say." She opened the center console and handed him his weapon. "But I'm not getting out of this truck without them seeing I'm not a friendly person."

"Sounds like a good plan to me." While Trent knew his way around a gun, he generally didn't point them at people. They were for protection from animals. And only if things went sideways.

They got out on opposite sides. Trent came around the front with his Glock up and his heart in his throat. Dove was on his left, weapon raised, looking a lot more confident than he felt.

Both men raised their hands.

"Mr. Mallor." The one on the right had the easy stillness of someone who'd been on the wrong end of a weapon before and knew how it went. "Ms. Quinn." He looked at Dove. "We're not a threat."

"You're trespassing," Trent said. "And how the hell do you know our names?"

"How about we start by giving ours?" one of the men said. "I'm Easton Ridge, and this is my brother, Lachlan."

"Everyone calls me Lach, and I'm a U.S. Marshal. I've worked—"

"I don't like marshals." Trent lifted his chin. He held his weapon steady, though he didn't much like pointing it at a human.

"Hopefully, you liked Slade, Dove's uncle," Lachlan said. "I'm so sorry for your loss, ma'am. Slade was a friend of ours and one of the reasons we're here."

Dove's weapon didn't waver. Neither did her stance. But she did inhale sharply.

"What are you doing at my gate?" Trent asked.

"We need to talk." Lach glanced between them. "About Garrett Dutton. About Sovereign Resources. About what's been happening here."

"I don't know you," Trent said. "And I sure as hell don't trust you."

"I trust you even less than he does." Dove raised her weapon. "You should know, I was a sniper in the Army. I could take you both out before my boyfriend here could get off a shot, and either of you had the chance to yell duck."

Lach chuckled. "I see you have the same sense of humor Slade had."

"I'm not going to say this again." Dove widened her stance. "It's time for you to leave."

"We're not gonna do that, ma'am," Easton said, holding up his hand before Trent could respond. "You're gonna want to hear what we have to say because we have what they're looking for."

Chapter Nineteen

Dove didn't trust men who were too comfortable in someone else's kitchen.

Lach had his boots crossed at the ankle, chair tilted back like he owned the floor under it, and a glass of Trent's good tequila, sweating rings onto the table. In front of him, he'd spread out a couple of folders. Nothing was written on the tabs. Nothing indicated what the pages inside held. And neither man guarded them with their hands or their posture.

Easton sat straight up in his chair, forearms on the wood, fingers curled around his glass, but he'd yet to take a sip.

Dove trusted that even less. She never accepted alcohol if she wasn't going to at least take a gulp or two. She honestly had no idea what to make of these two Wyoming ranchers. However, despite the cowboy aesthetic, they both still screamed military, government types. Granted, sometimes it was hard to beat that out of someone. She still carried herself a certain way, but the Aegis Network was the kind of organization that needed —desired—her specific skill set.

She stood in the hallway. Watching. Assessing. Analyzing. Like she would if she were three hundred yards away and looking through a scope. They weren't people. They were targets—things to be tracked until she needed to decide whether they were a threat.

She wasn't sure which way it would go.

Her phone buzzed.

Sterling: *Four brothers total. Easton runs Eagle Ridge Ranch. Other two are Holden—livestock commissioner—and Sutton, who runs a PI firm—all former military. Preliminary only, but these guys are legit. Photos, credentials, military background, what I could find, attached.*

She quickly scanned what was necessary for verification, then crossed to where Trent leaned against the counter, sipping his beverage. It was like the three men were standing on a dirt road in the middle of an old town at noon, waiting for someone to take the first shot. She held up the screen.

He read it. He didn't react one way or the other. Just took another sip of his drink.

She pocketed the phone, grabbed her glass off the counter, and dropped into the chair across from Easton. Trent stayed where he was, leaning against the sink with his tequila, watching the two men like he was plotting their demise.

She couldn't blame him. She wasn't so sure how she

felt about their appearance. About their connection to her uncle. About any of this. But right now, she had a job to do, and that's what she was gonna focus on. "Okay, gentleman. Shall we get down to business?"

"I want to start by thanking you both for hearing us out," Lach said.

Trent set his glass down. "There's been a lot that's happened, and I'd really appreciate it if you two would get to the point."

Lach looked at his brother before flipping open one of the folders.

Easton leaned forward. "For the last couple of years, Slade was secretly trying to build a case against Dutton."

"Why secretly?" Dove asked. "Does that mean he didn't have the support of the marshals office?"

"He didn't have anything concrete to go on," Lach said.

"What was he trying to do?" Trent asked.

"To connect Dutton as the leak in your father's protection detail twenty years ago." Easton stared at Trent. "He started this when he learned that Dutton was romantically linked to Courtney."

"When was that?" Dove asked.

"About five years ago." Lach flipped through some papers and pushed them toward Dove.

She took them between her fingers but didn't look at them.

"Every door Slade opened he found something. But the biggest one was Courtney and her father's money and how their names were buried six layers deep inside Sovereign Resources."

"We know all of that," Dove said.

Lach shuffled a few more papers around. "Sovereign Resources isn't just a mining company. They launder evidence. Physical evidence—documents, materials, things that need to disappear permanently. They do it for Courtney's clients, using the mining operation as cover. Bring things in as equipment or supplies. Process them in the shafts. Nothing comes out."

Trent didn't respond immediately. His thumb moved against the side of his glass. "Again, we've figured this out. We also know they want my land. What do you have that we don't?"

"When Parrish's dead man's cache surfaced, it filled in gaps Slade hadn't been able to close on his own." Lach pushed the thicker file across the table. "The feds have kept most of it quiet, but Dutton and Courtney are running scared because Parrish helped them launder evidence. Helped them hide bodies. He was on their payroll." He paused. "Which means, they know the net is closing."

"Panicked people do stupid things," Dove said.

"Dangerous things," Easton added.

Trent pushed off the counter and inched closer to the table. He tossed back a good gulp, before setting the glass down and lifting some of the papers off the table. "What are we missing that you're not telling me?"

"The dead man's cache is damaging to Courtney's clients, but not to her. And certainly not to Dutton."

Lach rubbed the back of his neck. "But Slade, right before he was murdered, connected the dots. He told us he was about to collect all the proof he needed to nail Dutton and Courtney."

"Are you sure?" Dove asked. "What is this proof, and where is it?" She reached for the file.

"It's not in any of this." Easton offered a weak smile. "We were in contact with Slade and told that he was going to meet with a source. He didn't give us details, just asked us to help with an asset. Unfortunately, we believe Slade was set up."

"So, we're back to square one," Dove said.

"No." Lach shook his head. "The asset that Slade asked us to look after was the source. One that can tie things back to Jack's case."

"How?" Trent asked. "And is that the proof?"

"Slade separated it, but it's better if you hear everything from the person who can connect it back to the past," Easton said.

Trent walked to the sink and braced both hands on the edge of it. Head down, staring at the drain. "I mean no disrespect but I'm struggling with all of this." His voice had gone quiet and that was somehow worse than the flat version. "You show up at my home when everything is upside down, and I'm just supposed to believe this?"

"I'd question it, too." Lach stood. "You need to understand that as soon as Slade heard Sovereign Resources was headed to this town, he was willing to put his job, his freedom on the line to make this right."

"What does that mean?" Fire rising in her belly, Dove flattened her hands on the table.

"Slade knew the past was about to repeat itself, and his source wasn't about to let that happen," Lach said. "They've been searching for answers to Jack's case for twenty years. It haunted Slade. Consumed him. All he wanted was to bring down the people who'd silenced Jack."

"When Sovereign Resources started filing for testing permits and asking for town hall meetings, that lit a bigger fire under Slade's ass." Easton pushed aside his glass. "But when Parrish's cache came to light, that added a ticking time bomb, and the clock is about to detonate."

"You're both still talking in circles, and it's pissing me off," Trent mumbled.

"Look, Slade isn't innocent in some things from twenty years ago, but what he did, he did to protect Jack and his family," Lach said.

"I'm about ready to toss you two out on your asses if you don't start making sense." Trent stared out the window.

"There's someone who wanted the chance to tell you part of this, themselves. Figured you had the right to hear it from them directly instead of reading it in a report or catching it on the morning news—and that's gonna happen whether we want it to or not." Easton stood and made his way across the room and stood next to Trent. "That person is outside. Near the dock. Waiting for you."

The refrigerator hummed. Somewhere out in the

moat, Dolly rolled through the water, her tail cutting a slow arc across the surface.

Dove watched Trent. The knuckles of his hands had gone white against the sink.

"This property is surrounded," she said to Lach. "Every entry point. My team has had eyes on you since you drove through the gate."

Easton turned and smiled. "We figured as much."

"Smart move. Slade would be proud." Lach picked up his glass. "Take Dove. Take half her team if you want. Point all the guns. Do what you have to do except shoot the man. All we ask is that you listen." He set the glass back down.

Trent didn't move for a long moment. Dove pushed back her chair, crossed the kitchen, and put her hand flat against his back. She felt the tension in him—coiled, barely-held in check—and didn't say a word. He straightened. Turned. His eyes met her gaze. "Grab your Glock."

She didn't need to be told that twice. Snagging her weapon, she followed Trent out the side door and over the bridge, nearly stumbling when a sudden realization crystalized in her mind. The prehistoric creatures thrashing about below were her friends. Her comrades. Her backup.

Chapter Twenty

The walkway groaned under his boots the way it always did—the low, familiar complaint from boards that had been expanding and contracting in the Florida heat for thirty years. Trent knew every pitch. Every soft spot. Every plank his father had laid by hand on a Saturday in October because the weather had finally broken enough to work outside without sweating through his shirt in the first ten minutes.

He'd walked this dock a thousand times. Tonight, it felt like the longest hundred yards of his life.

Dove moved beside him, her footsteps near-silent against his, her shoulder close enough that he could feel the warmth of her in the dark. Neither of them spoke. The night pressed in around the edges of the dock lights, thick and alive with the sound of the Glades settling into itself—frogs, crickets, and the distant splash of large fish moving through the bay.

Then came a thrash from the far edge of the moat. It was heavy, deliberate, the particular sound of a large animal rolling around in the water and mud like a small child stomping in puddles during a spring rain storm. And underneath it—a low, guttural noise that wasn't quite a bellow that he felt more in his chest than heard with his ears. It wasn't a gator giving a warning. It was more of a welcoming grunt.

Trent stopped dead in his tracks.

"What—" Dove started.

He raised his hand while his heart shot up to his throat. He stood still and let his eyes find the dark beyond what little glow was left from the porch lights. He didn't really need to adjust. He knew this property the way he knew his own heartbeat—every shadow, every shape, every place where the grass met the water and the moat curved out toward the far dock. He'd been reading this land since he was old enough to walk it alone.

But he stood there anyway, because part of him already knew what moved at the far edge of the moat, where the concrete lip gave way to a wide stretch of grass. Only, it was impossible.

The shadow was tall and broad through the shoulders. He stood at the water's edge with the easy stillness of a person who wasn't afraid of what lived in that water. Not many could come to Mallor's Landing and do that.

But what really shocked Trent was Dolly.

The twelve-foot alligator, roughly nine-hundred pounds of prehistoric territorial animal, was rolling around like she was a puppy that had been given a new chew toy.

This wasn't the slow drift she did when she was patrolling. Nor was it the aggressive display she put on for strangers who got too close. She rolled, her massive body turning in the shallows, tail sweeping in a wide arc through the water, the way she did when Trent came back from a trip and she heard his boots on the dock before she saw him. The way she'd done every single time his mother had walked this property in the last twenty years, right up until the month she got too sick to come outside.

The way she'd done, a long time ago, for someone else.

His throat closed. He rubbed his eyes.

Dolly didn't do that for people. She did it for family.

"Trent." Dove's voice was low and close to his ear. "You okay?"

He couldn't answer that.

He squeezed his eyes closed and counted to three before blinking them open again. The figure was still there. Still standing at the edge of the water, completely unbothered by the twelve-foot alligator performing what Trent could only describe as a greeting at his feet. The stranger had one hand hung loose at his side. The other rested, easy and familiar, on the top of Dolly's exposed flank as she rolled.

"Trent." Dove's hand found his arm. Then she went rigid at his side. "What the hell?" She drew her weapon, smooth and clean. "Show your face and keep your hands where I can see them."

The figure raised both hands slowly. Turned. And walked toward them.

He moved into the reach of the distant lights—unhurried, and seemingly unworried that he was on the wrong side of the moat. The light caught his face, and Trent's heart froze in his chest. His pulse soared. And his mind spun with a million questions.

All Trent could do was stand there with his mouth open and stare.

Stare at this man with the same wide nose. Same high cheek-bones. Same high forehead. Same shaggy hair that was always a little too long and a five-o'clock shadow.

He'd been looking at a version of it in the mirror his entire life.

The man stopped ten feet away, hands still in the air. "Hello, son."

The air in Trent's lungs became trapped. He couldn't release it, nor could he suck in more.

Son.

It was just a word. But staring at this man that he so strongly resembled, the word meant everything Trent had lost. That Trent had buried.

The ground beneath him didn't move. It held him steady while his insides began to tremble. An owl hooted. A frog croaked. The world around him indifferent and enormous. Everything was exactly where it was supposed to be, except for the man standing fifteen feet away. The one Trent and his mother had laid to rest twenty years ago.

Visions of that day raced across Trent's mind. It had been cloudy. Slightly chilly. Enough so that his mom had needed a sweater. She'd stood over that grave and cried for what seemed like hours.

Everything that Trent knew and understood tilted sideways all at once. Every possible emotion a man could have filtered through his heart. They competed for his attention, but he couldn't hold onto a single one.

Joy shot through him like electricity at the sight of his father. Flesh and blood and fucking breathing.

But then came rage, and behind that, the grief that had nowhere to go because the thing he'd been grieving was standing in front of him with a pulse, and underneath all of it, a confusion so deep it made him dizzy.

He breathed through it. Planted his boots on the walkway and breathed through it because if he didn't, he was going to do something he couldn't take back—and he didn't know yet if that something was throwing his arms around the man or putting his fist through his face.

Both were logical options.

"Lower your weapon," he said to Dove.

She didn't move. "I'm not gonna do that."

"Yes, you are."

"I'm not lowering anything until someone tells me what the hell is going on." She kept the Glock up, her stance wide, her eyes fixated on the man. "Because what I'm looking at doesn't make any sense."

He couldn't argue with that. His mind fought what his eyes saw.

He turned back to the figure—to his father. To the jaw he'd inherited and the eyes he hadn't and the shoulders that were broader than he remembered, his hair had grayed at the temples, and he had a few more wrinkles, but nothing else had changed, nothing, which was impossible. Twenty years was impossible. All of this was impossible.

"Prove to me that you're Jack Mallor," Trent said. His voice came out rougher than he intended. "Because my father has been dead for twenty years." The words crawled through his mouth like he was chewing glass. "And the man I knew—" he paused, wiggled his fingers to keep from fisting them and took in the deepest calming breath he could manage. "Wouldn't leave his wife and kid."

Jack—his father—looked at Trent with an expression that held twenty years of something Trent couldn't name and wasn't about to try.

"Coming back from the dead isn't as simple as people make it sound." His voice. That voice. Low and unhurried, with the particular timbre that had narrated Trent's entire childhood. "But if Dolly dancing for me isn't enough—" The corner of his mouth curved into a familiar half smile. "Then we can talk about the time you were six. Confident little boy. Always following me around and wanting to do whatever I did. I loved that. But your mother, she worried I gave you too much free rein." Jack shook his head and laughed. "One day, while my back was turned, you decided you were big enough to drive the Jeep."

Trent went absolutely still. He remembered that day as if it were yesterday.

"Your mother was inside. I was in the equipment shed. We'd been loading some tools to go fix the gate. You got it in your head, because your mother thought I needed to walk more, that you could drive it to the gate, and I could walk. I came out to the sound of the engine and watched you back that Jeep straight into that cypress tree up by the drive over there." Jack laughed. "Took out the whole left taillight. You tried so hard not to cry." Jack pointed to his mouth. "But your lower lip quivered, and you lost it when your mom came running out of the house."

"Mom yelled at you for leaving the keys in the Jeep. Yelled at me for doing something I knew I shouldn't. Then she scooped me up and hugged me so hard I thought my guts were gonna come out like a frog being squeezed."

"Exactly what you said to me when I tucked you in that night."

"And you told me next time to use the rearview mirror, and you gave me my first driving lesson right after the Jeep was fixed." Trent laughed. He hadn't meant to. It came out rough and short, but it came out, and across the fifteen feet between them, his father laughed, too—the same broken, helpless sound, as if neither of them had planned this, and neither of them could stop it.

Dove stared at both of them like they'd lost their minds entirely.

Trent reached over and put his hand over hers. Gently. The way you moved a weapon you weren't taking, just redirecting. She let him guide it down, slowly, her eyes still fixed on Jack—his father.

His fucking father.

"Give us some time alone," he said quietly.

"Absolutely not."

"Please. Just go inside."

"He could be an imposter." She kept her voice low, meant only for him. "Someone who did their homework knows the stories. Think about what's been happening. After everything today, I am not letting you walk toward a stranger in the dark."

He turned to face her.

In the moonlight, she looked exactly like—a woman running on no sleep and too much adrenaline and a grief she hadn't let herself feel yet, holding a weapon steady because that was the only thing she knew how to do when the world stopped making sense.

But Trent saw something entirely different. He saw the woman he wanted as a partner. The woman who had torn down every defense he'd ever constructed and shown him what it was like to really love someone.

And God, he loved her. He loved everything about her.

He cupped her face. Stared into her wide, blue eyes. "I'll talk to him on the porch," he said. "You can stand guard from inside. Your team will have eyes on us from the outside. It will be fine." He pressed his mouth to hers. Soft. Tender. Loving. It was a promise more than a kiss. "I want to speak with him alone. I need to do that."

She looked at him for a long moment. Then past him, at the man waiting at the end of the dock. "If you try anything," she said, raising her weapon, "I will kill you. I don't care who you are or who you used to be."

His father smiled. "I've been dead for twenty years. I'm used to it."

Dove lowered her weapon. "Be careful."

"I will," Trent said. "Let's go up to the porch."

"I've missed this place." His dad followed him along the walkway and over the bridge. A few gators made themselves known, while Dolly followed them, thrashing happily about.

"I could use a drink." Trent opened the porch door, letting Dove in first, then his father. "Would you like one?"

"Tequila, if you got it." His dad ran his fingers across his mom's favorite rocking chair, pausing for a moment.

"I'll get the bottle and a couple of glasses." Dove dragged a hand down his arm.

Inside, he could see the shapes of Lach and Easton through the kitchen window, Dove moving past them, snagging the liquor and rushing back through the door, setting everything down on the small table. "Buddy and Sterling aren't too far away. Cullen's out in the bay."

"Thanks." Trent kissed her cheek. He sat in the larger of the two chairs and poured the tequila.

"Your mother loved this chair." His father eased into

the rocker that he'd built with his own hands and sighed. "Your girlfriend, Dove, her uncle spoke so fondly of her. I talked with him the day he died, and he got a good chuckle out of the fact that the two of you found each other." His dad stretched out his legs, crossing his ankles, just like Trent remembered he used to do. "I told him it didn't surprise me by the way she looked at you at your mother's funeral."

Trent picked up his glass and stared at the liquid while he pondered that thought. "You were the man we chased."

"I was."

"Jesus," Trent mumbled. "You've been here all this time, and you couldn't tell me?"

"I didn't stay. I couldn't."

"Right." Trent lifted his drink, tossed back his head, and let the liquid burn. "Before we get into whatever the hell is going on." He turned and looked his father straight in the eye. "I need to know if you visited Mom before she died."

His father's hands wrapped around the glass. He looked down at it.

The silence stretched long enough that Trent heard Dolly slip back into the water at the far end of the moat. Heard the frogs start back up after going quiet when the voices had carried across the property.

"Yes," his father said.

One word. All the weight of twenty years inside it.

"Sneaking in to see her—the funeral..." His dad paused, let out a long breath and shook his head. "Probably the dumbest thing I've ever done. Given everything. Given how careful I had to be for so long." He lifted his eyes from the glass and Trent saw it there—the damage. The loss. The grief. Still fresh, somehow, despite the time. "But she was dying. And she was the love of my life. My everything. Maybe you can't understand. Maybe you can. But I never stopped loving her. Loving you. And I couldn't... couldn't let her go without saying goodbye."

Trent looked out at the moat. At the moon sitting flat on the surface of the dark water and the cypress trees black against the sky. He thought about the last days of his mother's life. The way she'd drifted in and out, present and then suddenly not, her eyes going somewhere he couldn't follow. The way the hospice nurse had said it was normal, the brain protecting itself, and he'd sat next to her bed and held her hand and talked about nothing because what else could he do.

And then one morning, she'd been calm. Not the medicated calm or the distant calm of someone slipping away. Something else. Something settled, like a question that had been asking itself for twenty years had finally gotten its answer.

He'd thought it was just the dying. The way bodies sometimes made peace with what was coming.

He turned back to his father. "It calmed her." His voice came out rough, and he didn't bother to try to smooth it. "I don't know if she knew it was real or if she thought she was dreaming, but it made the end easier for her."

His father bowed his head. His shoulders dropped in

a way that looked like twenty years of weight shifting, not lifting—just moving to a different place on the same body that had been carrying it all this time. His dad wiped one cheek. Then the other.

Neither of them said anything for a moment.

The Everglades breathed around them, patient and dark and completely indifferent to the fact that a dead man was sitting on a porch drinking tequila with the son he'd left behind.

Chapter Twenty-One

Twelve steps from the refrigerator to the hallway door. Six steps from the table to the sink. Five steps from the sink to the edge of the family room.

Dove had counted them enough times to know. But the worst part wasn't the waiting. Or not knowing whether they were in danger. It was the fact that she couldn't sit still, and that made her want to snag her Glock and shoot something. She needed to expend some unwanted energy.

"You're making me dizzy," Lach said.

"Do you think I care?" She turned at the hallway and came back. Paused, then made her way to the sink.

Through the kitchen window, the porch light threw a pale circle over father and son with a bottle of tequila between them. Trent's shoulders remained unnaturally still. The back of his father's head reminded her of a maniquin. Both men barely moved—as if their conversation required them to remain motionless.

"What the hell are they talking about out there?" she asked.

"Probably—"

"It was a rhetorical question," she said to Easton as she pulled out her phone and opened the text string with Buddy, Sterling, and Cullen, read the last three messages.

All clear.

Nothing moving.

Property quiet.

None of that necessarily meant anything good. Quiet was just the the pause before impact. Nothing was moving, just the snake coiled in the grass waiting to strike. And all clear just meant whoever was out there lurking in the shadows hadn't been seen yet. She knew this drill all too well. Nothing was ever what it seemed.

She shoved the phone back in her pocket and headed toward the family room.

"Could you please just sit down for five minutes?" Easton asked.

She stopped, spun on her heels, and looked across the kitchen at him with what she suspected wasn't her most charitable expression. "You want to tell me what's actually happening out there? Because from where I'm standing, all I see are two strangers and one of them is a dead man." She spread her hands. "You'll have to forgive me if I'm not immediately comforted."

Lach and Easton exchanged a look.

"Jack wanted to tell his son," Lach said. "So, we're doing this on his terms."

"He's had twenty years to tell it. I'd say he's a little too late. Not to mention, my uncle died protecting him, so I'd say I'm owed the courtesy."

"I know this is hard for you, but let them have their moment," Easton said. "And then we'll fill you in on everything."

"Right, because I'm supposed to trust you." She turned back to the window. The two figures on the porch hadn't moved. Trent's hand lifted, set his glass down, lifted again. The other man said something she couldn't hear, and Trent went still in that particular way he had when something landed somewhere deep.

Trent needed her. Or maybe she needed him. She had no idea, and it no longer mattered. She started for the door, but before she made it to the threshold, it opened.

Trent filled the frame, the porch light at his back, his expression serious, but there was a softness to it. "Come outside." His words were soft, gentle, even. But they did nothing to settle the tornado swirling in her gut.

She grabbed her glass off the counter and walked past Trent through the door without a word. Her pulse raced. Her breath was ragged. And her mind filled with a million questions that she had no answers to.

The night air assailed her skin in that heavy, wet way it did on the edge of the Everglades. She crossed to the table, picked up the bottle of tequila, and poured two fingers into her glass with the focus of someone who needed something to do with their hands. Then she dropped into the nearest chair.

Trent pulled his chair across the porch and sat down next to her. She appreciated the gesture.

Jack watched her, and she looked right back at him because she'd stared down worse things than a dead man drinking tequila on a porch surrounded by gators that she now considered her friends.

"I feel like I've known you your entire life," Jack said, rocking back and forth as if he belonged on this porch more than she did. Perhaps that was true—at one time. "When Slade and I first thought this was only gonna last a few years, he'd come visit, and he'd bring pictures of you. It was hard because I missed Trent so much it hurt, but boy, did Slade think the world of you.

Her eyes burned, but she wouldn't let the emotion that bubbled from her gut escape. She needed to remain detached. To be the person the Army had trained her to be for just a little while longer. "I have a million things I need answered," she started. "But why don't we start with why you had to stay dead for twenty years. And tell me why my uncle died protecting that secret."

Jack set his glass down and looked at the space between the table and the railing. "None of this was supposed to happen." His voice was low and weighted. "It was supposed to be temporary."

Dove shifted in her chair. "Mr. Mallor—"

"It's Jack."

"Okay. Jack." She pressed her palms flat on her

thighs. "With respect, I have heard a version of that sentence from men in positions of power my entire career and it has never once made me feel better about what came after it. So I'm going to need you to skip to the part where you actually tell us what happened."

Trent reached over and took her hand. "I've been listening to people give us the runaround for a few days now. I'm with her on this."

Jack looked at his son for a moment, then sat forward and rested his arms on his knees. "When the case against Edward Kirk and Armond Jackson fell apart and Slade found out about the hit on my life, he had less than a day to figure out what to do." Jack laced his fingers together. "He made a decision. He believed—and I believed—that he could fake my death, keep me out of sight, and use the time to find what the prosecution couldn't. The evidence that would actually stick." He leaned back, snagged his drink, and took a sip. "He knew the ME. Knew what the man would do for the right price. So we used him."

"Do I even want to know how he knew that?" Dove had always admired her uncle. He was smart, and she knew he'd sometimes skirted the rules, but that was a bit of a workaround.

"He didn't give me the details, and honestly, I didn't ask," Jack said. "Gulf Coast collapsed. Kirk walked away. And everything Slade tried to find turned out to be dead ends." He raised his glass before tipping back his head and tossing back the last few drops. "You can't bring a dead man back to life with nothing to show for it. And trust me, we argued about this for days, weeks, years. I wanted to come home. I wanted to see my boy graduate from high school. See him grow into a man. Be with the only woman I've ever loved. But as time went on, that became harder and harder for a lot of reasons."

"I have questions about all that." Trent traced a slow line across Dove's knuckles, back and forth, like he was keeping time. "But right now, I want to hear about Dutton."

"He was a young kid when I went to testify, and I barely spent any time with him. Wasn't even on our radar when we faked my death," Jack said. "But about five years ago. When we learned about his relationship with Courtney," Jack set the glass down. "That's when things started to shift. Courtney had built a practice in Tallahassee defending criminals, and those assholes needed evidence to disappear. She found a way to do that through Sovereign Resources." He stood, moved toward the railing, and glanced out at the water. "Legitimate mining operation on paper. But if you needed something gone—documents, physical evidence, bodies—Sovereign had the infrastructure. The equipment. The reach. A concierge service for anyone with enough money."

"We know all of that," Trent said. "Why can't anyone take them down?"

Jack leaned against the railing and folded his arms. "It took years to gather what we did, and most of it wasn't enough to build a case. It wouldn't have needed a fire, a dead witness, or another to recant their testimony for it to fall apart."

"So what changed?" Trent asked. "What made you come forward now?"

"Slade was close," Jack said. "Closer than he'd ever been. He had pieces that were finally, after twenty years, pointing to the same place. And then they started moving into this town. On this land." His hands tightened on the railing. "That's when I knew we were out of time."

"I still don't understand why now. Why not eight years ago? Or twelve?" Trent's voice had changed. Still controlled, but underneath the strength he always carried, no matter what was going on, a little boy lingered, and Dove wasn't sure the man could hold on. "Twenty years, Dad. Mom spent twenty years—"

"You think I don't know that?" Jack pounded his chest. "You think that it didn't chip away at me, too?"

"I'm just trying to understand," Trent said softly.

Jack sighed, as if he resigned himself to something. "Shortly before I agreed to let Slade fake my death, they threatened my family." Jack turned from the railing. He looked at Trent straight, the way Dove had noticed he did when the thing he was saying cost him. "I had to protect you and your mother and WITSEC wasn't an option. Not when the case was already falling apart." Jack spoke so fast, and his voice cracked on each word. "And then it became about protecting Slade's career. The only person we had on the inside who could still move, still access information, still build a case." He looked at his hands. "And then years went by. And they kept going by. There was nothing I could do but stay dead. If I came out of the shadows, there would have been consequences. Legal ones. I couldn't do that to you. Or your mother."

The porch was quiet except for the frogs, the water, and the low hum of the night.

"At some point," Jack said quietly, "a temporary decision becomes the only life you have left."

Dove had been watching Trent's face. Somewhere behind his clenched jaw, rage, frustration, grief, gave way to something deeper. Something truer. Something that two men who obviously loved each other still could build on.

Her heart dropped to her gut. She'd never have that with her uncle again. He was dead. Gone forever. A sudden need to call her parents filled her soul.

Jack rubbed his face with his palms. "Last year, things started to heat up. We had more and more information, but still no proof. And then Dove here left the Army, and both Slade and I worried about Trent and Linda."

"Excuse me?" Dove stared at Jack.

"Slade knew you were hurting and thought the Aegis Network would be a good fit for you and even better if you were down here and—"

"I was recruited," she interrupted Jack. "I was told I was hand-picked. That Buddy had specifically identified me as someone who—"

"Buddy did pick you," Jack said. "That part is true. Your record spoke for itself. Your skills. The work you'd done." He held her gaze. "But Slade may have put the idea in Buddy's ear first. And in the owners'."

The words landed like someone dropped a twenty-pound sledge on her head.

She looked at the tequila in her glass. Looked at the dark water beyond the railing and caught a glimpse of Dolly rolling through the moat. She paused, and Dove couldn't have sworn the damn gator smiled at her, as if to say, *I'm here for you, sister.* Right. Dove was losing her fucking mind.

She picked up the glass and drank.

"I'm still confused," Trent said. "I feel like all we've done is talk in circles."

"Slade had the documents connecting Courtney and her father to Sovereign's ownership. He had testimony from clients who'd used their evidence disposal service. Enough to open an investigation." Jack looked at Trent. "Not enough to bury them. And burial is what they deserve."

"Again, circles," Trent said.

"The last piece of this puzzle came when we learned Sovereign Resources was making a move on this property." Jack turned back toward the table. "Through the Hendersons." He sat back down. "Slade paid them a visit. Turned out Courtney had done the Henderson family a significant favor. Their son had been brought up on vehicular manslaughter charges that should have gone to trial. But Courtney buried it. Case closed." He spread his hands. "The Hendersons owed her. And this—pressuring you to sell, using what Karl gave them to threaten you—this was how they paid the debt."

Trent slowly rose . He crossed to the railing where

his father had stood, put his hands on it, and stared out at the moat, saying nothing for a long moment. Then he turned.

"You're telling me that for the last several weeks, while I've been losing sleep, thinking these people are trying to take my land—while I've been standing in my equipment shed, getting threatened— While Dove's house was getting torn apart—" He stared at his father. "The Hendersons have been working for your side this whole time?"

Jack nodded. "Not the entire time, but even after they flipped, they had to—"

"Don't." Trent held up one hand. "Don't tell me it was the only way. I've been hearing that for twenty years about everything." He wasn't shouting. That was the thing about Trent's anger—the quieter it got, the deeper it ran. "So everything... the threat? The photograph? Coming up to me at the town meeting with a smile and a warning—"

"They had to make it look good, so they had to do what was expected. They knew you'd never cave," Jack said.

Trent laughed. It didn't sound anything like the way he'd laughed at the Jeep story. Not even close.

"That was a dangerous game. Mom actually asked me if I wanted to sell. If I was happy here. She said she'd understand if I wanted to leave. To experience something else." He walked to the far end of the porch and stood there with his back to both of them, hands locked behind his head, staring at the night sky.

Dove couldn't stand it. She inched her way closer, looping an arm around his waist.

Trent wrapped his arm around her and kissed her temple. "Mom thought that since I kept insisting Dove and I were just friends, there was nothing holding me here. That I might walk away from the legacy when she passed.."

Jack chuckled.

"I don't see what's so funny." Trent glared.

"Your mother was always the smartest woman in any room," Jack said. "She'd known you'd turn down the offer just like she'd known you're in love with this lovely young woman." He smiled. "She told me all about how you fought your feelings for Dove, but she had faith, that in the end, you'd come to your senses. Looks like she was right."

"Mom was always annoyingly right," Trent said softly. He dropped his chin to the top of Dove's head. "I miss her."

"So do I," Jack said, turning toward the Everglades. "But we need to think about other things because once the exhumation results come back, and the news breaks that I'm not in that coffin—everything accelerates. Dutton. Courtney. All of them. They've been patient because they didn't have any reason not to be. And honestly, my remains not being in that coffin might not scare them."

Trent turned around and glanced at Dove. His expression had settled into determination. She knew that look, and Trent could be dangerous when he allowed himself to settle. "But it *will* make them nervous, and that will make them push harder," he said.

"That's what I'm guessing, too. And while I missed the last twenty years with the only woman I'll ever love, I'm not going to lose another second with my son." Jack stepped closer, resting his hand on Trent's shoulder. "Or the girl who stole his heart and already feels like family."

Dove's cheeks flushed. She could only hope that Trent's heart belonged to her, because she was so far gone she'd be lost without him.

Chapter Twenty-Two

The morning came in slow and easy, the kind of rising that made Trent forget, just for a minute, that the world outside Mallor's Landing had any problems. He had always loved how the sun lazily burned off the haze. Where the gators floated in from the bay and circled the moat, checking out the surroundings.

Trent sat at the kitchen table with a cup of coffee in his hand, his father across from him, and a plate of half gooey, half burnt muffins that Dove had made. It was strange that something he'd imagined ten thousand times over the last two decades could feel, in the actual living of it, more ordinary than he'd expected. Not less meaningful. Just ordinary. Like the man had simply returned after having been away for a while, and here they were—coffee cups between them and the Glades doing its morning thing outside the window.

"You want to know what I thought about every single day for twenty years?" Jack wrapped both hands around his mug. "Your mother's biscuits." He glanced at Dove. "No offense."

"None taken."

"She made biscuits that would make a grown man weep." Jack shook his head slowly. "I had a dream about them once. Woke up angry."

Dove laughed. "My mom's not the greatest cook. She tried, and we tried to be supportive, but a few times she got it so wrong, my dad would have to order pizza. I'm not much better than her, unfortunately."

"My mom loved your soup." Trent reached out, took her hand, and smiled.

"My dad taught me how to make that. It's not hard when you toss everything in one of those InstaPots."

"You know what he used to do?" Jack pointed at Trent with one finger. "He used to sneak down before sunrise, snag half the fresh biscuits, and bring them upstairs and eat them. Then he'd come skipping downstairs, and his mother would wave a spoon at him and ask him where they went, and do you know what this little firecracker had to say?"

"I can only imagine." Dove leaned forward, resting her elbows on the table.

"He would try to tell his mother that one of the gators or other wild animals must have snuck in and got to them."

"I was six, and I was hungry," Trent said.

"You were a biscuit bandit, is what you were." Jack leaned back. "But your mother thought it was so cute that she would always get up, make an extra batch just for

Trent." Jack ran his fingers across the table. "When he'd come down for his actual breakfast, she'd make a big deal about how Old Pete must have snuck in again."

"Old Pete?" Dove asked.

"A fifteen-foot gator that circled the moat for years," Trent said. "He died about ten years ago." He glanced at his dad. "I had to put him down. A fungal infection."

"That's too bad." His father shifted his gaze toward the window. "I see there are a lot of gators that have come and gone. "You've kept Mallor's Landing in good shape."

"It hasn't always been easy. I've hit bumps in the road, and I haven't always done the right thing." Trent didn't like admitting that to his father. However, his mother had told him that his father had always valued honesty above all else.

"Neither did I, and if your mom didn't tell you that, well, I'd be surprised."

"She told me about a few blunders in your youth."

"Linda always had a way of making dumb mistakes seem like nothing." His dad lifted his mug in salute before taking a sip.

"Agreed."

Dove's phone buzzed on the table. She looked at the screen, then looked at Trent. "That's Buddy. I need to go." She pushed back from the table and stood. "We're meeting Easton at Harvey's Cabins to go over everything Slade had. Figure out what's strong enough for the feds to use." She tucked the phone in her pocket. "Dawson and Lach are going to try to get the ME to hold off on releasing his statement about the remains. Buy us a little more time before this goes public."

"How long do you think they can hold it?" Jack asked.

"A day. Maybe two." She grabbed her jacket off the back of the chair. "But even if they can't, the worst that happens is it makes Dutton nervous. But he won't show it. He can't afford to look guilty. Besides, I doubt it would change what Courtney and Sovereign Resources are doing. It might make them a little less vocal, but pulling out would be stupid on their part. At least, right away."

"Be careful out there," Jack said.

"Always.'

"I'll walk you out." Trent followed her to the porch door.

The morning was already warm, the sun up and committed now, the kind of light that hit the water in the moat and turned it gold. Somewhere along the far bank, Dolly was making her slow morning patrol. "Dolly's gonna do her thing when you cross the bridge," Trent said.

Dove looked at the moat and then at Trent. "Define her thing."

"Roll around a little. Maybe bellow."

"Why?"

"Because she likes you. I told you. It's how she says hello and goodbye."

"She's a gator."

"She's Dolly. And contrary to popular belief, alligators do remember. They're smart. And they have feelings."

"Right." Dove pointed at him. "If I get eaten on the way to my truck, I'm haunting you for the rest of your life."

"You'd be the best thing that ever haunted this property." He took her hand and pulled her in. She came without resistance, which still surprised him every time. He cupped her face the way he had on the porch the morning before, her jaw fitting against his palm like it had always belonged there.

"I love you," he said.

She looked up at him. "You what?"

"I think you heard me."

"I suppose I did." She stuck her finger in her ear. "But you kind of just blurted it out like you say good morning."

"I should've said I love you when we woke up, but someone distracted me." He arched a brow. "Are you gonna leave me hanging? Or do you have a response?"

"I love you, too." She reached up ran her fingers through his hair. "Don't let your father go hungry. Don't be too hard on him. And don't do anything stupid while I'm gone."

"You sound like my mother."

"She was a smart woman, and she raised a really good son." She stepped off the porch.

He watched her cross the bridge. Dolly surfaced as she passed, rolled once, unhurried and enormous, and bellowed low at the morning sky. Dove kept walking without breaking stride, but shoulders went up around her ears, and he laughed.

He stood there until her truck disappeared down the drive and the dust settled back onto the road.

"She's a good woman," his father said.

Trent jumped. "Jesus, you scared me." He turned and went through the door his father held open. "Dove's the best."

"Slade couldn't ever shut up about her. I used to get jealous because he'd come to see me, and all I'd hear was Dove this, and Dove that, and I had no idea what you were doing. Every once in a while, Slade would get me a report, but it wasn't the same."

"I spent twenty years watching my friends with their dads and being angry at everyone that mine had been taken away."

"I'm sorry that—"

Trent held up his hand. "Yesterday, when I saw you, I was flooded with every emotion possible. Part of me wanted to throttle you for leaving me without a dad and honestly, I still do. But I didn't consider what the last twenty years might have been like for you." He strolled across the kitchen and held up the coffee pot.

His father nodded.

Trent refilled both mugs and sat back down across from his dad, and for a few minutes neither of them said anything. Just two men at a kitchen table with the Florida wilderness outside the window. There was more to say— there were years of it, piled up like a traffic jam—but none of it was urgent right now, and they both seemed to understand that.

"Dove's good for you," Jack said.

"I know."

"In some ways, she reminds me of your mother."

"That's what Fallon says."

"It's true." His father wrapped his hands around the mug. "Your mother never once backed down from a hard thing. She just faced it and figured out what to do next." He glanced toward the driveway. "That girl's the same way."

Trent opened his mouth to say something, but the sound of gravel crunching under rubber caught his attention.

"Are you expecting someone?" his dad asked.

"Nope." Trent went to the window.

A black SUV, one he didn't recognize, pulled down his driveway like it had every right to be there.

He had his phone out before the vehicle stopped. He texted Dove and Buddy.

Trent: *Vehicle coming down the drive. Don't recognize it.*

Dove: *Turning around. On my way.*

Buddy: *Heading to you now. I'll see where Cullen is. Keep Jack out of sight.*

Jack stood. "Why don't you meet them outside?" He pointed to Trent's weapon. "Maybe you should take that with you."

"Don't come out. There's a rifle in the closet."

"Not my first rodeo, kid."

Trent grabbed his phone off the table, holstered his weapon, walked out the side door, and made it halfway to the bridge before the SUV's engine had been shut off.

Seconds later, Garrett Dutton stepped out of the driver's side with an easy smile, like he was dropping by for a visit. Courtney Kirk came around the passenger side with a leather portfolio tucked under her arm, wearing heels that had absolutely no business on a gravel driveway, and yet she moved like the ground owed her something.

"Mr. Mallor." Dutton looked out at the property. "Wow. This place is breathtaking."

"Thank you," Trent said. "What can I do for you?"

"Mind if we come in?" He didn't wait for an answer. Just moved toward the wooden path.

Dolly didn't much like that. She made herself known by opening her mouth. A few other gators flanked her, doing the same thing.

Courtney stumbled. "Oh my," she whispered. "Can those things get to the house?"

"No ma'am. They can't. But if they swim out to the bay, they can get up on the driveway."

She gasped, clutching her portfolio and grabbing Dutton's arm.

"I think he's messing with you," Dutton said.

"No, sir. I'm not. This land is a natural habitat, and we sit on mostly freshwater. Gators are naturally drawn to this area, and I can't do much to change that. All I can do is protect my home. That's why we have the moat." Not entirely a lie, but not completely the truth, either. But they didn't need to know that.

"We'd like to discuss a business opportunity with you," Dutton said. "Maybe we can come in?"

"Sure." Trent turned, strolled up to the porch, and held the door.

They settled at the kitchen table, and Dutton looked around the room with appreciation. It almost felt like he was taking inventory of everything he saw.

Courtney set the portfolio on the table and opened it.

Dutton slid a single sheet of paper across the wood toward Trent. "I'll be direct," he said. "I want this property. And I believe in paying fair value for things." He tapped the paper. "That offer is more than fair. I think you'll find it's actually generous."

"Someone else already made an offer, and I refused."

"Yes, the Hendersons," Dutton said. "We're aware." He tapped his finger on the paper. "I urge you to look at this offer. It's more than you'll ever get for this place. Ever."

Trent looked at the number, but he didn't dare touch the paper. "My home isn't for sale."

"Everything's for sale at the right price," Dutton said, pleasantly. Like it was a simple fact of the world.

"Mallor's Landing has been in my family for three generations. And it's going to stay that way. No amount of money is going to change that."

Courtney folded her hands on the table, her long nails perfectly manicured. The only reason he knew anything about that was because for half a minute, he'd dated a chick who'd been obsessed with her nails.

"I understand how this being family land could make this emotional. I respect that," she said in a voice that sounded sweet and kind but had an edge that he didn't trust.

Or maybe it was the nails that could take his eyes out faster than Dolly could roll him under the water.

"But I also understand you're currently facing some very serious allegations. Illegal poaching. Evidence of criminal activity found on your property." She paused just long enough to take a breath and tuck a piece of hair behind her ear. "Charges like that could put you away for a few years. Cost you the permits it takes to run this place. Cost you everything you've built here." She pulled out another piece of paper. "I'm in a position to make those go away. All you have to do is sign both these agreements, and I, as your lawyer, will make sure you don't even have to set foot in a courtroom, much less have a stain on your record or reputation."

"First, I don't know what you're talking about," Trent said. "And second, my record is already questionable, so I'm not worried."

Dutton smiled. "This goes beyond fishing in unmarked waters or getting in a bar fight." He leaned back in the chair and looped his arm over the back of Courtney's. "These things have a way of moving forward whether we want them to or not. It's only a matter of time before formal charges are brought. And these aren't ones you want to snub your nose at. These are federal. These are the kinds of charges that—"

"Hey, Dutton."

Shit. Trent should've known his father wouldn't stay hidden or quiet. Trent certainly wouldn't have if someone had been trying to railroad his son. He swallowed. Odd thing to think right about now, but it was true. If Trent ever did have a kid, he wouldn't let anyone speak to him, or her, that way. Not without a fight. Didn't matter if they were grown or not.

His father strolled into the kitchen with the swagger that Trent had always remembered. Had always admired. Had always wished he had. His dad stopped at the edge of the table, looking down at the man who'd sold him out twenty years ago with the expression of someone who'd been waiting a very long time for this very moment.

Trent sat up a little taller and puffed out his chest.

"Long time no see," his dad said.

Dutton stared at him with wide eyes and parted lips.

Courtney wasn't handling the situation any better as she looked like she'd been frozen in time.

Trent wished he could take out his phone, take a picture, and send it to his friends.

"And really—" He pulled out the chair beside Trent and sat down. "You're resorting to blackmail these days?" He shook his head and made a tsk noise. "With my son, no less."

Dutton stared. Whatever he'd walked in here expecting, it was obvious by the way he looked between father and son, this wasn't it.

Courtney stiffened, and she cleared her throat. "This is unexpected."

"Well, they did just dig up my grave the other day." His father winked.

"You being alive creates potential legal complications for you personally. I'd tread carefully if I were you," Courtney said.

"I'd be more worried about how my being alive might bring some attention to your father, as well to what you're planning on doing here in Calusa Cove with Sovereign Resources," Jack said. "You know, history repeating itself and all."

A phone buzzed. Courtney reached into her bag and pulled it out. She tapped the screen, showed it quickly to Dutton, then set it on the table, face down.

Trent pushed back his chair, stood, and walked to the window. He stared out at the moat. A couple of gators had climbed up on the grassy section of the yard near the dock to sun themselves. He contemplated how much he could push Dutton and Courtney. This wasn't his wheelhouse. And while his father had known Dutton twenty years ago, he had no real experience with the man in present day.

"Because of you, my girlfriend's uncle is dead," Trent said.

"We heard about Slade." Dutton nodded, like he might actually give a damn. "He was a good marshal. I enjoyed working with him, but we had nothing to do with his murder."

"That, I don't believe," Trent's dad said. "I'm sure my son and Dove agree with me on that point."

"And I'm not selling Mallor's Landing," Trent added.

"Yes, you are." Dutton picked up the offer from the

table and held it out. "You will sign it. Today." He'd shed any semblance of congeniality and civility. "Or Dove doesn't make it to your driveway."

* * *

Dove glanced at the dashboard. It had only been twenty minutes since she'd left Mallor's Landing, but the fact that she hadn't heard anything from Trent regarding his visitors spiked her pulse.

She turned down the access road, which curved through a tight row of cypress trees with branches hanging low enough to drag across the truck's roof. She thought coming through the north side of the property, past the Alligator Farm, across the walking path, and past the graveyard would be best, since she could hide her vehicle, take cover, and get a good look at what was going on inside the main house. Only, it was taking longer than she anticipated.

On the side of the dirt road, she could see the iron fence of the family cemetery through the trees, the old stones catching what light filtered through the canopy.

She focused her gaze on the hairpin turn coming up, looking to avoid the big pot hole.

"Shit." Just as she came around the corner, she had to slam on the brakes. "What the hell?" A dark SUV sat sideways in the road. Three men stood in front. All holding weapons at their side. Not a pleasant greeting from people who didn't belong.

The engine hummed as she stared at Karl standing between two men she'd never seen before. Slowly, she lifted her phone off the seat and pulled up Buddy's contact information.

Buddy: 3 *gunman access road, Mallor's Landing. Need back-up.*

"Get out of the car with your hands up," one of the men yelled.

Yeah, she'd get out, but she was bringing her weapon with her. She shoved the gearshift into park, stuffed her phone into her back pocket, lifted the center armrest, and gripped her Glock.

Fuck. Another SUV eased in behind her.

Slowly, she opened the door and slipped out.

The air was thick and wet, the way it always was this deep into the property, where the mud and standing water and the green smell of cypress baked in the morning heat. A bird cut across the road ahead and disappeared into the tree line.

Karl stepped forward, raising his weapon. "I'll take that."

"I don't think so," she said, raising hers to match his. She knew she was outnumbered and outgunned. She didn't stand a chance. She'd get one, maybe two shots off. And they'd be good ones, dropping two dead. But then she'd be dead.

Not going to happen today. But she wasn't going to make this easy for them.

"Look, lady." One of the other men inched forward.

"We can do this the easy way. Or the hard way. Now hand over the gun."

Karl took a few more bold steps forward. One hand pointing his gun at her chest. The other, he held palm out. "Come on, Dove. I don't want to hurt you."

Now, that made her want to laugh. But she placed her weapon in Karl's hand. "What are you doing out here?" she asked.

"You'll find out soon enough." He curled his nasty little fingers around her biceps. "You're gonna need to come with us."

"If I'm gonna do that, I want to know why." She resisted the urge to jerk her arm away. Not a good move with two guns pointed in her direction and no clue how far away Buddy was—not to mention if he was coming in hot or with a low profile. She hoped the latter.

"Not for me to tell." Karl squeezed her arm and yanked her toward the SUV.

She sized up the two men. One of them had opened the rear driver's side door. They both wore dark slacks, white shirts, dark sport coats, sunglasses. They were clean-cut. Reminded her of Secret Service. But they weren't. They could be a protection detail. But if they worked for the government, they were highly stupid to be dressed like that while kidnapping a civilian.

"In you go," Karl said.

"Make me."

The man who'd opened the door took one step forward, raised his hand, grabbed her hair, and slammed the side of her face into the side of the SUV.

"You fucking asshole." She lifted her fingers to her cheek and then looked at them. A small amount of blood stained her skin. Her cheek throbbed. Her eyes watered, and stars danced like someone rearranged the sky.

"Get in, or the next one will be worse," the man said.

She glanced over her shoulder at Karl. "If you think these people are going to take care of you after this is over, you're crazy," she said. "You sold out a friend for nothing."

"You don't know shit." Karl pulled a zip tie from his back pocket. "We'd better tie her up. She can't be trusted." He grabbed her arms and slapped the plastic around her skin.

The guy who'd made her face bleed lifted her off the ground and shoved her in the SUV, slamming the door behind her.

Karl climbed in next to her while the other two took the front seats. She twisted her wrists and flexed her fingers. She wasn't getting out of the zip tie anytime soon. Looking out the window, she scanned the area in her sight. She knew what to search for. Knew the signs of human intrusion in the brush. No matter how well hidden, there were always signs. Leaves, or tall grass, moving in the wrong direction. Animals scurrying because something spooked them. Or in this case, a signal from Buddy.

Only problem, she could only search from one side of the vehicle.

The first scan showed no signs of Buddy. She kept her breathing slow and controlled and began the pass as the vehicle inched forward, and that's when she saw it. A small flat-bottom boat with a two-stroke trolling down the channel that snaked through this part of the property about one hundred and fifty feet out. The boat was maybe twelve feet, and the engine no more than fifteen horsepower.

From this distance, she couldn't see any real recognizable markings on the boat. And it was impossible to see who was in the boat. Except, the man lifted his hat, ran his hand across the top of his head, and then readjusted his cap. After that, he lifted his fishing pole and jerked it in a very specific direction and it wasn't toward him, which would've been the proper technique.

The hat adjustment screamed Cullen. He did that all the time. And he'd pointed toward the observation tower, not the house.

"Where are you taking me?" she asked, watching the small boat do a loop inside the channel and head toward the bay in front of the main house.

No one in the vehicle answered her.

"Excuse me," she said. "I'd like to know where—"

"Say one more word, and I'll give you a reason to be quiet." Karl lifted his gun and arched a brow.

Her cheek turned to fire at the thought. She faced the window. The channel curved further away from her, but she could still see the boat. Still see the man sitting on the bench, hand on the throttle, looking forward, as if he hadn't a care in the world.

The iron fence of the Mallor gravesite slid past. The cypress closed in, swallowing the road behind them.

She pulled her wrists apart—slow, small, testing—and felt the flex cuff hold. She ran the math—the way she always did when everything went sideways. What she had. What they didn't know she had. What she needed to stay alive long enough to use it.

She'd been in worse spots than this—and survived.

Chapter Twenty-Three

The words *won't make it to your driveway,* filled Trent's brain. They bounced around in his mind for a couple of seconds before they stuck. "What did you say?" he managed, as the rage began to bubble in his gut.

Courtney tapped her fingers on the papers sitting in the center of the table. "All you need to do is sign the purchase offer. Walk away with a good chunk of money in your pocket, and your freedom."

"Or what, exactly?" Trent asked. "And where's Dove?'

"She's fine," Dutton said. "And she'll stay that way as long as you sign."

Trent stood, knocking over the chair. He hit the table hard enough to rattle everything on it. "What did you do with her?" He stared at Dutton across the kitchen. "If you've hurt her, I swear to God—"

"Easy." His father rose and placed a hand on his shoulder.

He shrugged it off. "I'll fucking kill him if anyone lays a hand on her." He didn't turn to look at his dad. He kept his gaze on Dutton.

Who dared to tilt his head and smirk, sitting in his chair like a man with nothing to prove and nothing to lose. He looked at his watch then toward the window. "She's fine." He lifted his chin toward the driveway. "Look. Here she comes."

Trent raced toward the sidedoor and curled his fingers around the knob.

"I wouldn't do that if I were you," Dutton said.

The sound of chairs scraping on the floor and footsteps shuffling grated on Trent's ears. He turned, and his heart dropped to his toes. Dutton held a weapon to his father's head. "You're a fucking bastard."

Courtney stood, pointing a gun at Trent. She held it steady while standing in his kitchen in her ridiculous four-inch heels.

"Step away from the door." Courtney waved her pistol. "Go sit on the sofa."

Trent lifted his hands and reluctantly did as instructed. He wasn't giving up. He wasn't waving the white flag. He was just regrouping.

Dutton pushed his father out of the kitchen and into the family room. "You too, old man."

Through the picture window, Trent watched two dark SUVs pull to a stop in the main parking area not far from the bridge. Men with guns slipped from the vehicles.

One of those men was Karl.

Trent clasped his hands in his lap. He felt his knuckles connecting with Karl's face as if it were really happening.

Karl moved to the driver's side rear and opened the door.

Dove eased out of the vehicle. Her hands were bound in front of her. She walked without being dragged—that was something. That was Dove—refusing to be pulled around like cargo.

"You alright?" his dad asked softly.

"Ask me again after she walks through that door." Trent cracked his knuckles—something he hadn't done in years.

The men in suits took various positions around the outside of the house. All five of them held automatic weapons. All of them kept their distance from the moat and bridge.

The side door opened, and Karl came through first, hand on Dove's arm, moving her into the family room the way you'd move something you owned. One of the armed men filed in behind them.

Trent locked gazes with Dove. However, a second later, his focus shifted to her left cheek. Blood had started to dry and crust on the side of her face. Bruising had formed on her cheek and around her eye.

He jumped from the sofa and was across the room before anyone could do anything about it.

Except Karl, who stepped in front of him, shoving a gun against his chest.

"Get the fuck out of my way," Trent said behind gritted teeth.

"Go ahead." Dutton waved his hand. "Give the love birds a minute. Can't hurt."

Karl moved, but not too far, and he kept his grubby fingers on her elbow. Asshole.

"Hey." He cupped Dove's face. She flinched when his fingers grazed her cheekbone, and his jaw locked so hard his back teeth ached.

"It's not that bad." She stared at him with steady eyes.

"Who hit you?"

"The SUV."

"I'm serious."

"Right now, it doesn't matter." Her voice was quiet, but it had an edge. "Before these guys jumped me, I saw the gator you patched up a little bit ago. The one you named Two-Stroke. He was headed out to the bay. Looked good."

"I'm so glad." Only, Trent had never named a gator Two-Stroke. Not to mention, he hadn't patched one up in at least six weeks. Trent had to assume that was code for someone was out there watching. His best guess was that Cullen was out on the water.

He looked down at her hands and then turned to Dutton. "Untie her."

"Sure, why not," Dutton said. "Go ahead, Karl. Cut her loose."

"Are you crazy?" Karl asked. "She's nuts, and she used to be a sniper."

"She doesn't have a gun. She's not going anywhere. Not with the firepower that I brought. We're fine," Dutton said.

Karl took out a pocket knife and cut her free. He took a few steps back and leaned against the wall by the side door, weapon in hand.

"Sit down, both of you," Dutton said.

Trent took Dove by the hand and guided her to the sofa, wedging her between him and his father.

Courtney's heels clicked on the floor as she placed the paperwork on the coffee table with a pen. "Time to sign."

"I'm never gonna do that." Trent kept his fingers laced tightly through Dove's.

"Sign it, and we'll let you walk away with enough money to start over wherever you want," Courtney said. "If you don't, well, that's a different story."

"We'll take the different story." Jack sat up taller. "Because whatever it is, you're not going to get away with it. Not this time."

"We didn't want it to come to this. We really didn't. But you've made this more complicated than it needed to be, and now we're out of patience." Dutton sat on the edge of the coffee table. The one that had been his mother's. The same one that she'd kick his ass for anything other than his clean feet wrapped in equally clean socks being on it.

"Come to what?" Jack actually lifted his feet and

placed them on that very coffee table like a man who'd been in worse situations and had made it out. Maybe because he had. "Because I don't see a scenario where you come out smelling like roses, especially if you have to dispose of us."

"If it comes to us having to do this the hard way," Courtney said. "We don't have to get rid of anything or anyone."

"No?" Jack questioned. "Because you've got a bunch of armed men on private property, and I don't think they came here to admire the gators." He tilted his head. "The feds are already looking at Sovereign Resources. That's not a rumor—that's a fact. Whatever case Slade was building, he gave them enough to start asking the right questions. And Slade's murder?" Jack lifted his hand and stared at his nails like he was contemplating whether they needed trimming or not. "You think that doesn't come back to you eventually? A former US Marshal, shot twice in a parking lot right before the world finds out my body wasn't in that casket? And let's not forget, you were one of the other few marshals tasked with my detail. People are already asking questions."

Courtney and Dutton stole a glance at each other. Whatever passed between them, Trent couldn't read.

Trent leaned forward, making eye contact with Dove, then his father.

Twenty years ago, his dad had been dead. For twenty years, Trent had run this land either with his mother or alone. They'd handled every hard thing that had come their way because there'd been no one else. And now here was his father, alive, sitting on the very sofa that Trent remembered him purchasing and carrying in from the truck. And here was the woman Trent loved with a bruise and cut on her face, and there was no fucking way Trent was going to lose either one of them.

Not today.

Courtney folded her arms and tapped her toe on the floor. "Everything is working out just fine," she said. "You think the world finding out Jack is alive is a problem for us?" She shook her head. "It's not. Because the world will also find out that he faked his death—ish the help of a sitting US Marshal." She paused and leaned closer. "Slade broke the law to hide a witness to a crime that never happened. The courts would look at it as a fabrication for some kind of profit. And Slade would've had to bribe at least one official, if not more, to make Jack's death look real. That's gonna come back and bite someone in the ass."

"Not me," Jack said.

"Oh, but it's not going help your case." She smiled serenely. "Especially when you're dead, and/or missing—again. I mean, twenty years later, it's all coming apart. You see, we can spin this any way we need to. Like, let's say, Jack panicked because he didn't want to be brought back from the dead. Killed the one man who could expose him." She looked at Dove. "And this one—she discovered the truth. Came to confront him. Had words with Trent. And well..." She lifted one shoulder. "Crime of passion. Or maybe an accident. You know how accidents can happen on properties like this. Everyone knows that."

"Wow. You've created quite the plan in a short period of time." Trent stared at her, a little in awe of the smooth, practiced way she'd assembled that story, the way every piece fit against every other piece like she'd been building it for a while. There were holes. But those holes might not need to be filled if there were no bodies, or if those bodies couldn't speak for themselves.

His dad leaned forward, pressed his hands on his knees and laughed. The kind of laugh that rattled a man's chest. "That's an interesting plot twist," his father said when he'd settled. "But it doesn't explain why I'd kill Slade. I have no motive. None. I owed him everything. And the second anyone starts digging into why my death had to be faked in the first place—and they will, because that's how these things go—they'll find the ME who did it. A Dr. Raymond Weiss. The same one who'd gotten a little tired of Edward Kirk threatening him."

Trent shifted his gaze to Dutton, who narrowed his stare.

"You don't know what you're talking about," Courtney said.

"But I do," Trent's father said. "Your father might have been able to keep his hands from getting dirty. His name might have never appeared in Parrish's Cache and Weiss couldn't prove anything. But he kept records. And he gave them to Slade, who gave them to me, and I gave them to someone else for safekeeping." His dad shrugged.

"But you know, if you want to take your chances and kill us off, bury our bodies, good luck."

"And no one is going to believe Dove and I killed each other," Trent said. "It's absurd."

"Not a problem you have to worry about." Dutton pointed his gun at Dove.

Trent sucked in a breath and slowly let it go.

"But at the end of the day, I'm the one holding the cards," Dutton said.

The song *Born on the Bayou*, by Creedence Clearwater Revival, came alive in the room.

Trent knew that ringtone. It belonged to Karl and his phone.

Karl dug into his pocket.

"Who the fuck is it?" Dutton asked.

"No one important," Karl said, staring at his screen.

"Not what I asked." Dutton glared.

"Cullen Monroe. A guy I grew up with." Karl stared at Trent.

Trent didn't move a muscle. He didn't breathe. He had no idea what Cullen's play was, but he suspected Cullen wasn't the only one out there, and that had to be a good thing.

"Answer it, and put it on speaker," Dutton said.

Karl tapped the screen. "What do you want, Cullen? I'm kind of busy."

"I can see that." Cullen's voice filled the kitchen. "Why don't y'all come on outside. And I mean all of you."

Dutton inched closer and tapped the screen. "Who is this guy?"

"Trent and I went to high school with him. He left town right after to join the Marines. He came back a couple of years ago, not quite right in the head," Karl said. "He's close with Trent and Dove."

"He can go to hell," Dutton said.

"Not sure where you think I am, but I'm not home and like I said, I'm busy."

"I know. You're at Trent's. You're with Dove, Trent, and I'm guessing Jack as well. Along with a politician and—"

"You don't know who you're messing with, young man," Dutton said. "But I'm sure my protection detail mentioned we were conducting important business in here. Please leave."

"I really think you want to step outside," Cullen said. "And if I were you, I'd bring everyone. Don't make me come in and get you. That'll just upset me." The line went dead.

"That kid has some set of balls on him." Dutton strolled toward the picture window and glanced outside. Then he looked over his shoulder before moving to the kitchen window. "Courtney, we've got a problem."

Trent pushed to a standing position.

"Sit the fuck down." Dutton pointed his weapon. "I won't hesitate to put a bullet between your eyes."

Trent held his hands up, but he didn't back down.

Both Dutton and Courtney moved to the side door.

"All right. We're heading outside," Dutton said. "Karl, you've got the girl. Courtney, you've got Jack. I'll take Trent. If any one of them does something stupid, shoot them. I'm tired of this shit. No more playing nice. We're taking this property, and we're putting an end to it. And if I have to add one more crazy Marine to the list, then so be it."

Trent took Dove's hand and squeezed it. "It's gonna be okay."

"That's my line," she whispered.

Dutton walked them out the side door and across the porch—Trent and Dutton first, Dove and Karl behind him, Jack and Courtney behind her—each pressing a weapon into their side while each of them held their hands up in the air.

Cullen stood in the driveway with a grin that had no business being that wide, given the circumstances. He held his rifle in his arms but not pointed at anyone. He stood there with a wide stance and an easy confidence that Trent wasn't sure he'd ever seen from the man.

On the ground behind him, all five of Dutton's men sat zip-tied back-to-back in a line as if they were waiting for an execution.

And on the bank of the moat, Dolly had hauled herself halfway out of the water, her tail still cutting slow arcs in the shallows, her massive head swinging toward the group with the patient, ancient attention of something that had been on this earth long before any of them and planned to be here long after.

Clarkson was right behind her. The pale scar on her flank caught the morning light as she pulled herself up the bank, her head low, her eyes fixed on the gathering near the bridge with an expression—if you could call it that—that suggested she was deciding whether the flesh in front of her was too big to consume.

It was a dangerous look from a gator, especially if that gator felt threatened, and Clarkson was a wild beast who, while she trusted Trent, would still take off his leg if he moved in a manner that frightened her.

"Let my men go," Dutton said.

Cullen chuckled. "That's not gonna happen. You're gonna step away from my friends and hand over your weapons."

"It's one against three," Courtney said. "You lose every time."

"Do I?" Cullen adjusted his stance. "You don't know who I brought with me, or where they are. I could have a shooter on the observation platform. I could have someone hiding in the reeds. Not to mention the gators who are working pretty hard to cross the moat to come and say hello."

Dutton turned. "Shit."

"I'd put those weapons down," Trent said, without taking his eyes off his gators. "And I'd do it slow. Real slow." He glanced over his shoulder at Dutton, who was staring at Dolly with the particular expression of a man whose plans had just developed a significant complication. "She can move a lot faster than you think, and her hind legs just wiggled over the edge."

"If she comes at me, I'll shoot her," Dutton says.

"There are anywhere from ten to twenty gators in that moat at any given time. Not to mention a second one just managed to climb where she isn't supposed to be able to. One shot isn't going to put them down." Trent took a chance and stepped away from Dutton. "Dolly, the big one. She's mostly friendly, but she doesn't take too kindly to strangers, and she can be incredibly territorial. Not to mention she gets all the other ones riled up."

"I don't like agreeing with Trent." Karl took a slow step toward the bridge. "But I've been around alligators my whole life. We don't want to be here right now."

"What do you suggest we do?" Courtney asked.

Trent completely separated himself from Dutton. "I'll create a diversion while everyone else makes their way into the house. Once I've got them back on the right side of the moat, we can go back to killing each—"

"That won't be necessary," Cullen said. "Dawson and that other US Marshal are down at the gate waiting for my signal." He lifted his rifle, pointing it toward the observation deck. "Buddy's up there. Sterling's around the other side of the house."

Trent looked up toward Buddy. "Don't kill my gators unless I'm the one about to die, got it?" Trent blew out a puff of air as he took a step backward, since Clarkson was closing in a little faster than Dolly.

Cullen moved toward the five men kneeling on the ground with their hands bound. "Let's go. Slow and easy. Nobody runs because if you do that, those gators will bite your limbs off." He helped the first man to his feet, rifle slung over his shoulder. He kept his movements precise and so did the man he was helping.

Dove helped the second man, lifting him by the arm,

talking low and calm like she'd done this a thousand times. Jack took the third.

Trent kept his gaze glued to Clarkson.

She'd stopped about six feet from the group, her head swinging back and forth, tail doing that slow, deliberate sweep that meant she was still determining something. Her nostrils flared. She could smell the strangers. The fear. Maybe even the blood from Dove's face.

None of that was good.

"Easy, girl." Trent kept his voice low and even. "No one wants to hurt you."

Out of the corner of his eye, he caught movement. Slow at first, and then all of a sudden, Courtney broke off in a full run toward the SUVs, heels hitting the gravel.

Clarkson's head snapped toward the movement, and she opened her mouth, making a deep, guttural grunt.

"Stop running," Trent said as calmly as he could. While he wanted these people in jail, he didn't want them attacked by a gator.

Clarkson shot forward like something mechanical—low and fast, covering ground in that terrifying burst that people never believed until they saw it. Courtney screamed.

"Fuck," Trent mumbled.

Karl lunged. He grabbed Clarkson's tail with both hands and spun hard, throwing his weight into it, but the gator shifted. She did, however, pause, turning her head. She repositioned herself, facing Karl, hissing through her open mouth.

"Don't. Move," Trent said.

"Wasn't planning on it." Karl held his hands up and stared Clarkson down like he'd done it a million times, which he had.

Dolly bellowed.

The sound rolled across the property like a wave, and every other gator in the moat joined in. Trent turned. Dolly had committed—all twelve feet of her driving toward Dutton, who'd backed himself against the second SUV with nowhere to go.

Shit. Trent hadn't even seen Dutton move.

Cullen stepped between them, waving his arms wide. "Hey. Hey. Come on, big girl. Over here."

Dolly didn't care about Cullen.

Dove got in front of Dutton and spread her arms the way she'd seen Trent do it, planting her feet, making herself large. "Over here, sweetheart." Her voice dropped to that low register. "Come on, Dolly. It's okay."

Dolly slowed. Her head swung toward Dove.

Dutton raised his weapon.

"Don't you fucking dare," Trent said.

The shot cracked across the property.

Dolly lurched. A sound came out of her that Trent had never heard before—not a bellow, not a hiss, it almost sounded like a gargled cry—and she spun sideways, tail whipping.

Trent raced in her direction.

"You shot my gator." He got between Dutton and Dolly without thinking about it, without any plan except that Dutton was not firing again. "You shot her."

Dutton yanked open the driver's side door. "It's not a pet."

Pop. Pop.

Dutten jumped. Courtney gasped. The SUV sank as the tires exploded. Trent glanced over his shoulder and saw Buddy wave from the observation deck. "Watch out. Dolly's on the move, and Clarkson's right behind her.

"I got Clarkson." Cullen waved his hands and stomped his feet.

Clarkson turned her head but didn't move.

Trent had nothing left that resembled patience.

Dolly had flattened herself on the ground. But that was only temporary.

Trent pointed at Dutton. "Get to the porch. Right now. You move anywhere else, and I promise you this gator is the least of your problems."

Dutton took Courtney's hand and moved to the porch.

Trent turned back to his animals.

Clarkson wasn't interested in Cullen and had Karl pinned against the SUV, mouth open, waiting. Jack had worked his way around the far side, arms out, moving slow. Cullen came in from the other angle.

"I don't think she'll charge if he doesn't move," Trent called. "Give me a second."

He got to Dolly first. She'd begun circling, agitated, tail still sweeping hard. He could see the wound now—high on the tail, entry and exit both visible, bleeding but not pumping.

His shoulders dropped about an inch.

"Hey." He crouched down to her level and put out his hand. "Hey, old girl. I see you. Let me look."

She turned her head toward him. One amber eye, ancient and furious.

"I know." He kept his hand out. "I know. You're okay."

She stilled. Not calm—still hot, still agitated—but she let him move closer.

Dove appeared beside him. She crouched the same way he did, held her hand out the same way, and spoke in the same low register. "Come on, Dolly. It's okay. You're okay."

Dolly's tail slowed.

Trent glanced at Dove. She was watching the gator the way he'd tried to teach her—patient, steady, no sudden movement, letting the animal decide on her own.

He looked back at Dolly.

The wound wasn't bad. Clean through the thick part of the tail, well clear of anything vital. She'd end up with a scar, and she'd be sore. She'd be in a mood for a good week, but she'd be fine.

"Back to the water," he said softly. "Come on. Go on home."

Dolly held for another moment. Then she turned and moved toward the moat, slow and dignified, like the whole thing had been her idea from the start.

He stayed crouched until she slid off the bank and into the water.

Behind him, he heard Cullen utilizing that same low and steady timbre that everyone who'd ever been raised with gators used. Jack echoed it, and the two of them worked Clarkson back toward the moat one patient step at a time until a splash told him she was back where she belonged.

Karl slid down the side of the SUV and sat in the gravel with his head in his hands.

Trent stood.

Buddy climbed down from the observation platform, rifle across his back, and Sterling came around from the far side of the house, and from the end of the drive, tires screamed on the pavement as Dawson's cruiser rolled in hot, another vehicle right behind it.

Dawson was out before the car stopped rocking. Chloe was right behind him. And from the passenger seat, Lach Ridge unfolded himself from the vehicle.

They didn't need much direction, though Buddy gave it to them anyway, even though his FBI days were long behind him.

Dutton sat on the porch steps with his hands up while Dawson cuffed him, reciting his rights in the flat, practiced tone of someone who'd done it enough times that the words were automatic. Chloe moved Courtney to the second vehicle, portfolio still somehow under her arm, mascara tracking down her face. Lach walked Karl to the patrol car without a word, and Karl went without argument, which told Trent everything about how much fight the man had left.

He almost felt sorry for Karl. Almost was the keyword.

Trent stood in the middle of his driveway and watched the people who'd tried to destroy him—and who had a hand in taking away his father twenty years ago—get what they deserved. He knew this was only the beginning. He knew how the law worked. Charges would be filed, both local and federal. Dutton and Courtney—they'd fight them. And they had the means.

Karl? Something told Trent that Dawson might be able to get him to turn on them for the right reduction of his sentence, and he hoped that would be the play. Why Trent still had a soft spot for Karl, he had no idea, but he did. He supposed years of running barefoot together in a place as special as the Glades did that to people.

Trent rubbed the back of his neck and glanced around. Three generations of Mallors had worked this land. His grandfather had carved it out of the Glades with nothing but stubbornness and a tolerance for heat. His father had loved it enough to testify for it, to die for it—or to disappear for it, which had turned out to be the same thing. His mother had kept it alive through grief and tight budgets and sheer refusal to quit.

And now here it was. Still standing. Still his.

Dove stepped up beside him. She didn't say anything. Just stood there with her shoulder against his arm and the morning light catching gold on the side of her face where the bruising had started to settle in around the cut.

His father appeared on his other side.

The three of them stood there watching Dawson's people work, watching Cullen joke with Buddy near the moat, watching Dolly drift past in the water below like nothing had happened, like she hadn't just taken a bullet and kept moving.

"Hell of a morning," his father said.

"Yeah." Trent looked at the moat. At the house. At the land running all the way down to where the Glades opened up and went forever. "It was."

Dove laced her fingers through his.

He looked down at their hands. Then up at his father, who was watching him with the same expression he'd had in the kitchen that morning—warm and quiet and twenty years of an absence that had finally found its way home.

"Your mother had the most beautiful wedding dress," his father said.

"Excuse me?" Trent stared at his dad. "We nearly died, and you're thinking about mom's wedding dress?"

"I'm wondering if that dress is still in the closet because ever since you were born, she kept telling me that she was never gonna be the mother of the bride, and she just hoped that maybe your bride would humor her and wear that dress." His father laughed. It wasn't boisterous. Or loud. Or even humorous. But it was real and it was the same laugh Trent had been carrying in his memory for two decades even if it was slightly worn around the edges with grief but still recognizable.

"Um, we're not discussing this right now. Or any time all that soon," Dove said. "I think we need to let things settle for a bit."

Trent leaned over and kissed her unbruised cheek. "Mom tried to get me to realize how much I cared for Dove the moment she learned she could cook chicken and rice soup." Trent smiled. "Mom was always right about everything."

"She told me within the first two hours of us meeting that we were gonna get married. I thought she was crazy. We were married three weeks later." Jack looked out at the water. "Your mother was always right. Always."

Trent had nothing to add to that. He just held onto Dove's hand and stood between the two of them in the morning sun on the land that was still his and let that be enough.

Chapter Twenty-Four

A month later...

A month ago, Dove would have said she wasn't a dock person.

She'd have said the humidity was oppressive and the bugs were relentless and the sounds the Glades made at night were the kind that kept a person's nervous system alert long past the point where alert was useful. She'd have said that sitting on a wooden dock in the dark, surrounded by water that contained animals capable of removing limbs, wasn't her idea of a good evening.

She'd have been wrong.

The sky over Mallor's Landing was doing something she still didn't have words for—the way the stars came out here, without any artificial light to compete with them. The water caught the reflection and held it, and the entire world turned into something that looked like it had been painted by someone who'd never learned restraint.

Her mother sat beside her in one of Trent's Adirondack chairs, a glass of wine in her hand, her eyes open wide.

"I have to say," Rose said. "This isn't how I pictured this place. It's more spectacular than you described."

"It is," Dove agreed.

Her father, Stanley, had positioned himself as far from the edge of the water as the dock would allow and was doing his level best to look casual about it. He'd spent eight years in the Army and had done things that would make most people's hair go white. But he was deeply, genuinely concerned about the alligators.

"They can't get up here," Trent said, for the third time.

"You said that about the bank," Stanley said.

"The bank is different."

"How?"

"The bank is their territory. The dock is mine." Trent leaned back in his chair and propped his feet up on the railing with the ease of a man who'd been doing this his entire life. "They know the difference."

"That's not true." Stanley looked at the water. Something moved out in the darkness, and he shifted an inch closer to the center of the dock without acknowledging whatever lurked below.

"Dad, Trent's teasing you." Dove pressed her lips together, suppressing a laugh. "The alligators can't climb the bank, and they can't get up on the dock."

"But it's Florida, so where there's water, there are gators." Jack sat on the cooler at the far end, a beer in his hand, watching Stanley with open amusement. In the last month, she'd learned that Jack found most things quietly amusing, and that he expressed this through a particular half-smile he'd clearly passed directly to his son.

Trent chuckled. "Let's not forget the snakes."

"I can't believe my daughter wants to live in this state," her father said.

"My brother loved it here." Her mom sighed. "He said the wildlife just made it all the more exciting."

That brought Dove's thoughts back to everything that had happened.

The last four weeks had been filled with emotions no one knew what to do with. Trent and Jack had gone through a laundry list of feelings. One minute Trent would be angry and lashing out at his father as if Jack had purposely abandoned him, and the next minute, Trent would be acting like a teenager demanding his father's attention.

Jack had his own issues. He struggled every day with the fact his wife was gone and that he'd lost twenty years of his son's life. But together, these two men worked diligently to have a semblance of a father-son relationship. Most of the time it was like twenty years hadn't passed and they were so much alike. But they still had a lot to work through. However, Dove knew they would. The one thing Trent and Jack had that others didn't was mutual respect for the tough decisions they'd made in the name of family.

Dove could see how twenty years apart had affected them. However, every day, they lived and laughed a little more.

The formal charges against Dutton and Courtney had come down three weeks ago. Conspiracy, obstruction, and a list of federal offenses that the DOJ had been quietly building since her uncle had first handed them the lead. Edward Kirk—Courtney's father, the man behind Gulf Coast Energy Partners twenty years ago—had been pulled out of his comfortable retirement to answer for his part in it, too. He wasn't going to get away with anything, and he, too, would face a litany of charges.

Raymond Weiss, the ME who'd signed Jack's death certificate, would be testifying against all three in exchange for immunity. Karl had taken a deal—reduced sentence, full cooperation—and was somewhere in protective custody doing what Karl had always done best, which was looking out for himself.

Sovereign Resources had been shut down. No permits. No mining. No limestone extraction coming to the Calusa Cove watershed or anywhere near it.

The Henderssons had signed formal affidavits, and their testimony would be the final piece that put everyone away.

The town had exhaled. The Glades had kept doing what the Glades always did, which was exist without caring about any of it.

"The party was beautiful," her mother said. "Aaron would have loved it."

"He would've complained about the playlist," Dove said.

Her mother laughed. "He always complained about playlists. That man had opinions about music, and his opinions were wrong. It's why I chose it—just to annoy him in death."

"Aaron had opinions about everything," Stanley said. "And he never kept them to himself. Oddly, I'll miss that about him"

"So true." Her mother turned her glass in her hands. "That was the best part of him—and the most annoying."

Dove looked out at the water. Her uncle's memorial had been at a hall in Fort Lauderdale with a hundred people she recognized and a hundred more she didn't. Someone had put together a slideshow that started with a photo of her uncle at about twenty-two that looked so much like she'd felt when she was twenty-two—all sharp edges and something to prove—that she'd had to look away for a minute and find Trent's hand in the dark.

He'd given it to her without being asked.

She still thought about that. About how Trent was always just there when she needed him and often when she didn't. He knew her needs and desires, and while they fought like every other couple, he never held on to those arguments. He always apologized when necessary and sometimes when it wasn't.

For two people who didn't have relationships, theirs was easy. Comfortable. It was like her favorite sweater. A little worn around the edges. Faded in color. But it fit her like nothing else ever would.

"So." Her mother's voice shifted—not dramatically, but enough. Dove recognized that tone. The one her mom deployed when she'd been building toward something and had decided the time had come whether Dove was ready or not. "You mentioned at the service that you had some news."

Dove glanced at Trent. Boy, did she have some news to share. It wasn't the news her mother was referring to, but it was the news Dove would start with.

Trent smiled, taking her hand. They'd discussed this with Jack last week. He wasn't surprised. It's not like Dove stayed at her house these days at all anymore.

"Trent and I decided to move in together," she said. "So, I'll be living here at Mallor's Landing from now on. I even got my landlord to let me out of my lease." She spoke so fast she could barely breathe. But she always did that when she was nervous, and the real news made her want to go find Dolly and roll in the mud with her.

Her mother looked over her shoulder at the moat. Then at the dock. Then, at the cypress trees that closed in on three sides of the property in the dark.

"With the alligators," Stanley said.

"With Trent," Dove said. "The alligators come with the property."

"I'm starting to think she likes the gators more than me," Trent said. "Same with the land."

"Maybe," Dove said, and she meant it in a way that surprised her every time she thought about it. She'd moved to Calusa Cove for a job, for a change, for the practical reason that Buddy needed someone and she needed somewhere to be. She hadn't expected to find something that felt like hers. She hadn't expected to find Trent. To fall in love. To become all domesticated in a way that made her mother want to knit booties. "I can't imagine being anywhere else."

Her mother looked at her for a long moment—the way mothers looked at a daughter when they were trying to figure out if there was more meaning beneath the surface. If there was something else to be said.

Dove's throat grew dry. She snagged her water and took a sip.

"Well," her mother said. "It's beautiful, and you two seem very happy."

"It is, and we are," Dove agreed.

"I don't mean to ask a weird question, but where exactly will Jack be?" Stanley asked.

"I'm fixing up the old house my parents used to live in," Jack said. "Back corner of the property. Far enough that I won't hear things I'm not supposed to hear." He took a long pull of his beer. "Close enough to annoy everyone regularly."

"That sounds about right," Trent said. "I loved having my grandparents so close, but I remember mom complaining every time Grandma showed up in *her* kitchen."

"It was my mom's kitchen before your mother's," Jack said. "We all tried living in that house together until you were two. It was great when you were born. We loved the help, but it was a lot. So, your grandfather turned the old garage where he used to keep his boat, the Margaret, the one he named after your grandmother, into a lovely little home for them."

"I remember that damn boat. It was a beater, that's for sure," Trent said.

"The hull rotted out when you were maybe four, and we replaced it." Jack looked at the property the way Dove had noticed him looking at it when he often thought of his late wife, like a man reading a book he'd been missing for a long time. "I'm looking forward to being here when the grandchildren come around."

Dove coughed. There was no way Jack could've known. She hadn't even told Trent yet, and she'd only confirmed it with the doctor yesterday.

Trent cleared his throat. "On that note." He dropped his feet from the railing and sat forward. He looked at her in the way he looked at her when it was just the two of them and the rest of the world had stopped being relevant. "I've been trying to figure out the right time to do this for a week," he said. "But I've come to understand that with you, there isn't a right time. There's just—now, or not yet, and I'm done with not yet."

Dove stared at him with her heart in her throat.

He reached into his pocket.

Her mother made a sound.

"What are you doing?" Dove asked.

"I'm getting to that." He held up one hand. "I've spent most of my life believing that the things worth having were the things I'd already fought for. This land. These animals. The people in this town who know me well enough and still like me anyway." He took her hand. "Then you showed up and hated my moat, and argued with everything I said, and somehow that turned into the best thing that ever happened to me."

"I didn't hate the moat," she said.

"You called it a ditch with ambition."

"That isn't a lie."

"I'm not having that conversation again—not when I'm trying to ask you if you'll marry me?"

The ring sat in his palm—simple, nothing like what she would have picked out for herself and somehow exactly right.

Her mother made the sound again, louder.

Her father put down his beer.

Jack was very still at the end of the dock, watching his son with an expression that had nothing restrained about it at all.

"Yes," Dove said. "Obviously, yes."

Trent exhaled. Like he'd been holding that breath longer than just tonight, longer than just this month—like he'd been holding it for the entire wild, impossible run of this last month and had finally found somewhere safe to let it go.

He slid the ring onto her finger, stood and pulled her up with him. He cupped her chin. "I love you," he whispered.

"I love you, too."

He kissed her, slow and gentle. It wasn't long, but it was passionate.

Her mother jumped out of her chair. "Oh, my God." She practically shoved Trent out of the way. "I'm sorry. I honestly never thought I'd see this day." She hugged Dove so hard, she couldn't breathe.

Her dad took Trent's hand and Jack hung back for exactly two seconds before he put his arm around his son from the other side, and for a moment all five of them stood on the dock in the dark over the water with the stars glittering in the sky.

But Dove couldn't let another day go by without telling Trent and since he proposed in front of the family, she might as well make this a family thing. "I have something I need to tell everyone, and it's kind of a big deal."

Trent took her hands. "Bigger than getting married?

She decided to just blurt it out. "I'm pregnant."

Trent's face went through approximately four separate expressions in the span of two seconds. Surprise, calculation, something that was trying to be composed and wasn't, and then something that was so far past composed...shock.

He reached behind him and lowered himself.

But there was nothing behind him, and Trent went backward off the dock and hit the water with a sound that sent every gator in the moat to the far bank.

"Trent." Dove was at the edge of the dock. "Trent."

His head came up. He was in about four feet of water, sitting on the bottom, staring up at her with hair and mud plastered across his forehead. He brushed it from his face. "You're pregnant," he said.

"Yes."

"We're having a baby."

"That's what pregnant means," she said.

His father burst out laughing. Her father joined in.

Her mother cried. It was that happy cry, but there were still tears, and Dove had been making her mom cry since she graduated from high school.

Trent sat in the water for a few more seconds. He didn't smile. He didn't frown. Nothing. "Holy shit," he said.

"We need to watch our language," her mother said. "Good practice for when the little one arrives."

Jack reached down and took Trent's hand. "Let's get you out of that water before a gator decides you're dinner."

Trent took his dad's hand and jumped up on the dock, dripping, still wearing that expression, and Dove put her hands on either side of his face the way he'd done to her at least a hundred times.

"You okay?" she asked.

"I think so." His hands came up and covered hers. Warm, even soaking wet. "Yeah." He turned his face into her palm for a moment. "Yeah, I'm good."

"You fell in the water."

"Shock will do that to a man." He smiled. "We're having a baby."

"We are," she said.

"My mom was right about you." He kissed her hard, ignoring the fact that their parents were standing right there. And honestly, she didn't care. There was a time and a place, and this was certainly the time.

Behind them, the Glades settled into its nighttime

rhythm. Something moved in the moat and bellowed. Dolly, most likely, doing her slow circuit.

The stars held their position overhead, indifferent and endless.

Dove rested her head on Trent's chest and closed her eyes.

Calusa Cove. Mallor's Landing. The ditch with ambition, and the man who'd named his alligators. The land that had started to feel, against all reasonable expectation, like the first place she'd ever chosen on purpose.

This was home.

About Jen Talty

Jen Talty is the *USA Today* Bestselling Author of Contemporary Romance, Romantic Suspense, and Paranormal Romance. In the fall of 2020, her short story was selected and featured in a 1001 Dark Nights Anthology.

Regardless of the genre, her goal is to take you on a ride that will leave you floating under the sun with warmth in your heart. She writes stories about broken heroes and heroines who aren't necessarily looking for romance, but in the end, they find the kind of love books are written about :).

She first started writing while carting her kids to one hockey rink after the other, averaging 170 games per year between 3 kids in 2 countries and 5 states. Her first book, IN TWO WEEKS was originally published in 2007. In 2010 she helped form a publishing company (Cool Gus Publishing) with *NY Times* Bestselling Author Bob Mayer where she ran the technical side of the business through 2016.

Jen is currently enjoying the next phase of her life...the

empty nester! She and her husband reside in Jupiter, Florida.

Grab a glass of vino, kick back, relax, and let the romance roll in...

Sign up for my *Newsletter* (https://dl.bookfunnel. com/82gm8b9k4y). *where I often give away free books before publication.*

Join my private Facebook group *(https://www.facebook. com/groups/191706547909047/) where I post exclusive excerpts and discuss all things murder and love!*

Never miss a new release. Follow me on Amazon:amazon.com/author/jentalty
And on Bookbub: bookbub.com/authors/jen-talty

Also by Jen Talty

Brand New Series
Collaboration with Kris Norris!!!!!
The BLACK HOLLOW series.
Hollow Point (written by Kris Norris)
Hollow Code (written by Jen Talty

Also a Brand New Series!
The Aegis Network: The Everglades Division
Hunted in Calusa Cove
Shadows in Calusa Cove
Deception in Calusa Cove

Welcome to...Everglades Overwatch!
Secrets in Calusa Cove
Pirates in Calusa Cove
Murder in Calusa Cove
Betrayal in Calusa Cove

www.ingramcontent.com/pod-product-compliance
Lightning Source LLC
Chambersburg PA
CBHW011930050726
47590CB00011B/3226